BRIE'S SUBMISSION

Claim Me

D1248944

Red Phoenix

Claim Me: Brie's Submission
9th of the Brie Series

Edited by Amy Parker, Proofed by Becki Wyer and Marilyn Cooper
Cover by Shanoff Designs
Phoenix symbol by Nicole Delfs

Adult Reading Material (18+)

Dedication

To MrRed:
My love and devotion to the man
who not only changed my life,
but also believed in me.

Huge hugs to my fans! To have people relate to my
characters as real people and to celebrate their big
moments with me? Well, I don't think there is anything
more satisfying or wonderful for an author.
Thank you, my friends!

YOU CAN ALSO BUY THE AUDIO BOOK!

Claim Me #9

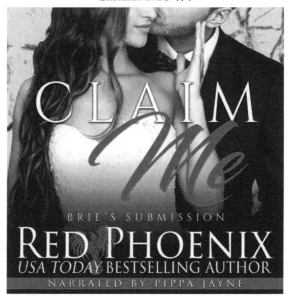

SIGN UP FOR MY NEWSLETTER HERE FOR THE LATEST RED PHOENIX UPDATES

FOLLOW ME ON INSTAGRAM

INSTAGRAM.COM/REDPHOENIXAUTHOR

SALES, GIVEAWAYS, NEW RELEASES, PREORDER LINKS, AND MORE! SIGN UP HERE

REDPHOENIXAUTHOR.COM/NEWSLETTER-SIGNUP

CONTENTS

The Wolf Surrenders 1

Ghosts of the Past 21

Tono Experiences Flight 33

The Cat's Out of the Bag 43

A Good Day 61

Positive Force 80

Baron's Sultry Session 95

Come to Me 108

Heartbreak 123

Cold Reception 136

Betrayal 148

The Limo Ride 163

White Russian 175

Goodbye 190

La Famiglia 201

I Do 212

The Dance 232

Exchange of Souls 249

(Special Bonus) 16 Years Earlier Master's POV 261

Coming Next 279

About the Author 280

Other Red Phoenix Books 283

Connect with Red on Substance B 287

The Wolf Surrenders

F aelan's parents met them in the downstairs lobby.
"Mr. and Mrs. Wallace, this is Ren Nosaka," Brie said, introducing him to the anxious couple.

Mr. Wallace shook Tono's hand energetically. "I can't tell you how grateful we are. What you are doing for us is… Words can't express the depth of our gratitude."

Before Tono could respond, Mrs. Wallace held out a jar of preserves. "I can't…" She broke into tears and thrust the jar at him.

Tono took it and gently placed his arm around her shoulder. Brie saw the woman begin to relax, responding to the peace he exuded. "It is my pleasure to help a friend."

Faelan's mother looked at him, shocked. "You know my son?"

"I do. He's a good man."

"I'm sorry to say he's never mentioned you to us."

Tono's smile was charming when he replied, "I'm not surprised. Although your son is a good man, he is also exceedingly arrogant."

Faelan's parents broke out in unexpected laughter and Brie joined in. It felt good to laugh under such stressful circumstances.

"How did Todd seem to you today?" Brie asked his mother, once the laughter died down.

"He wouldn't speak to us, but he seemed calmer. More at peace than he's been in a long time."

Tono nodded. "Good. If you don't mind, I would like Miss Bennett and I to speak to him alone. If all goes well, we will invite you to join us later."

"By all means," Mr. Wallace answered.

Tono went to the nurse's desk first, and was handed a huge stack of papers to fill out. He spoke to the staff for quite a while before nodding to Brie to join him.

"It looks like Wallace has indicated to the staff that he will decline my offer. Shall we go change his mind?"

"Let's," Brie answered, feeling more confident with Tono beside her.

The look on Faelan's face when Tono walked through the door was priceless. "What the hell are you doing here?"

Brie smiled to herself as she shut the door behind them. Those were the exact words she'd used the day Faelan had surprised her at the Training Center. She took it as a positive sign.

"I am your donor, Mr. Wallace."

"Like hell you are," Faelan said, struggling to sit up on his own.

The difference in him from yesterday to today was startling. Anger seemed to be a good motivator for Blue

Eyes. Brie walked over to help him, but he glared at her with those ocean blues. "Get away. You should have told me."

"I just found out myself," she protested.

Tono sat down and stared at Faelan, waiting patiently for him to calm down.

"Come join me, Brie," Tono suggested, pulling a chair next to his.

Brie left Faelan's side and sat down, unable to hide the smile that threatened to escape.

"What are you grinning about?" Faelan snarled.

"I'm just glad to see you're feeling better today."

"I'm not feeling better, I'm dying. Are you really that dense?"

Brie giggled.

Faelan punched the controls on the bed so that he slowly moved into a sitting position. "Laugh at me again," he demanded.

A remark Mary would make came to Brie's mind, but she kept it to herself, struggling to keep her smile from widening even more.

"You're unbelievable, Brie," Faelan growled.

"What's unbelievable is that you're planning to turn down the surgery," Tono stated.

"Yes, I decided last night. I don't want someone else's kidney and I refuse to spend my life on dialysis. What I really want is to die."

"And yet you have a willing donor and the chance to reverse your circumstances. Why would you turn that away?"

"I didn't ask for your help, old man."

Tono smiled. "You must be referring to the difference in maturity between us, since I'm only five years your senior."

"Brie, get him out of here," Faelan said, glaring at her.

Tono answered evenly, "But I wish to help."

"I don't want it!" Faelan insisted, pounding his fist on the bed.

Tono's demeanor did not change. "Explain why."

Faelan gave him an icy stare. "I want to die, damn it! I already told you that."

"But you don't have to."

Faelan roared furiously, "I said I don't want your help!" When he broke into a fit of coughing afterwards, he scowled at Tono as if it were his fault.

"Why are you refusing a new kidney, which will ensure your health and prosperity?"

Faelan looked at Brie, those big blue eyes beseeching her to agree with him. "It's not worth the risk to him." When Tono argued the point, he snarled, "Do I have to spell it out to you? *I'm* not worth the risk."

"Tell me why."

Faelan growled in frustration. "Go and live your life, Nosaka. Have kids, get old and croak at the age of a hundred. That's what you are meant to do."

"And you?"

"I was supposed to die years ago. I shouldn't be here, and fate has finally seen fit to finish the job."

"Mr. Wallace, you are as stubborn and strong as you were the day I met you. Nothing has changed except your attitude."

"You have no idea what you're talking about."

Brie broke in. "I disagree. That man who came to me at the Training Center and introduced himself as Faelan sits before me now. It's the same man who earned the respect of the subs in our community despite his lack of experience. The very same man who won my friend's heart."

Faelan's eyes flickered with pain at her mention of Mary.

Brie continued, "You have no idea the number of people you have influenced and who genuinely care about you."

"It is your duty to go through with this operation," Tono maintained. "Fate saved you the day of the crash, and has saved you again with a suitable donor. To give up now does not honor the man you've become."

Faelan clapped his hands sarcastically. "Oh, those are very pretty words, Mr. Nosaka."

Brie stood and walked over to the bed, deciding now was the time to lay all her cards on the table. "You should know that Mary left the commune. She's been going to therapy and working hard to break the chains of her past."

Faelan's eyes softened as he asked, "Mary's okay, then?"

"Yes and no."

"Why? What's wrong?"

Brie's lips trembled. "She misses you."

He rolled his eyes. "Well, she'll get over it."

"No, she won't. Mary confessed that she's in love with you."

Faelan closed his eyes and laid his head back on the pillow.

"If something happened to you…" Brie's voice broke and she needed a moment to regain her composure. "I don't know if she could survive it. That's why you can't give up. You just can't!"

He didn't respond to her plea, so Brie sat back down next to Tono. They waited in silence, letting Faelan war with his soul.

Brie lay down that night, surprised that she didn't feel the need to cry. She had been certain when she'd watched Sir leave that morning that her pillow would be stained with tears that night. Instead, her heart was full of joy because Faelan had agreed to go through with the surgery.

Brie had been given specific instructions by Sir for her nightly ritual while in Denver. It started with journaling to him, but *not* in her fantasy journal. He had stressed that this time apart would be challenging for them both, and it was vital they stay connected.

"I don't want to miss the varying emotions you'll experience while I'm gone. The only way for me to know them is if you share them faithfully each night. I promise to do the same for you." Sir had handed Brie a new journal and held up his as well. "This is our commitment to each other while we're separated."

Brie took the new journal from the nightstand and

opened it to the first page. It comforted her to know that Sir was doing the same on the other side of the world.

Dear Sir,

Today was quite a rollercoaster! I'm sure you were grinning on your trip to China, knowing how surprised I would be when I saw Tono. Such a flood of emotions, Sir—happiness at his return, anger that his mother was so unkind to him, fear about the surgery ahead, and sadness that he is still alone. I found out it did not work out with Chikako—I was secretly hoping it would.

We tried to talk in the car on the way to the hospital, but it proved too challenging for me so I had to pull to the side of the road to ensure no ducklings were harmed in the driving of the vehicle.

When Tono shared his plans to remain in the States, I wanted to shout for joy! I don't think he's had a moment of peace since his father died. He tries to hide it, but I can tell the toll it's taken, and my heart hurts for him.

As much as I wasn't prepared for Tono, you should have seen Todd. Wow! He became irate (which I found amusing). In a matter of seconds he went from being the sick and weak individual we saw to an angry bull.

It took Tono's wisdom and patience for Todd to finally agree to go through with the surgery.

I'm so thrilled right now I can barely contain myself. He was ready to give up, and now he is getting ready for the fight of his life.

But all this makes me think of you, Sir. How you are facing the exact opposite situation with your mother. Know that my heart is with you, my love surrounds you, and my thoughts are yours.

Love, Brie

Brie closed her journal, laying it back on the nightstand. Sir had given her a second task for her nightly ritual. With a nervous smile, she opened the drawer of the nightstand and pulled out the Hitachi.

Sir had handed her the Magic Wand along with a small box of toys. "You must choose a different instrument to challenge yourself with each night. Imagine your Master controls it, and discover the one that brings you the most pleasure. When I return, it will be the first one I use on you."

His sexy promise made her giddy to try, even though he had picked some demanding instruments. She opened the box and grinned as she examined her choices. She was about to grab the shiny metal clothespins, but her hand drifted over to the Wartenberg Wheel. She knew Sir personally enjoyed the tool, and wanted to see if she could learn to appreciate its spiky caress.

Brie got up and went to her suitcase, pulling out a T-shirt of Sir's. She'd brought it so she could sleep with Sir's scent every night, but she'd enjoyed the way Rytsar had employed it in Russia.

She figured it would enhance the experience and draw her even closer to her Master. Brie plugged in the Magic Wand and laid the shirt on the pillow. She then picked up the wicked little wheel and scrutinized it. "Your job is to bring me pleasure."

Taking a deep breath, she pulled down her panties and turned on the vibrator, placing it against her clit. The delicious vibration sent instant shivers through her. Her body knew this toy well and responded quickly as soon as she imagined Sir was watching over her.

She pulled it away, scolding herself. "Not so fast, woman."

Brie placed the Hitachi back on her mound, and closed her eyes so she could fantasize as she played with the challenging caress of the wheel.

Sir wanted to take her in the garden…

He escorted her to the center of the huge rose garden and laid out a blanket on the grass. "Take off your clothes, téa."

It was a beautiful Colorado day with blue skies and warm sunshine. As she undressed, Brie noticed a slight breeze and her nipples hardened in response.

Sir noticed and commented. "Your nipples are anticipating our play, I see."

"My whole body anticipates your touch," she confessed.

"Lie down, then, so I can begin."

She lay on his blanket, opening her legs expectantly as he removed his shirt.

"No, téa, close those lovely legs. I have something else in mind."

She was surprised by his command, but demurely closed her legs and waited.

Sir pulled out shears from his pocket and started cutting the stems of the most stunning roses in the garden. He seemed very particular about the ones he chose. After gathering a number of them, he stuffed the shears in his back pocket and meticulously removed the leaves from each stem.

She watched in fascination, wondering what he had planned for her. When he was done, Sir laid the flowers beside her and sucked the blood from his fingers. "Roses are beautiful but treacherous flowers."

"They are, Master," she agreed.

"Are you ready to be caressed by such a treacherous blossom?"

She nodded eagerly. "Please."

He picked up a large pink bloom and put it to her nose. "Take in its scent. Know its full character."

She breathed in its fragrance deeply, intoxicated by the sweet perfume.

Sir lightly trailed the soft petals over her stomach, causing a delightful tickling sensation. She purred with pleasure, anxious for more.

Brie rolled the wheel across her stomach and goosebumps rose on her skin. She laid her head back, breathing rapidly, pretending that Sir was dragging the large thorns of the rose across her stomach, causing her to squirm and whimper.

"I told you it's a cruel flower."

He leaned forward and kissed the area that had received its harsh attention. His warm lips caused her stomach to tremble in pleasure.

Brie felt the very real pulsation between her legs announcing her body's enjoyment of the fantasy. She pulled the wand away and forced her heart rate to slow back down. She was determined to make her body work for that orgasm, just as Sir would.

She stared at the spikes on the wheel, deciding that she could take more pressure if she prepared herself for it.

Pressing the vibrating Hitachi harder against her clit, she closed her eyes again, imagining Sir kissing her on the lips as the sun beat down on her skin, his tongue running over her teeth before darting in and claiming her.

Brie moaned, the pressure of his lips and the taste of his mouth very real to her.

Sir picked up another rose, a light purple one with tiny thorns. "A wicked thing, this one. So delicate and inviting…" He let her smell it, the fragrance spicy, like cloves.

The silky petals teased her as they skimmed across her breasts, especially when he ran them over her nipples. However, a cold chill followed, knowing that the thorns would soon take their place.

"Are you ready, téa?"

She turned her head and smashed her face into his shirt, taking in Sir's scent as she moved the Wand to the perfect spot to make her come quickly.

Sir kissed her breasts before he trailed the tiny thorns across them…

Brie ran the wheel over her breasts and gasped each

time it came into contact with her sensitive nipples. "Oh!" she moaned. Brie lifted both instruments from her, panting from the effort.

One more pass and she knew she would come. She deeply inhaled Sir's scent before she gave in to the sensation of the wheel and wand. "Oh, oh, ooooooohhh…." she cried, tears coming to her eyes as she allowed the powerful release.

"Good girl," he whispered in her ear.

Brie opened her eyes. She could have sworn she'd heard his voice, but was disappointed to find herself all alone. She turned off the Magic Wand and laid the wheel beside her, panting with pure satisfaction.

That was when she heard the subtle squeak of a floorboard outside her room. She turned her head to see the movement of a shadow under the door before it disappeared.

Brie blushed, wondering how loud she had been. She quietly put her toys back in the drawer but kept Sir's shirt beside her, curling up in the bed and sighing.

"Good night, Sir. Until tomorrow night…"

She woke up to the savory smell of Tono's favorite breakfast and emerged from her room to find him dishing up a bowl for her.

"Good morning, sleepyhead."

She looked at the clock and protested, "It's only six in the morning, Tono. I don't think that qualifies me as a sleepyhead."

"We have too much to do to waste even a minute," he said with a gentle smile as he handed the bowl to her.

Master Anderson stumbled into the kitchen, rubbing his eyes. "Why the racket at this ungodly hour?"

Tono proceeded to dish him up a bowl as well. "I did my best with the ingredients on hand. I hope you enjoy it."

Master Anderson stared at the mixture of rice, egg and vegetables. "There is no doubt I appreciate a hearty meal in the morning, but not this early."

"Brie needs to get to the hospital to check on Wallace. I was also wondering if I might use your facilities in the next day or two. I only need a single room. I would like to show her what I've been working on."

Brie perked up. "Oh, Tono, do you mind if I film it?"

"Not at all. I'd be honored."

"I suggest you use the auditorium so it can be filmed on stage."

She turned to Master Anderson and beamed. "That would be perfect! Thank you."

"I have another favor to ask," Tono said.

"Certainly," Master Anderson replied agreeably.

"Could I use Lea, or will she be working this week?"

"She does have work all week, but if you do it in the afternoon, there's no reason she shouldn't be able to take part. Of course, you'll have to run it by her first."

"I'll phone her," Brie piped up. "I have to give her a hard time for not calling me yet."

Master Anderson gave her a guilty half-grin. "That

would be my fault, young Brie. I asked her to leave you alone the first two days. Thane wanted it to be just the three of us the night you arrived, and I knew yesterday the Boy would need extra tending after meeting with his donor."

"You're lucky you said something, or I would have ridden Lea's ass for being a crappy friend. Dang, she's probably as anxious as I am to get together."

Master Anderson slid his phone over to her with a sly grin. "Let's find out."

Brie knew he was counting on the earliness of the hour to be a deterrent for Lea's enthusiasm, but she was curious as well to see how her best friend would react to such an early call. She picked up his cell phone and dialed the number.

When it went to voice mail, she hung up and called again. Just before it switched to voicemail again, Lea picked up and cried, "Noooooooooooooooooo!"

"No what?" Brie giggled.

"Wait. Brie? Is that you?"

"Yeppers. What the hell are you sleeping in for?"

"I didn't go to bed until two-thirty, girlfriend."

"Three and a half hours of sleep should be more than enough."

Lea gave her a long raspberry.

"Dang, I've missed you, woman," Brie confessed.

"I missed you too, although I forgot what a pain you can be."

"Don't blame me—Master Anderson was the one who told me to call."

"No wonder his number showed up on my phone."

Master Anderson told Brie, "Inform Ms. Taylor that any plans for retribution had better be tempered by the knowledge that I am allowing her to film with you."

"What was that?" Lea asked.

"Master Anderson is going to let you scene with Tono!"

"Wait… Did you say Tono? What's he doing back in the States?"

"He's Todd's donor."

"Get out!"

"Seems they share the same rare blood type," Brie told her, smiling at Tono.

"Man, Faelan's been so negative about the transplant I didn't think he was going to go through with it."

"Luckily, Tono is a very convincing man."

"Oh yes, he is," Lea purred.

Brie grinned into the phone. "Lucky for you, he wants to show off his new rope tricks. Do you mind if I film the session?"

Lea squealed. "Of course not, Brie! But you'd better hang up now, because I'll need my beauty sleep if I'm going to be on camera. Last thing I need is to have the dark circles under my eyes distracting people from my gorgeous boobs."

"Diva," Brie teased. She stared at Tono critically and commented, "You know, Tono doesn't have dark circles, and he's suffering from jetlag."

"I need my sleep, Stinky Cheese."

"Fine, but you'd better be perky when I see you, Miss Thing."

"No worries, I'll be perky like virgin tits."

Brie giggled. "Before I let you go, I have a joke for you."

"No way. Lay it on me, girlfriend."

"How do you know you're kinky?"

"Tell me, tell me!"

"You know you're kinky if your favorite dessert is hot-cross buns and you don't even like sweets."

Silence met her punch line.

Brie protested. "Seriously, Lea, I laugh at your stupid jokes."

"Oh wait, was that supposed to be the joke?"

"You weenie!"

Lea giggled hysterically.

"You're a butt. Go back to bed," Brie said, hanging up on Lea's wild laughter.

She shook her head, sliding the phone back to Master Anderson. "After all the bad jokes she's made me endure…"

"In her defense, it wasn't funny," Tono stated.

"It's not supposed to be funny, Tono. That's the whole point."

Master Anderson chuckled. "She got you good."

"You're as evil as she is," Brie grumbled, shoveling rice into her mouth, but inside she was laughing.

One point for you, Lea the Lame.

Before they left for the hospital, Brie made one more quick call. "Hey, Autumn, it's Brie. I know it's early, but I'm in town and a dear friend of mine has agreed to do a Kinbaku demonstration for my film. Only hitch is that it'll be happening in the next couple of days. I would love for you to see it. Lea is going to be his partner for the scene, and I think you would enjoy seeing her in action."

"Oh, my goodness, Brie, thanks for the invitation, and I don't want to seem ungrateful, but I don't want to be in your film."

Brie laughed. "Don't worry, the camera will be focused solely on Tono and Lea. Let me sweeten the pot by promising no one else will be there."

Autumn asked hesitantly, "Are they going to have sex?"

"No, this is simply bondage. His rope art is breathtaking. You don't want to miss it."

"You're sure I won't get in the way?"

"Not at all. You'll be keeping me company while they perform."

"Well, if that's the case, I would love to come. I've got a few days of vacation left from work, so it shouldn't be a problem. Just tell me where and when."

After talking to Autumn, Brie grabbed her purse so she could leave with Tono, and they headed to the hospital.

Faelan was in a foul mood when Brie arrived. While Tono met with the surgeon performing the operation, Brie faced the angry brute alone.

"Good morning, Todd. I see you haven't eaten yet," she stated, looking at his untouched tray of food.

Faelan glared at her. "Turn around and leave."

"What's all the hostility for?"

"I feel like shit and I want to be left alone."

"I'll be happy to leave after you eat a solid meal."

"I'm not hungry," he growled.

"Hungry or not, you have to give your body the nutrients it needs to heal after the operation."

"Fine, I'll eat later," he said dismissively.

"Fine, you'll eat now," Brie answered, taking his fork and stabbing the rubbery eggs with the tines. "Here you go…" she said, handing him the fork.

He folded his arms and glared at her.

"Now, Todd, we can do this the easy way or the hard way. You can eat these eggs like a big boy, or I will be forced to take drastic measures."

His glare burned like acid, but Brie met it without cringing. "Last chance or suffer the consequences, big guy."

When he didn't budge, she put the fork down and left. She heard him snort in triumph as she closed the door. Did he seriously think he'd won?

Brie talked to the nurse in charge, who readily agreed to her request. "His refusal to eat has been a sticking point with me. If this works, I'll thank you personally."

A few minutes later, Brie returned with a covered dish and smiled sweetly at Faelan. "Do you know what happens to big bad Doms who refuse to eat their food?" She removed his breakfast tray, replacing it with her new dish. Brie lifted the lid with a flourish. "They get spoon fed like a little baby."

He looked down at the oatmeal and snarled in disgust.

"Last chance, Todd. Will it be eggs or oatmeal?"

"Neither," he huffed, looking towards the window.

"Fine, oatmeal it is."

Brie scooped up a spoonful and made airplane noises as she brought it to his lips.

"Get that away from me."

"Come on, Wolffie, don't make me bring out the big guns."

He clamped his mouth shut and ignored her.

Not in the least bit discouraged, she rolled the tray out of the way and lowered the railing on his bed. Being mindful of the many tubes and monitors connected to him, she carefully mounted the bed and straddled him.

She heard the beeping of the heart monitor increase, and hoped it wouldn't trigger any alarms at the nurse's station.

Faelan stared at her in disbelief as she leaned forward and sensually grazed his lips with the spoon.

"Come on, open those pouty lips and eat this for Mary."

His blue eyes stared at her, unblinking.

Brie was sure he was going to call security and order her to leave, but to her relief he slowly parted his lips. She smiled as she fed him the first bite. "Good job." After he'd finished the whole bowl, Brie pulled out the piece of candy she'd been saving.

"For being so good, you deserve a piece of chocolate," she announced, holding it out to him. Chocolate held a special place in her heart after her auction session with him. She'd never forgotten the driving beat as they'd performed their chocolate dance together.

Brie proceeded to unwrap the candy and put it to his lips. "You earned it." When he wouldn't take a bite, she bit into the decadent chocolate and purred, "Best chocolate in the world…"

She lifted it to his lips again and was pleased when he opened his mouth, taking the bite.

"Isn't it sooooo good?"

He chewed it and swallowed, his eyes never leaving hers. "Brie."

"Yes?"

"Why are you doing this? Why has Davis bothered to do all this for me?"

She stared at him in shock. "Not only are you my friend, but you trained with Sir. We both care about what happens to you."

He rolled his eyes, but she could tell it meant something to him.

Brie licked her fingers to get the last of the rich chocolate and smiled at Faelan. "When I saw you and Mary together at the commune, I was so happy."

"How is Mary—really?"

"She's working hard to be whole again, but as strong as she is, she cries whenever she talks about you."

"I want to believe it, Brie."

"I would never lie to you."

He touched her cheek lightly. "No, blossom, you never have."

Ghosts of the Past

"Brie, there's something I feel I must do before I leave Denver, but I would like you to join me," Master Anderson stated.

She tilted her head, curious what he was asking of her. "Of course, Master Anderson, I would love to. But what's this about?"

"Thane suggested closure would help me break away from Denver cleanly."

She looked at him with sympathy, "Is this about Amy?"

Master Anderson closed his eyes. When he opened them again, she saw intense pain reflected in his jade-colored gaze. "Not just Amy."

"Do you mean her husband?"

He nodded.

"That's a huge step," she said, feeling only compassion for the man.

"The move is forcing it on me. If Thane's right, it must be done before I leave."

"I think you're doing the right thing."

"I don't want her feeling sorry for me, so that's where you come in. Since Amy already believes we're a couple, do you mind continuing that ruse a while longer?"

Brie smiled. "Not at all, Master Anderson. I'll speak to Sir about it tonight."

"Good. I've set it up to meet them at lunch tomorrow. I should warn you that their baby will be joining us."

"Aww…"

"Not 'aww'," he reprimanded. "It will only be a distraction."

She shook her head. "I must respectfully correct you, Master Anderson. The baby is not an *it*."

He smiled, his green eyes showing a hint of the old spark. "Fine, the child is not an *it*, but he'll be a distraction."

"Oh, so they had a little boy and not a girl?"

Master Anderson nodded, complaining, "I hope it doesn't cry through the whole damn lunch."

Brie gave him a disapproving look.

He sighed angrily. "I meant he."

"I know you did," she said with a gentle smile. "I think this meeting is long overdue," she added, wrapping her arms around Master Anderson's muscular waist.

Master Anderson took Brie to the Italian café where they'd run into Amy before. He explained as he helped her out of the truck, "I figure I might as well confront her at our favorite restaurant."

Brie took his hand in hers. "You're not confronting Amy, you're letting her go."

She saw the flicker of pain return, but he nodded. "That's right, I'm letting her go."

The redhead waved the two over as soon as they entered the establishment. Master Anderson escorted Brie to the table, whispering, "I want you to address me as Master."

Brie was surprised by the request but answered amiably, "Of course, Master."

Amy and Troy stood as they approached. There was no disputing that they were a striking couple. Amy, with her long red hair, sun-kissed freckles and big green eyes, and Troy, who was her perfect complement with his dark hair, dark eyes and five o' clock shadow. But it was the man's smile that caught Brie's attention—it was genuine and kind.

Troy shook Master Anderson's hand first. "It's good to see you, Brad." He looked at Brie and took her hand with a warm, firm grip. "And a pleasure to meet you, Miss Bennett."

She smiled, responding to his natural charm. "Please call me Brie."

Amy walked over to Master Anderson and gave him a tentative hug. "I can't tell you how glad I am that you asked us to lunch, especially at our favorite restaurant."

Brie saw him tense as she hugged him, but Master Anderson forced a smile. "It's good to see you again, Amy. Been far too long."

Amy hugged Brie next. "Great to see you again, too."

"Likewise. I see your bun is out of the oven."

Amy giggled. "Yes, he is!"

Troy lifted the baby carrier, saying apologetically, "I'm sorry, he just fell asleep."

Brie peeked under the hood of the carrier and grinned, whispering, "What a handsome little guy." She looked up at Master Anderson, who was staring warily at the baby. "Don't you think so, Master?"

She noticed that Troy shifted uneasily upon hearing her call Master Anderson by that title.

"Yes, Brie, he looks to be a healthy child. That's what's important, right?" Master Anderson said, chuckling uncomfortably.

Brie suspected the forced laughter stemmed from his uneasiness, so she joined in by giggling, hoping the others wouldn't notice. "Yes, and he's a cutie, Amy. A real charmer."

"Such a good baby too," Amy said proudly, looking down at her sleeping child. "Brandon has been a dream come true for us."

Troy carefully placed the carrier on the chair between the two of them before asking, "Would either of you care for some wine?"

"Please," Brad answered without hesitation.

Troy raised his hand and the server immediately came over. "Yes, Mr. Dawson?"

"Our friends would like some wine."

The waitress stared brazenly at Master Anderson when she asked, "Which would you prefer, sir?"

She actually blushed when he turned his full attention on her. "I've always been partial to the house wine here."

The woman bowed her head slightly, a flirtatious smile spreading on her lips. "You wouldn't happen to be Brad Anderson, would you?"

"I am. Do I know you?"

"No, but one of our servers does. Mandy described you to a T." The girl laughed coyly. "Oh, won't she be crying tomorrow when she finds out you were here."

"Please give Mandy my best regards." Master Anderson turned and asked Brie, "And what you would like, my pet?"

The waitress stared unabashedly at the collar around Brie's neck. There was no doubt she knew *exactly* who he was.

Brie smiled affectionately at Master Anderson, wanting everyone at the table to know how much she cared for the man. "I'd be honored to have whatever you're having, Master."

"Perfect. Bring a carafe and glasses for everyone."

Amy held up her hand. "Please, none for me." When Master Anderson questioned her on it, she explained with a blush, "I'm still breastfeeding."

"Ah…" He glanced at Brie, looking chagrined.

"So, you still have quite the reputation here," Brie said after the waitress left, wrapping her arm around his muscular one. "I'm not sure if I should feel jealous or proud, Master."

Master Anderson kissed the top of her head. "No need for jealousy, my pet. No one holds a candle to you."

Troy's unease increased and an uncomfortable silence settled over the table until Amy burst out, "Oh, my goodness! Is that an engagement ring I see on your finger?"

Brie looked down at her glittering diamond and then at Master Anderson, curious how he would handle it.

He smirked, obviously thrown off by the discovery but not one to back down. "It's true, a marriage is in our near future."

Amy grinned. "I'm so happy for you both! It's plain to see how much you're in love with each other."

Brie blushed when Master Anderson took her hand and kissed it. He looked deeply into her eyes and said, "Brie's a rare gem."

Troy interrupted. "Brad, I don't mean to sound rude, but this feels like a setup to me."

Master Anderson nodded, a look of newfound respect on his face. "You're right, Troy. I do have an ulterior motive for this meeting."

"Which is?"

Master Anderson kissed Brie's hand again before setting it on his muscular thigh. "I'm moving to Los Angeles and doubt I will return." He glanced at Amy. "I wanted to clear the air between us before I left Denver."

"I've wanted that too, Brad. I care about you and hate having this 'strangeness' between us," Amy said, relief on her face.

Master Anderson turned back to Troy and stated, "I owe you an apology."

Troy seemed taken aback. "That's probably the last thing I expected you to say."

"Well, I've had a lot of time to think. Although I can justify my actions back then, the fact is I acted dishonorably and it has haunted me since."

Troy stared at Master Anderson as if he were seeing the man for the first time. "Again, you surprise me."

"I suppose you could say that I've gotten a little older and wiser."

"Brad," Amy said with compassion, "I understood why you did what you did, based on the little you knew of Troy. Every time you and I got together it seemed like I was recovering from losing him."

"I only wanted to protect you, Amy."

Her smile held a hint of sadness when she answered, "I know."

Master Anderson addressed Troy again. "It appears you really are as good a man as she claimed."

Troy seemed troubled by the admission, and took a sip of wine before replying. "I suppose I owe you an apology as well."

"How so?"

"Amy always insisted you were acting in her best interests, but I didn't believe it. I've never liked you."

Master Anderson actually smiled. "Understandable. We *were* rivals."

"It was more than that." He glanced at Brie and asked, "Do you mind if I speak frankly?"

"Not at all," Brie encouraged.

"Brad, I've never forgiven you for what you did to Amy. When I saw the bruises I wanted to kill you."

Master Anderson threw back his head and laughed. "Finally, the truth comes out."

"It was no laughing matter to me," Troy stated angrily.

"You do realize it was consensual."

Troy glanced at Amy. "She said as much, but I've never understood it—how a man could hurt a woman like that."

"Maybe I can provide some clarity," Brie offered. She lifted Master Anderson's strong, masculine hand and held it in both of hers before continuing. "This man has the unique ability to please a woman on a level she never knew existed. It is done with respect and a deep-seated desire to please her. Any marks left behind are something to be cherished, because they remind her of that special encounter."

This time it was Amy who shifted uncomfortably in her seat. Brie knew she must be remembering her encounters with Master Anderson and thought, *Poor girl, you probably haven't known that kind of satisfaction since.*

"Thank you, Brie," Troy said. "I've never had it explained to me that way before." He looked apologetically at Amy. "Although you tried to tell me that on several occasions."

"I'm grateful Brie was able to shed some light on it," Amy said, a blush creeping over her cheeks.

Troy addressed Master Anderson again. "So I must apologize for hating you. It appears there was no cause."

Master Anderson shook his head. "Let's be honest. You had a legitimate reason for hating me. I did everything in my power to win her over." He looked directly at Amy while still speaking to him. "And if I'm completely honest, I'm still in love with her."

Amy gasped, tears filling her eyes as she abruptly stood up and murmured, "If you'll excuse me." She ran off to the bathroom before Troy could stop her.

He sat back down, glaring at Master Anderson. "What was the point of that?"

"I wanted to be open, to lay it all out there so Amy and I could experience the closure we both seek."

"Did you honestly think that confession would help any of us?"

Master Anderson shrugged. "If you think for one second she doesn't know I still love her, you're only kidding yourself."

"What about Brie? Don't you have any regard for your fiancée's feelings, or is she supposed to accept it because you're her *Master*?" Troy said with disgust.

"She knows exactly how I feel, Mr. Dawson. Just because I still care about Amy doesn't change how I feel about Brie. That is one important skill you lack. I know how to communicate openly with my partner."

Troy's eyes narrowed. "I beg to differ."

"I'm curious, Dawson," Master Anderson said. "Why did you agree to meet with me today?"

"Because I love Amy and I knew she needed this."

"Admirable."

Amy returned to the table, smiling apologetically. "I'm sorry about that."

After she sat down, Troy took her hand. "Were you aware he still had feelings for you?"

She cringed, but answered, "I wasn't sure…"

"Come on, Amy," Master Anderson urged.

"I *did* suspect there might be something," the redhead admitted, looking down at her lap, her face turning a deep shade of crimson.

"Does it affect how you feel about Troy?" Master Anderson asked.

Her head popped up and she answered defiantly, "Of course not."

"Then why did you run?" Troy asked gently.

"It was so uncomfortable, my love. I didn't want you to be hurt by his words." She kissed Troy on the lips, then glanced at Master Anderson. "And I hate knowing I hurt you."

She shifted her gaze to Brie. "I'm sorry for hurting him."

Brie grinned. "You followed your heart, Amy. There's no reason to apologize for that."

She smiled gratefully. "Thank you for saying that, Brie, because you're right, I had no other choice. I *had* to follow my heart."

Master Anderson pushed his chair back. "So there we have it, the truth laid out in all its ugly yet glorious beauty."

"What are we supposed to do with it?" Troy questioned.

"Accept it, I suppose. I will always love Amy, but I have a new respect for you and I'm glad to see she's happy."

Amy nodded. "And I'm glad that you're getting married soon and will experience the same happiness. Who knows? Our kids may even play together someday."

"Oh no, we're *not* having kids." Master Anderson stated, grasping Brie's chin and kissing her passionately on the lips. "She and I have no interest in messy diapers."

Amy laughed at his assertion. "We'll see about that…"

The waitress came up with the check and whispered to Master Anderson, "If you ever need an extra partner or anything, my number's inside."

He opened the check and handed back her number. "I could never do that to Mandy. I hope you understand."

The woman took the paper, muttering, "Of course," before she rushed off.

Troy raised his eyebrow. "Does that happen often?"

Brie laid her head on Master Anderson's beefy shoulder. "More than you know, but he always lets them down gently."

Troy grunted. "I suppose I had you pegged all wrong, Brad. Thank you for this meeting today. It has been enlightening, to say the least."

"For me as well," Master Anderson agreed.

As soon as the baby started to fuss, Master Anderson stood and held out his hand to Troy. "So, we'd better be going. I wish you both well."

Troy took his hand and shook it heartily. "I wish you success in your marriage, as well as the move to California."

Amy picked up her crying child, cradling him against her chest, and the boy instantly quieted. Brie thought the interaction was beautiful and smiled at Amy.

"We would love an invite to the wedding," Amy begged.

Master Anderson shook his head. "Sorry, Mrs. Dawson, the wedding won't be held in Colorado. However, I appreciate the sentiment."

His casual statement caught Brie's attention. Was it possible that Master Anderson knew where her wedding would be? Surely, Sir must have told him... "I'm curious about the location, Master..."

Amy's eyes sparkled with intrigue. "You mean you don't know where your own wedding will be?"

Brie shook her head, smiling at Master Anderson. "But I'd *sure* love a hint."

Master Anderson laughter filled the restaurant. "My lips are sealed, pet. I'm not spoiling the surprise for you."

"Drat," she pouted.

When the baby fussed again, Brie walked over to Troy. "It has certainly been a pleasure meeting you, Mr. Dawson. I must say you have a lovely wife and the cutest little boy."

"Thank you. I've enjoyed sharing lunch with you. I hope our paths cross again."

"Me too," she said with sincerity.

Brie hugged Amy next, the baby between them. "You have a beautiful family."

"Thanks, Brie. It's been a real treat getting to know you better."

"I feel the same way."

"Come, pet," Master Anderson commanded.

Brie played with the collar around her neck so that Troy noticed, and purred, "My pleasure, Master."

She trusted Troy would take the hint, hoping Amy might enjoy a little side of kink in the near future...

Tono Experiences Flight

B rie was shaking with excitement as she pulled up to the Academy.

Tono laughed beside her. "You're behaving like a little kid at Christmas."

"That's exactly how I feel, Tono," she giggled. "You know me so well—you always have." She reached over and opened the glove box, pulling out the small container that held the orchid comb he'd given her. "I never film without it."

Tono opened the box and lifted out the delicate white orchid, admiring the flower. "Do you mind if I put it in your hair?"

"Please, it would be my honor."

He smiled as he carefully placed it in her hair, his lips coming dangerously close to hers in the process. In another time and place, she would have leaned forward to kiss those lips, but neither of them made a move towards the other.

Tono sat back to admire it when he was finished. "It looks as good in your dark hair as I'd hoped."

Brie lightly touched the petals and smiled. "Thank you, Tono. I've gotten many compliments on it."

"It's unique, like you."

She gazed into his chocolate-brown eyes, trembling with joy. Something was going to happen today, she could feel it in her bones.

He looked at her questioningly. "What's got you so anxious?"

"I'm not sure. Maybe because I get to film you today? I never thought I would have the chance again and you know I love watching you in your element. The icing on the cake is that I get to hang with Lea and you get to meet Autumn. I think this is mounting up to be the perfect storm of happiness."

Tono looked at her curiously. "I didn't realize Autumn was coming."

"I hope you don't mind. I invited her as soon as I knew you would be partnering with Lea." Brie got out of the car and popped the trunk, handing Tono his heavy duffel bag full of jute. He slung it over his shoulder and offered to take some of her equipment, while Brie explained, "This is a rare chance for her to see what Lea does. Plus Autumn is such a graceful person on the ice, I'm certain she'll fall in love with your art."

"If you think she'll enjoy it, I'm fine with her watching."

Brie stopped pulling out her camera equipment from the car for a moment to warn him, "She's *really* shy, Tono. Autumn has never seen bondage of any kind, so this is a huge step for her. Don't be offended if she hides from you."

Tono gave her a half-smile. "I'll keep that in mind when we meet."

Brie picked up the rest of the equipment, bumping shoulders with him. "I can't believe you're really here with me!"

As they walked towards the school, she thought back to the dream she'd had about Tono a few nights earlier, and realized that it must have been her soul hinting at their upcoming reunion. The soul connection she had with him was truly rare and beautiful.

While Brie set up her camera equipment in the auditorium, Tono laid out all his rope on the stage. He then hung the black lights that would add to his unique performance. "I've chosen a toned-down version of my act, since you'll be filming it for the documentary."

"That's perfect, I thin—"

Hands covered Brie's eyes as big boobs pressed against her back. "Guess who?"

"Pamela Anderson?"

Lea giggled as she turned Brie around. "Aren't you cute?"

Brie noticed that Lea was wearing the red kimono she'd worn for Brie's twenty-third birthday surprise. Seeing it brought back a flood of pleasant memories involving the three of them... She grabbed her best friend, squeezing the breath out of Lea. "Oh, I've missed you!"

Lea gave as good as she got, and the two were left gasping for air by the time they were done.

Then Lea turned to Tono, bowing formally. "I'm thrilled to be working with you again, Tono Nosaka."

"I'm looking forward to it as well, Ms. Taylor."

Lea grinned, bursting out, "By the way, I've got a joke for you."

Brie groaned. "Why am I not surprised?"

Lea was not deterred by her lack of enthusiasm. "So, God, in all His wisdom, promised the Dominants that good and obedient subs would be found in all the corners of the Earth…then He made the world round."

Tono chuckled lightly.

"A+ for me!" Lea squealed.

Brie teased her, "Forced to grade your own jokes these days?"

"Hey, I'm the only one who judges them fairly."

Brie hugged Lea again, her heart overflowing with happiness. She wanted so desperately to beg Lea to come back to LA, but knew the decision was not an easy one for her friend. In the end, what Brie honestly wanted was for Lea to remain true to her heart, even if it meant staying in Denver.

"So, Tono Nosaka, is there anything I need to know about this scene today?" Lea asked.

He led her up onto the stage and went over the progression of the rope ties. Brie went back to setting up. She looked through the camera's lens, focusing it on her best friend, and watched Lea nod enthusiastically while Tono explained the scene to her. Brie felt a twinge of jealousy knowing that her girlfriend was going to experience flight with the jute Master.

Once again, woman, you owe me one.

Brie nearly jumped out of her skin when she felt an unexpected tap on her shoulder. She turned to see

Autumn, dressed in blue jeans and a T-shirt, wearing a thin veil that covered the lower half of her face.

"I'm sorry, Brie. I didn't mean to startle you like that."

"Oh, no, that's okay." She giggled, hugging Autumn tightly. "I'm glad you made it!"

"Me too. I've wanted to see what Lea does here."

"Well, you're in luck, because you'll also get to see Ren Nosaka, a world-renowned Kinbaku artist. Since they're going over the scene right now, why don't you sit beside me and we can chat while I finish setting up?"

Autumn quietly took a seat, admiring the comfortable leather auditorium chair. "I didn't realize the school was going to be such a fancy place."

"Master Anderson believes in quality."

"I see that." Autumn watched as Brie finished making the final adjustments to her equipment, and commented, "You must enjoy making films."

"I love it!" Brie answered, not holding back the excitement she felt towards her craft.

Lea heard them talking and looked down from the stage. "Is that Autumn?"

"In the flesh!"

Lea let out a joyous squeal as she ran down the steps. She hugged Autumn tight, looking over her shoulder at Brie. "You sneaky devil."

Brie shrugged. "Once in a lifetime opportunity. Couldn't let Autumn miss out, now, could I?" She then asked, "Autumn, would you like to meet the man who is going to make Lea fly today?"

She seemed startled by the suggestion and sat back

down. "Oh no, I would prefer not to, Brie. Let me just sit here and watch."

"If you're sure," Lea stated, "then it's time to get this party started!"

"Let's," Brie agreed. She called up to Tono, "Are you ready?"

He gave her a thumbs-up, looping the first rope through the hanging metal ring above him. While Lea rejoined Tono on the stage, Brie readied the auditorium lights with a remote control, turning them down except for one solitary beam that shone from above, highlighting the couple.

She whispered to Autumn, "I'll need you to be quiet through the entire performance. My mic will pick it up anything you say."

"Got it."

Even though Tono hadn't given the signal to start, Brie turned on the camera to capture this moment. It was one of her favorite parts whenever she'd scened with Tono—the process of becoming in sync with each other before the formal scene began. Brie suspected movie-goers might find it as romantic as she did.

Lea knelt on the jute mat he'd placed on the floor, and Tono settled behind her with his hands on her shoulders. He leaned forward and whispered in her ear. Brie knew that he was instructing her to breathe with him, as he slowly embraced her in his arms. Brie closed her eyes, slowing her own breath, and soon felt soothing peace enter her soul. She was amazed Tono still held that kind of power over her.

Brie opened her eyes to find him staring at her

through the lens, waiting for her to begin the count-down. She blushed, held up her fingers and silently counted down from five before cuing the music.

The musical piece Tono had chosen for the performance was a combination of traditional flute and low bass drums. It started off dramatically but soon slowed to a sensual beat, drawing Brie into its erotic spell as Tono and Lea swayed to the captivating rhythm.

Brie adjusted the lighting, dimming it to a soft glow as she turned up the black lights, so the dyed jute could reveal its intense colors. She bit her lip as she watched Tono pick up the first bundle of rope and begin binding Lea in a rope harness of fluorescent purple. His movements were graceful, sensuous and precise.

Brie's skin tingled as if she could feel the jute caressing her own skin with its magical touch.

The next color Tono chose was a bright pink, which he used to bind Lea's wrists and legs. He pressed her gently to the floor, continuing his binding by tying Lea in a pose reminiscent of a dancing ballerina.

Tono stood, grabbed the glowing yellow rope from the metal ring above him, and secured Lea's bonds to it. Brie leaned over, whispering to Autumn, "Lea's about to fly."

The two watched with rapt attention as Tono took the strands of rope and pulled on them with such skill that Lea was lifted gracefully from the ground, as if floating by her own power. He tied the jute off and cradled her face, kissing her on the lips before pushing against her shoulder to start her twirling in circles.

"Head back," he commanded.

Lea threw her head back and the pose was complete, the ballerina caught in mid-air.

Brie heard Autumn gasp loudly, and smiled to herself. She didn't reprimand the girl, because the vision before them was extraordinary and poignant. Gasping was a totally appropriate response that the audience would echo.

Tono continued, binding Lea in several different positions. Each was reminiscent of the last but building upon it, becoming more complicated and challenging as he progressed. The bindings the Asian Dom created accentuated Lea's sexuality while remaining elegant, artfully emphasizing her female form as she floated gracefully above the stage.

The entire performance was breathtaking and romantic, enhanced by his occasional kisses and light touches throughout the scene. By the time Tono finished, Brie had fallen completely under his spell—along with Lea.

Brie turned off the camera and sighed quietly to herself. *That was pure perfection, Tono…*

Autumn clapped enthusiastically, the moment Brie stepped away from her camera. "Bravo, bravo!"

Lea was still coming down from subspace after the scene, and was a little slow as she attempted to walk down the steps of the stage. Tono took her by the arm and guided her, sitting her next to Autumn.

"Mr. Nosaka, that was incredible!" Autumn gushed, standing up to face him. "I've never seen anything like it, never imagined anything like it even existed."

Tono held out his hand to shake hers. "Thank you

for the kind words. I'm Ren Nosaka."

She tilted her head, looking questioningly at him. "But Lea always calls you Tono Nosaka."

"That's my title because we work together. Tono means Master in Japanese."

"Oh!" She giggled nervously. "Well, that explains that."

To ease her obvious embarrassment, Brie asked, "What did you enjoy most about the performance, Autumn?"

"All of it! The rope, the music, the overall character of the dance—and it did feel like a dance to me. But what I loved most is that it also possesses the effortlessness found in ice skating."

Brie noticed Tono staring intently at Autumn, and then he did something she would never have imagined the gentle Dom would. Tono reached over and gently tugged on Autumn's veil so that it fell to one side, exposing her face.

"That's much better," he complimented.

Autumn stared at him in shock, but no words of protest escaped her lips. She automatically went to cover the scar on her face with her hand, but let it drop to her side.

"Brie told me you're like poetry on the ice," he said kindly. "I would like to see you skate sometime."

She laughed, shaking her head. "I'm not nearly as graceful as you made Lea today."

"I could teach to you to fly, Autumn."

Her eyes widened as if she was enamored by the thought, but she quickly backpedaled. "Oh no, Mr. Nosaka. It wouldn't be the same." She knocked on her artificial leg. "I would look ridiculous up there."

"You wouldn't wear it," he said with a confident smile.

A flush crept up Autumn's face when she answered, "I couldn't possibly, Mr. Nosaka."

"Please call me Ren."

"Okay…Ren," she said, nervously twirling a strand of her hair with her finger.

Brie turned her attention to Tono and was struck by the change in his countenance. His eyes were sparkling and his smile melt-worthy. Was it possible a new romance was budding before her eyes?

Oh, please, please let it be so… she thought.

The Cat's Out of the Bag

It had been a particularly hard day, fighting to keep Faelan's spirits up the day before his surgery. Brie returned to Master Anderson's home early, collapsing on his couch.

"Bad day?"

"Sometimes I think Todd actually beats me in the stubborn department, and that's saying a lot," she groaned, dragging her hands over her face in frustration. "That boy is killing me…"

Master Anderson sat down beside her. "Maybe you need a nice bullwhip session to get the tension out."

"I hate to break it to you, Master Anderson, but I find your bullwhip is a tension-maker, not a tension-taker."

He laughed. "A cooking session, then?"

"Again, tension-maker."

"A sure-fire tension releaser is rough sex, but since a good romp in the hay is out of the question, how about joining me in a practical joke?"

"We're not pranking Ms. Clark again, are we?"

"No, my plans are far bigger, young Brie."

She looked at him warily, but the distraction was desperately needed. "Count me in."

"Good. You'll be acting as my plant to help engage the others involved. I simply need you to react to what you see—overreacting would be even better."

"Am I required to wear a ridiculous outfit?"

"No, but you'll need to dress in businesslike attire. You're going as one of the investors I'm meeting with tonight."

"Sounds a tad boring."

"Boring?" He laughed. "Never! I live for this stuff."

"Hmm… I suddenly understand why you prank others so often. You're in serious need of a permanent sub. By your own admission, 'If a romp in the hay is not an option, pranking is the next best thing'."

He shook his head, grinning. "Touché, young Brie, touché."

Due to the upcoming surgery, Tono chose to remain at Master Anderson's house to meditate. "I must ready my mind and body," he explained, when Brie asked if he wanted to join them.

"Of course, Tono. Would you rather I stay here with you?"

"No, a solitary evening would be beneficial to me."

"I support whatever you need," Brie said, letting out an anxious sigh.

"Why the heavy heart?" he asked, tucking a stray curl behind her ear.

"I'm worried about you—about both you and Todd."

"Whatever happens is supposed to happen," Tono assured her. "I've lived that truth my whole life."

She was hesitant to express her deepest fear to him. "But Tono, this surgery carries serious risks."

"There is no point in worrying about what *might* happen. If tomorrow is my last day—"

Brie was about to protest, but he put his fingers to her lips. "What would you want to say to me?"

Her lip trembled. She didn't want to contemplate the worst out loud, but when he lifted his fingers she took the opportunity to speak from the heart. "Knowing you has changed my life, Tono Nosaka. You've become a part of me."

"As you are a part of me. I tell you this with a full heart. If I were to die tomorrow, I would have no regrets. I've lived a full life. There would be no reason to mourn."

"But I would mourn, Tono."

"And you would look back on this day and know that I'm okay."

Brie closed her eyes, struggling not to cry. Tono responded to her unspoken pain by whispering, "No regrets…"

Brie arrived at the Denver Academy with Master Anderson an hour before the Submissive Training course began. "It's imperative that I have everything ready," he explained, "but you can't help, because I want your reaction to be as genuine as possible."

"What do you want me to do until then?"

"Keep Baron company. He's extremely allergi—No, never mind. Just go to the teacher's lounge. You'll find him there."

Brie liked the assignment he'd given her and asked no more questions. She found Baron reading a newspaper while sipping a cup of coffee. He put the paper down when she entered the room. "What a pleasant surprise."

"Master Anderson sent me. He said you might be a little bored while he sets up whatever this thing is that he's setting up."

Baron smirked. "That man is always hatching something. We're lucky he doesn't possess an evil bone in his body, or we'd all be in serious trouble."

She sat down next to him, scooting her chair closer. "A little bird told me you're planning to return to LA."

He folded his newspaper and set it on the table. "I am. I was willing to stick it out here with Master Anderson, but the moment he informed the staff he was heading back to California, I volunteered to follow."

"I can't tell you how happy that makes me. LA hasn't been the same without you."

"I miss the old haunts, and never really found my groove here."

"Will it be hard returning to the places that remind you of Adrianna?"

"I plan to move somewhere new—a fresh start in the city where she and I fell in love."

Brie smiled, putting her hand on his. "She would like that."

There was a sneeze on the other side of the door just before it opened. Ms. Clark waltzed in, her high heels clicking rapidly as she hurried to grab a tissue before she sneezed again. "Why does he do this to us?" she grumbled, wiping her nose.

Baron's chuckle was deep and easy. "I can't complain—Anderson keeps things interesting here."

Ms. Clark gave Brie an unexpected smile. "So, Miss Bennett, I see you're back with us."

"I'm only here tonight to help Master Anderson. I'm planning on being at the hospital most of this trip to look after Mr. Wallace and Tono."

"We're all praying for them, kitten," Baron said compassionately.

"Thank you. I'm sure it will go well, but—"

"There are no buts, Miss Bennett. They will both be fine," Ms. Clark interjected.

Brie nodded, knowing there was no solace to be found with Ms. Clark.

The Domme changed the subject by asking her, "Are you almost done filming the second documentary?"

Brie didn't mind the shift in the discussion and answered, "I'm close." She turned to Baron. "That reminds me. I would really love to film you, Baron. Would you be willing?"

"Let me think on it. I saw how Faelan was hounded by desperate subs after your first film came out. I'm not interested in that kind of attention."

"I'll respect whatever you decide," Brie answered, still hoping he would consent.

"Miss Bennett," Ms. Clark barked, "I would like to have a private conversation with you at some point while you're here."

Brie's heart rate shot up when she turned to face the Domme, Rytsar's warning coming to her mind. "What about?" she asked lightly.

Ms. Clark inclined her head toward Baron. "It's *private*."

Stalling for time before she gave a definitive answer, Brie replied, "Before I commit, I'd like to talk to Sir."

"If you feel you must," the Domme stated dismissively, before sneezing into her tissue. "The hell I put up with working under that man."

Baron laughed. "You know you love it, Samantha. Why else would you join in?"

"I only do it because I respect Brad as my Headmaster," Ms. Clark said defensively, but then her lips curled into a dangerous smile. "Of course, seeing the reaction of his intended victims is always entertaining."

Master Anderson popped his head in, addressing Brie. "Are you ready? The show is about to begin." He handed her a pair of glasses, as well as a tablet and stylus. "We need you looking the investor part. Just write down anything that sounds important while I give my sales pitch.

"As for you, Baron," Master Anderson added, "remain here until Lisa confirms the facility has been cleared. You'll be heading the panel during my absence tonight."

"Good luck," Baron replied.

"With fifty—" Master Anderson looked at Brie and stopped short, shrugging his shoulders. "What could possibly go wrong?"

"Not a thing," Baron said, chuckling.

When Brie slipped on the plastic frames, Master Anderson whistled in appreciation. "I knew you'd make an enchanting geek, Miss Bennett." He rushed her out of the room, explaining, "The first of the investors should be arriving any minute."

Master Anderson escorted her to the front entrance, telling his secretary, "Lisa, I have a last-minute addition to our list of investors. A Kristoffer Larson will be joining us."

"Certainly, Master Anderson."

He smiled mischievously when he shared, "Gunnar Larson and I have an 'accidental' encounter planned. It should prove entertaining."

"Of course," Lisa answered, grinning to herself as she dutifully added the name to her list.

He whispered to Brie, "We have a little love connection in the works. Gunnar suspects Kristoffer and one of our current students—a cute little redhead named Pamela that I've had my eye on—might be the perfect match. Gunnar's hopeful a nudge in the right direction might set things in motion for these two unsuspecting colleagues. Tonight, we'll see if his instincts prove right."

"That's so romantic," Brie cooed.

"But it's not why you're here," Master Anderson explained. He opened his mouth to say more, then groaned, as if not telling her was a great sacrifice to him. "No, I can't say another word, damn it!"

She laughed, loving that he was fighting not to divulge any more of his devious plan. "I can't wait to see what you've got planned, Master Anderson."

Brie took on her businesswoman persona the moment the first investor entered the school. She held her back straight and crossed one leg in front of the other to make for a more pleasing form to the eye.

Master Anderson strode over to greet the first man, his whole demeanor suddenly morphing into that of a serious business owner. "Welcome to the Denver Academy, Mr. Rodriguez…"

Brie watched in admiration as he interacted with each individual as they came in. They not only responded to his obvious knowledge of the business, but his natural charisma. She noticed, however, that he kept glancing towards the front doors, stalling for time.

The moment a middle-aged gentleman with a solemn disposition entered the school, Master Anderson strode over, holding out his hand. "Ah, you must be Kristoffer Larson. Glad you could make it—I was beginning to worry. I know Gunnar voiced particular interest in this property."

The man did not smile as he shook Master Anderson's hand. "I apologize for being late. There was a five-car pileup on I-70 near Georgetown. It couldn't be helped."

Brie watched covertly as they talked. She was struck by the contrast between the two men. Master Anderson was tall and muscular, with jet-black hair, chiseled good looks, and a winning smile, whereas Mr. Larson was leaner, but toned, with shoulder-length blond hair slightly gray at the temples, furrowed brows, and a somber expression on his handsome face.

Observing the man more closely, however, Brie noticed that Mr. Larson seemed unsettled, as if something were weighing on him. When he caught her staring, his gaze held hers because of the intensity of those piercing blue eyes—a Dom for sure.

She smiled apologetically, pretending to adjust her glasses before turning her focus back to Master Anderson. There was no doubt in Brie's mind that the serious-minded man could benefit from Master Anderson's friendly nudging. *Oh, Mr. Larson, you have no idea what you're in for tonight…*

"Before we enter the school proper," Master Anderson said, standing at the front to address the group, "let me explain the concept behind the Denver Academy. While we run both a Submissive and a Dominant Training Program, tonight I will focus solely on the submissive aspect. Our training consists of an intensive six-week course that tests and refines the men and women chosen to attend our classes. Each night they begin with a formal lesson, then they move on to a practice session critiqued by a panel of Dominants, and finish with a personalized practicum centered around the individual's interests and talents. At the end of each week of the course, we hold an auction attended by vetted Dominants from the community. They take our students for an extended excursion outside the walls of the school, where the submissives receive additional practice and a written critique by the winning Dominant. In every way, we strive to prepare our students to become skilled submissives who are not only confident in their talents, but also highly sought-after by the BDSM community worldwide."

"Isn't there a school like that in California?" one of the investors asked.

Master Anderson nodded. "You are correct, and our curriculum is based off of that highly successful program."

The man who'd asked the question scribbled in his notebook, so Brie followed suit, using her stylus to type in the information on her tablet, hoping she would appear like a serious investor.

Master Anderson continued, "We take the privacy of our students seriously, but I've informed the class of tonight's agenda and they've graciously agreed to allow an observation of the lesson."

Brie trembled as Master Anderson led them down the hall to the first classroom on the right. She fondly remembered the excitement of being a student, and warm feelings of nostalgia washed over her as she listened to the teacher's confident voice lecturing on the other side of the door.

Master Anderson instructed in a low, commanding tone, "Please line up against the wall to the left as you enter, and remain quiet. I'll answer any questions you have *after* we exit the room." He opened the door and the group was treated to an anatomy lesson—one that Brie remembered well.

Pamela, the pretty redhead Master Anderson had

spoken of, was standing in front of the class beside a muscular male. Both were completely naked.

Brie snuck a peek at Mr. Larson, who seemed to be scanning the classroom and making mental notes, until he spied the redhead and his eyes opened wide in surprise. He shifted his feet, which inadvertently garnered the attention of the woman. When their eyes met, a pink hue crept over Pamela's face. She quickly turned back to face her classmates, pretending she hadn't recognized him, and Brie didn't miss the worried look in her eyes or the slight frown on her lips before she set them in a firm, straight line.

"Mr. Avery, please come up to the front of the class and name the anatomy of both sexes."

One of the male submissives stood up from his desk and took the wooden pointer the teacher handed him. Brie smiled to herself, recalling when Boa had stood before her as she'd pointed to his impressive manhood while naming each part.

To Pamela's credit, she showed the same confidence Boa had. Any sign of her earlier distress was gone as she focused on the back wall of the classroom, her head held high but at a respectful angle.

Brie stared at Pamela unashamedly, admiring the beautiful contrast of her red pubic hair against her pale white skin. She suspected Mr. Larson was appreciating that triangle of curls as well, or perhaps that Mr. Avery was pointing out the pink areola of her breast near her very erect nipple. Mr. Larson surreptitiously loosened his tie before undoing the first button of his collar. The attraction he felt for her was obvious to Brie, and she couldn't help wondering how things would play out between them when they met again outside the school walls.

The group was ushered out of the room once Mr. Avery had successfully named the various body parts of both sexes. Brie noticed that Mr. Larson was the last to leave, and smiled to herself. While Master Anderson answered questions in the hallway, she casually glanced at Mr. Larson again. The man's attention returned several times to the door they had just exited. Even though he hadn't been taking written notes during the tour, he was obviously no longer making mental notes either.

Master Anderson noticed his distraction as well, and winked at Brie.

The next stop on the tour was the row of practice rooms specially furnished and designed to accommodate specific kinds of play. "You will note that a fully functioning kitchen is utilized in our training as well. We want every graduating student to please their Master's full range of appetites. I have seen firsthand that some of the submissives we train are in dire need of such instruction." Master Anderson glanced briefly in Brie's direction, chuckling loudly as he continued down the hall.

"And this is my crowning glory," he announced, as he opened the doors to the luxurious theater-in-the-round. The dramatic reveal was met with appreciative whistles from the crowd.

"The practicums are the heart of this training program. It was important for me to invest accordingly. We have state-of-the-art lighting and sound systems, as well as fine leather seats for the students and trainers. If you look above the stage, you will notice a variety of equipment hanging from the ceiling, which is lowered for use as needed during training."

"This is quite a remarkable setup you have," Mr. Larson stated, once again engaged with the tour.

"Thank you. It's my belief that to create superior graduates, you must utilize superior equipment and hire only the best trainers. There's no reason the Denver Academy can't become as renowned as the Submissive Training Center in LA."

For the last part of the tour, Master Anderson guided them to a large, open room with an impressive assortment of BDSM furniture and suspension equipment. "Unlike the Training Center in California, this warehouse is large enough to include a dungeon area especially designed for the use of the bullwhip. The area itself is perfect for community gatherings and special events, and can be an added revenue generator when classes aren't in session."

A stern-looking female raised her hand and asked, "Does all this equipment come with the school?"

"Yes, everything you see here is included with your purchase of the Academy. As an added bonus, you will also receive the experience and talent of the staff members who remain."

Mr. Larson tucked a strand of his blond hair behind his ear before asking, "Will training continue for the current class of students if the center changes hands within the next six weeks?"

"Rest assured, Mr. Larson, as Headmaster of the

school I will not be abandoning my current students. Only after this class has graduated will the transfer of ownership take place."

The object of Pamela's attentions narrowed his eyes and nodded curtly. Brie was certain his interest in the future of the students was for purely personal reasons.

Score!

There was quiet murmuring among the investors when Ms. Clark walked into the room, dressed in a slim, black business suit, her high heels clicking seductively as she joined the large group.

Master Anderson introduced the Mistress to the potential investors. "This is Samantha Clark, a long-standing faculty member of the Submissive Training Center. She understands the program inside and out, and will remain part of the training panel after I'm gone." More murmurs erupted and Master Anderson responded by adding, "You need to be aware that I've asked several staff members to stay in order to ensure the quality of the program remains consistent. As part of the contract, I will also have the program evaluated each year to confirm that the Denver Academy continues to meet the high standards I have set."

"That's highly unusual," a shorter man wearing thick plastic frames complained beside Brie.

Master Anderson smiled broadly. "This is a highly unusual school."

Suddenly a door opened on the far side of the dungeon and a hefty man entered carrying a large cardboard box—followed by a steady stream of cats.

"Not again!" Master Anderson cried in frustration.

"What the hell?" the man beside Brie exclaimed.

Brie looked around in utter shock as at least fifty cats stormed the dungeon. Master Anderson growled, barking commands to his staff. He sounded properly exasperated when he apologized to the group. "Could you please excuse me for a moment?"

Brie feigned a look of horror, even though she was giggling inside. *Cats? Really?*

One of the staff members picked up a bullwhip from the wall and started swinging it at the creatures.

Master Anderson yelled at him, "For God's sake, Ryan, put that down now. You might hit one of the damn things."

An orange tabby rubbed against Brie's leg and she screamed loudly, clutching the short man beside her for protection. "I hate cats," she whined. "They're too much like giant rats!"

The group of investors became more agitated with her antics as the entire Academy staff—minus Baron—arrived to descend on the cats.

Ms. Clark picked up a crop and tried to herd the cats in one direction, hissing, "Shoo, shoo…"

"Ms. Taylor," Master Anderson yelled at Lea, "I need a little help here!"

Lea grabbed two paddles off the wall and tried to direct the clowder of cats back into the far corner, where Master Anderson stood ready to grab them. She waved the paddles wildly, saying in a deep, manly voice, "This is your captain speaking, please find your way to the nearest exit."

"Make the awful things go away," Brie begged, continuing to cower against the man next to her while she watched the reigning chaos with delight.

To her surprise, Mr. Larson took her antics seriously and reached down to remove the cat from her ankle, idly stroking its neck while he watched the bedlam around them. She noticed a wedding band on his finger and wondered why Gunnar Larson and Master Anderson were trying to hook up a married man.

But the cats soon distracted her again as they scattered, some even climbing onto the equipment to avoid capture. Brie noticed a fluffy white Persian sitting primly on a spanking bench, licking its paw as if it didn't have a care in the world. Ms. Clark tried unsuccessfully to sneak up on the beast, but her high heels gave her away. The moment she was close enough to grab it, the cat jumped down dismissively and disappeared under the bondage table.

Finally, the man who had let the cats in managed to catch one standing on the top of a St. Andrew's cross. He held it up proudly for all to see.

"Good job, Nathan," Master Anderson called out.

The man walked to the door, struggling to hold on to the squirming creature. When he opened the door to throw it out, three more cats ran in to take its place.

Mr. Larson shook his head, smiling for the first time. "Herding cats? You can't be serious, Mr. Anderson."

"What?" Master Anderson asked innocently, holding two mewing kittens in his muscular arms.

Larson raised his eyebrow, a knowing smirk on his face.

Master Anderson handed the tiny felines over to Ms.

Clark and pointed at him. "I *knew* I liked you for a reason." He reached out to take the tabby from Mr. Larson's hands, before whistling loudly.

A new door opened and, as if by magic, the cats headed towards it. When Master Anderson set the tabby down to follow its comrades, the feline rubbed against Mr. Larson's dark pants leg, leaving a patch of white-and-orange fur to mark its territory.

Before it left, Mr. Larson bent to give it one last ear-rub with his large but gentle hand, almost making Brie want to purr herself. To his credit, he didn't even attempt to brush the fur from his once-impeccable suit.

Turning her gaze toward the retreating cats, Brie nearly lost it when the Persian sauntered past Ms. Clark, its head held high in a dismissive manner as it strolled towards the door.

Master Anderson crossed his arms, staring intently at the group of investors as the door closed with a resounding clang. "This was simply my way of illustrating how investing can be a lot like herding cats unless you know what you're doing. This Academy is growing, and will continue to grow at a steady rate with the right person heading it. You may think that you came tonight to decide whether this is the right investment for you, but you'd be only partially correct. I will not hand over this business unless I feel confident that you are worthy to own this training center."

"Well played, Mr. Anderson," Mr. Larson replied, clapping his hands in admiration. Brie joined in the applause with everyone else, impressed by the meaning behind his little stunt.

It was easy to see that Master Anderson had won them over with his unconventional methods, and he was peppered with questions as he led them to a meeting room to lay out the numbers in black and white.

Master Anderson was absolutely brilliant, so that by the time he'd finished, many of the investors had voiced interest in becoming the new owner of the Denver Academy. Brie noticed, however, that one investor kept glancing at the door. It appeared that Mr. Larson was far more interested in a certain red-headed trainee within the walls of the school than in Gunnar Larson's financial future.

Brie gave Master Anderson a slight bow of her head when he looked in her direction, wanting to show her gratitude at being included in the evening's events.

It had been exactly what her heart needed.

A Good Day

B rie arrived home late from the Academy and knew the next day was going to be brutal. Still, she faithfully wrote to Sir in her journal, adding a brief fantasy rather than challenging herself with a toy. She hoped Sir would not only understand, but employ it at some future date.

The Intruder

I'm woken by a strong hand covering my mouth.

"Don't scream, or I'll hurt you."

My mind sifts through the fogginess of sleep, quickly becoming alert when it registers that this man does not smell or sound like my fiancé.

"Please don't hurt me," I plead when he takes his hand away.

"Lie still and I won't have to."

I start trembling, my body thrown into the primal fight-or-flight instinct when he rips the blanket from me and whistles his admiration at my nearly naked body.

The hand returns to my mouth as he starts to caress me with the other. I can only stare at this frighteningly beautiful stranger as he invades me with his touch, squeezing my breasts and pinching my nipples before his hand heads lower.

I feel him tug at my panties, but I refuse to cooperate, squeezing my thighs together. It proves to be of no consequence, as he rips the material from my body and tosses it aside. I whimper in terror and hear him chuckle in response.

Knowing that he hungers for my fear, I remain silent, even when he forces his fingers between my legs.

His middle finger grazes over my clit, demanding entrance into my sex, but my pussy is dry and tight. I attempt to bite the hand covering my mouth, but he growls in anger and moves it from my mouth to my throat, pressing against my windpipe.

The action effectively quiets my protests.

"Open those legs."

I resist until the blood starts pounding in my ears, my body desperate for the oxygen it needs. I spread my legs for him and he rewards my obedience by easing the pressure around my neck.

He forces his fingers inside, and I squirm but make no sound.

"Good girl," he praises, as if I am his pet.

My body is initially resistant to his manipulations, so he changes tactics, unzipping his pants. He repositions himself, straddling my chest and presenting me with his rigid manhood.

When I turn my head, he responds by increasing the pressure around my throat. "Come on, baby, open that mouth and suck that cock like a good girl."

I shake my head, but when the pressure on my throat increases, I open my mouth reluctantly.

"That's it," he murmurs, forcing his large shaft between my lips. "I want to see it disappear down that pretty little throat."

He releases his hold on my neck, grasping my hair with both hands as he forces me to take all of him. I am left gagging on his cock, and try to pull away, but he holds my head still, telling me, "I want you to choke on it."

To my horror, he reaches between my legs and discovers I am wet. He looks at me, a knowing smile on his lips, but says nothing.

When he tires of my mouth, he announces, "I'm going to fuck you hard."

"No!"

He laughs wickedly. "I never leave a wet pussy unsatisfied."

The man grabs my wrists in one hand and lifts them over my head as he settles between my legs. I feel the head of his penis pressing against my opening and I cry out.

"Make no mistake, I'm going to give this body exactly what it wants…"

Brie closed her journal and slipped it under her pillow, wanting to feel closer to Sir. She closed her eyes and eventually drifted off to sleep.

The alarm went off far too soon, but Brie dutifully dragged herself out of bed and dressed. Checking her phone, she was relieved to see a text from Sir, sent while she was sleeping.

Thinking of you today. Be strong.

She texted back.

I will, Sir. Love you.

She stuffed the phone into her purse, then walked out of the room, looking for Tono. She found him sitting cross-legged out on the patio. She opened the sliding glass door and asked, "Do you mind if I join you?"

"Please," he answered, patting the ground beside him.

She knelt down and looked at the colors of dawn making their appearance in the eastern sky. The vibrant hues were spectacular, but did little to calm Brie's nerves.

"How are you?" she asked.

"At peace. And you?"

She smiled sadly. "Not so much."

"Clear your mind," he ordered gently.

She closed her eyes and listened to the birds singing as they greeted the new day. It was easy finding peace beside Tono, and it didn't take long before her spirits were lifted.

"Thank you, Tono."

"Today will be a good day," he stated, as he leaned over and gave her a hug.

She wrapped her arms around him, resting her chin on his shoulder. "Yes, it will," she agreed.

They headed to the hospital early so that he could be prepped for surgery. Once Tono was settled in his room, Brie left to check on Faelan.

She noticed he had a grimace on his face when she entered the room, but it disappeared as soon as he turned towards her. "Well, look what the cat dragged in."

At the mention of the word cat, she laughed softly. "Did you hear what happened last night?"

"Yes. Lea called to wish me luck and filled me in."

Brie shook her head, thinking back on the night's events. "It was nuts, Todd."

"Sounds like it."

She took his hand, gazing into those ocean-blue eyes, and saw a look of foreboding in them. "How are you doing this morning?"

"I don't want to do this, Brie. I'm only consenting for the sake of others, not myself."

She lifted his hand to her cheek and admitted, "I don't care what your motivation is as long as you go through with the surgery."

"How is Nosaka doing?"

"He's at peace. There's no doubt he wants to do this."

Faelan broke eye contact and looked out of the window. "He's a brave man."

"Yes, he is. I think his courage comes from knowing this will save your life."

He looked at her again. "I don't like being on the receiving end."

She kissed his hand and laid it back on the bed. "I know."

"If anything happens…"

Brie shook her head. "Don't."

He ignored her plea. "If anything happens, let Mary know she was my last thought."

Brie looked at the ceiling to hold back the tears. Once she had them under control, she looked him in the eye again. "I promise to tell her if needed, *but* I won't have to. The surgery is going to be a success."

"And one more thing."

"What else?"

"Thank you."

Brie smiled. "I'll have you know there'll be a piece of chocolate waiting for you when you wake up."

"I'd prefer to wake up to heavy bass."

She winked, giggling. "I'm sure that can be arranged as well…"

Faelan's parents entered the room, so Brie took her leave, hugging them both on her way out. She could see the excitement and hope radiating in his mother's eyes.

"This is really happening," Mrs. Wallace exclaimed.

"Yes, it is!" Brie answered, matching the woman's enthusiasm.

"We can't thank you enough for all you've done."

"Ren Nosaka is the hero here."

Mr. Wallace spoke up. "We just finished visiting with him, Miss Bennett. What a remarkable young man."

"I wholeheartedly agree," she said. "I'm headed back to him now."

As she was leaving, Faelan called out, "Brie." She turned and smiled at him. "Don't forget what I said."

She knew what he was referring to, but refused to consider that he might not survive the surgery, and answered, "Heavy bass. You've got it!"

Brie returned to Tono and found him surrounded by jars of preserves. "Wow, Todd's mother sure has been busy."

Tono chuckled as he looked them over. "It's a virtual fortress of fruit."

She picked a jar up, examining the homemade label

crafted with care and smiled. "This appears to be a fortress of fruit protection made with love."

"I like that sentiment."

"His parents are so excited, Tono. I don't think they believed this day would ever come."

"How is the Boy?"

"Struggling, but still going through with it." Brie put the jar down and walked over to him. The reality of what was about to happen hit her full force.

"How are you, Brie?"

"Good."

He laughed softly. "Why do you bother lying to me?"

Brie shook her head, tears welling up in her eyes.

"It's okay. You can voice it out loud."

"I'm still afraid for you."

Tono stared at her for a moment, then motioned Brie to him. "Listen to my heart." Brie pulled down the railing and rested her head lightly on his chest. His slow, steady heartbeat resonated in his chest, declaring his vitality and strength. The sound of it soothed her growing fears.

She lifted her head and smiled at him. "It's strong."

"Remember that when you sit in the waiting room." Her fears suddenly seemed foolish as she stared into his warm gaze. He reminded her, "I will be okay."

Brie nodded.

She gave him one last kiss on the cheek for luck when Flora, one of his attending nurses, came in and announced that he was being taken to the operating room. Brie headed to the waiting room still riding high on Tono's confidence, and burst out in giggles when she saw Master Anderson, Lea and Autumn waiting for her.

"I didn't expect you guys to be here!"

"Before he left, Thane insisted I stand in his place today," Master Anderson explained.

She ran to hug him, thankful for his added strength while she waited through the dual surgeries.

Brie looked upwards and silently said, *Thank you, Sir!* before giving Lea and Autumn both hugs. "You guys are the best."

Autumn held up two 'Get Well' signs she was holding. "I thought we could hang these up in their rooms."

Lea looked at them and grinned. "Hey, we could have a little fun decorating their hospital rooms. What do you think?"

"Sounds a lot more fun than sitting around here worrying," Brie replied.

"We should go to a party store if we want to do this properly," Lea insisted.

Master Anderson sat down. "I'll stay here and hold the fort."

Brie's eyes lit up. "Fort? Oh, that gives me a great idea for Tono."

The girls giggled and chatted as they made their way to the elevator. Two hours later, Brie was placing the final touch, a little flag on the top turret of the fortress she'd created out of Tono's jars of preserves. "He's going to love this!" she stated proudly, stepping away from the windowsill to admire her creation.

"Brie," Master Anderson said, walking into the room, his voice tense with worry. "You need to come. Something's happening. I'm noticing a lot of activity."

Brie's stomach sank, her whole body becoming numb as she rushed out of the room. She ignored the shouts of the nurses as she scooted through the closing doors of the restricted area and ran down the hallway until she found the operating room with all the commotion.

She stared through the glass window to see Tono surrounded by a crowd of nurses and doctors. Alarms were blaring as they rushed about, but her eyes were glued to the heart monitor—her worst fears realized as she watched the straight line move across the screen.

"Tono…"

Time stopped. She felt the numbness consume her body while she watched helplessly as the paddles were brought out. His chest lifted from the table as the electricity was applied, but he lay back down limp and unmoving, the line continuing with cruel conviction.

Brie turned away and slowly slid down the wall, hugging her knees to her chest as she struggled to breathe. All thought faded into darkness as fear took hold of her. She heard faint voices insisting she leave the area, but she did not respond until she felt the strong arms of Master Anderson lifting her.

"He's gone," she whimpered.

Master Anderson said nothing as he carried her to the waiting room and cradled her in his protective arms. Lea and Autumn sat on either side of her, crying silently, but she was in too much shock to shed a tear.

Tono.

Master Anderson understood his role well and held her even tighter, sharing his strength while reminding her that she was not alone.

A short time later, Flora came into the room and walked straight over to Brie. She stood up to face the nurse, even though she was afraid of what Flora had to say.

"The surgeon wants you to know that Mr. Nosaka has been revived and his vitals are reading normal. Dr. Shepherd will speak to you later, once the surgery is complete. He expects Mr. Nosaka should be moving to the recovery room in the next hour or so."

"Can I see him then?" Brie managed to choke out.

"No, I'm afraid not—he'll need to be closely monitored—but once the doctor gives his consent, you will be sent for."

Brie touched her arm, needing her reassurance. "He's okay, Flora?"

"Everything appears normal, Miss Bennett. Mr. Nosaka is a healthy man, and Dr. Shepherd remains optimistic he'll make a full recovery."

Once the nurse had left the room, Brie finally broke down, letting out all the pent-up fear and pain that had been building inside her. It was a cathartic release in the arms of her friends.

Both surgeries were successful, but it was hours later before Brie was allowed to see Tono. He was still being closely monitored, but the surgeon surprised her by agreeing to let her visit him briefly.

She moved the curtain aside and was stunned to see Tono gracing her with a faint smile, tubes running everywhere from him. The nurse monitoring his vitals pointed to where Brie could stand.

She moved to his side, her heart in her throat as she stared down at him.

He gazed up at her—the two speaking volumes without words. When he lifted his hand weakly, she grabbed it, holding on to it with both hands.

Brie swallowed hard to get rid of the lump in her throat so she could speak. "You left me, Tono."

"But I came back," he whispered hoarsely.

Brie kissed his hand, covering it with fresh tears. "I was so scared."

"It's okay."

Her lip trembled as she nodded.

"The Boy?"

"He's in recovery too."

"Good."

"It's best that you keep this short," the nurse said curtly. "The doctor only agreed because Mr. Nosaka insisted on it."

Brie leaned over and gently kissed him on the cheek. "Thank you."

"I could feel your fear."

"Now you will only feel my healing thoughts."

After she left him, a second nurse directed her to another bed in the recovery area. "Mr. and Mrs. Wallace have asked that you speak to their son."

When Brie pulled back the curtain, she was shocked by the contrast between Tono and Faelan. His skin was ashen in color, and he looked despondent.

"The surgery was a success," she reminded him.

Faelan looked at her with such agony that she hurried to his side. "What's wrong?"

"Nosaka almost died."

"I was just with him. He's fine. You don't have to worry."

"He should never have taken the risk."

"But he did, and now your body has a healthy kidney. This is a good day," she insisted.

"How can you say that when his heart stopped on the operating table?" Faelan closed his eyes, the devastating pain easy to read on his face. "I almost killed another man today."

The overwhelming guilt he carried hit Brie. "Todd, don't."

He opened his eyes. "I'm not worth another man's life."

"Tono believes you were worth the risk."

"And he almost died because of it. I'm nowhere near as good a man as he is. Not even close."

For the first time since knowing Faelan, Brie heard humbleness—not arrogance—coming from his lips. "You most definitely were worth the risk he took, based solely on what you just said."

"What?" he growled. "You enjoy seeing me grovel?"

"No, I like seeing you humble. It's a positive step."

He gave her an icy stare. "Get out."

"Normally I'd be offended, but I kind of like it when you're feisty."

"Out. Now."

"Fine, but heavy bass and chocolates are waiting in your room. Not that you deserve it."

He snarled as she left, but it was music to Brie's ears. She was convinced that Faelan would be okay.

Brie dug her phone out of her purse, needing to hear Sir's voice, and was disappointed not to have any messages or texts from him. She tried to call, but it immediately clicked over to voicemail, so she was forced to leave a message.

"Please call, Sir. I *need* you."

After spending time with Lea, Autumn and Master Anderson at an old-fashioned diner across from the hospital, Brie excused herself. Food held no interest for her—all she could think of was Tono.

"I hate to cut this short, you guys, but I'm heading back to the hospital."

"Wait, Brie," Lea said. "Before you go I have a little funny you can share with Tono."

Brie knew it would be bad, but suspected Tono might appreciate it. "Hit me."

"I love *everything* about pain play except for one thing."

"What's that?"

"The pain part."

Brie snorted as she shook her head. "Is that even a joke?"

"It made you laugh." Lea grinned.

Autumn giggled. "Hey, I liked it."

Brie looked at her incredulously. "But Autumn, you like all of her jokes."

"Because they're funny!"

"Girl, I need to take you to see a real comedy act. You have no idea what funny is."

Autumn looked shyly at Brie. "I have one I think he might like."

Brie assumed it would be terrible, but urged her to share anyway. "I'm sure Tono will enjoy it. Give it to me."

"What's round and tastes like an orange?"

"Hmm…" Brie thought for a moment, but nothing came to mind. "You've got me stumped."

"An orange."

Master Anderson burst out laughing. "I like that, Miss Autumn. Simple but effective. You have my seal of approval."

Brie shook her head in disbelief. The fact that Lea and Autumn were equally unfunny was astonishing to her.

After promising Master Anderson she would return to his house soon to get some rest, Brie made her way back over to the hospital. She was happy to find that Tono had been taken to his room by then—a positive sign.

When she walked in, she noticed that most of the tubes and monitors had been removed. "You look more like yourself, Tono."

He nodded, managing a pained smile. "Don't feel like it yet."

"It really hurts, huh?"

"The drugs help, but it only takes the edge off."

"I wish I could do something to help you."

"I know what would help."

"Anything, Tono."

"Come lie with me."

She looked back at the door, worried. "Do you think it's allowed?"

"I don't care."

Tono grunted as he scooted over to make room for her. His heart monitor shot up, but quickly calmed down as he worked through the pain.

"Oh, Tono," Brie whimpered. "I can't stand seeing you in agony."

"Come, then," he insisted.

Brie lowered the railing and carefully lay down, covering them both with the extra blanket before settling down beside him.

"I feel better already, toriko."

She noticed he'd used her sub name, but at that moment it was exactly what she needed to hear. She'd almost lost him…

As she lay there with Tono, listening to the reassuring rhythm of his heartbeat, she was haunted by the image of his lifeless body lying on the operating table and the tears started to flow.

"There's no reason to cry," he gently chided.

"Today I came face to face with how fragile life is."

"It *is* fragile, which is why every moment must be savored."

Brie looked up at him. "This experience highlighted just how much you mean to me." She settled back, laying her head lightly on his chest.

He kissed the top of her head. Again the heart monitor jumped as he worked through the pain caused by the effort, but it quickly returned to its slow, steady beat.

"Have you decided where you'll be headed after you recover?" Brie ventured.

"I'm beginning to think Denver might be a good place to settle."

Brie snuck a peek at him. "Is that because a certain ice skater lives here?"

He chuckled, then groaned loudly. "Laughing hurts."

"Then I'd better save Lea and Autumn's jokes for another time."

"Feel free to share them."

"No, although they aren't funny, I would never risk hurting you." Brie grinned knowingly at him. "So you *like* Autumn, don't you?"

He smiled. "I would like to know her better."

"I bet you're unaware that she helped decorate the room. She made that for you."

He glanced at the sign that read, *Get Well Soon, Master Ren Nosaka!*

"Did she now? That was thoughtful of her." He looked over at the fruit fortress Brie had built on the windowsill. "I appreciated my fortress of protection as well."

"It seems you really needed it today." Brie settled back down again, smiling to herself. "Considering all that's happened, this has ended up being a good day."

"A very good day," he agreed, holding her closer.

"Tono?"

"Yes, toriko?"

"The world is a much better place with you in it."

When Brie returned to Master Anderson's home, she found a big bowl of soup waiting for her. "I want to warm your belly before I put you to bed, young Brie. I noticed how little you ate at the diner."

She smiled apologetically. "But I'm not hungry."

Master Anderson pulled out a chair and directed her to sit. "Still, you will eat my soup even if I have to force feed you. I can't shirk the duty Thane entrusted me with."

Brie frowned as she took out her phone to check it again. "You know, I haven't heard from him all day."

He handed her the spoon. "Take a bite and I'll tell you why."

Brie brought a spoonful of the warm soup to her lips and slurped it, purring at the soothing meld of broth and herbs swirling on her tongue.

"One more," he insisted.

She would have protested, but it tasted so good that she obliged.

"I got a call from his sister this evening. Apparently Thane's phone disappeared—most likely stolen—although the tracking on it shows that it's still in the hotel. The theft wasn't discovered until late in the afternoon, after they returned from visiting his mother. He's torn apart his room looking for it. From the little his sister shared, it sounds as if things are going badly over there."

Brie's heart dropped at the knowledge Sir might have

experienced a day as difficult as hers. She hadn't considered it, and felt terrible now for being short-sighted. "How is Sir?"

"I don't know. The connection kept cutting out, so we had to keep the phone call short. Thane has no idea what happened with Nosaka today, which may be for the best—considering."

Brie's concern showed on her face.

"Another bite," he insisted.

She swallowed another spoonful, pondering what he'd said. "I wonder why Sir didn't call me using her phone?"

"I was told he tried several times but the calls failed to go through."

It relieved Brie to know that Sir had made an attempt. She looked down at her soup, the day's events weighing heavily on her. "I don't know how I would have survived today without your strength, Master Anderson."

"I'm grateful to have been of service, but I also owed you one. It's fortunate Tono Nosaka survived the operation. Not only because he is a good man, but because losing him would have devastated many people in my circle. Hell, I don't know if the Wolf Pup could have survived the guilt."

"You're not kidding. He's taking it hard enough as it is."

"I hope he doesn't waste Nosaka's sacrifice."

"I'll do everything in my power to make sure that doesn't happen, Master Anderson."

He took the utensil from her and fed her himself. "This must come from him. You are not responsible for what happens."

She nodded, taking the next spoonful he offered her.

"After I finish with you here, I want you to take a warm shower and go straight to bed. That's an order."

She smiled. "Thank you, Master Anderson. For everything."

"You have been strong, but I have a feeling you will be tested even further by Thane's situation. Don't lose heart, and if all else fails, eat a good soup. It will see you through."

He wiped her mouth with a napkin once the whole bowl had been finished, then dismissed her. Brie did as he commanded, and was surprised when he came to tuck her in.

"Straight to sleep," he ordered as he covered her with blankets.

Brie called out as he was leaving, "Sweet dreams, Master Anderson."

"Same to you, young Brie." He gave her a wink before turning off the light.

Once the door was shut, she turned on her phone for added light and pulled out her journal so she could write. She told Sir everything that had happened that day from the moment she woke up to now, sharing her hopes and fears to the smallest details, like Lea and Autumn's awful jokes. She wanted him to feel he had been there with her the entire day, and desperately hoped he would do the same for her.

Afterwards, she grabbed Sir's shirt and pressed it against her cheek. Brie was fearful of what was coming, but she fell asleep determined to meet it with courage.

Positive Force

B rie woke up to the subtle sound of her phone vibrating. She checked it and saw that Sir had texted her from Lilly's phone. She dialed the number immediately.

"Sir, I'm so glad to reach you!"

"Shouldn't you be asleep?" he asked. She was instantly alarmed because the tone of his voice sounded distant, cold.

"I was asleep, Sir, but I've been waiting for your call and woke when you messaged me."

"I didn't mean to wake you," Sir said irritably, as if he regretted texting her.

"But I'm *glad* you did. I needed to hear your voice."

He paused for a moment before replying, "Last night was rough. I'm still recovering from it."

"What happened?"

He chuckled angrily. "I don't know what kind of local concoction I drank, but I'm suffering from an intense headache today, and my memory of the evening has been compromised."

Brie was deeply concerned. Sir wasn't the kind of man to drown his sorrows with liquor. "Were you with Lilly last night?"

"She insisted we get out of the hotel and celebrate."

"Celebrate what?" Brie was surprised having assumed things were not going well.

"Lilly saw my mother open her eyes briefly." He let out a low groan. "It's the last thing I need, Brie—the possibility that the Beast might recover."

She couldn't help questioning Lilly's claim. "Do you think it's possible she might have imagined it? We both know how close she was with your mother."

"I have considered it, trust me. However, the only way to be sure is to have another scan for brain activity. I can't cut life support until that question has been resolved. Based on Lilly's excitement yesterday, I'm afraid she'll be crushed when the results of the scan come in— and I can't even consider the alternative."

"It's so sad, Sir. Either way, one of you is going to suffer."

"Yes."

When Sir didn't say anything more and didn't ask about the surgeries, Brie decided to share what had happened to Tono. Her voice caught when she said, "We…almost lost Tono."

"What do you mean you almost lost him?"

"His heart stopped on the operating table." Tears rolled down her cheeks as she thought back on that moment. "They were able to revive him, but—"

"But what?"

"I saw it. I saw Tono's lifeless body, Sir." She broke

down sobbing, unable to say more.

"I trust Brad was with you."

She swallowed hard several times before she could quiet her sobs. "He was, Sir, and he was wonderful support. However, he isn't you."

Sir didn't reply. As the silence stretched, Brie feared the phone connection had been lost.

"Sir?"

"I'm sorry I wasn't there for you."

She suddenly regretted saying anything because of the pain she heard in his voice. "I'm fine, Sir. I don't know what I would have done if Tono had died, but he didn't."

"How is Nosaka now?"

"When I left him last night he was in pain, but in good spirits."

"And Wallace?"

"The fact that Tono's heart stopped has really messed him up."

"I'm not surprised. Wallace has lived with the guilt of that young man's death for most of his life. I can only imagine what effect Nosaka's own brush with death has had on him."

"It's bad, Sir. He looked so despondent after the surgery. I don't think he'll ever forgive himself."

"If anyone can center Wallace, Nosaka is the man to do it." Sir abruptly changed subjects. "Have you had time to work on the film?"

"I've filmed Tono's scene. I hope to shoot Baron in the next day or two, but he says he needs permission from you."

"Why would he require permission?"

"Baron wants to reenact the scene he and I did together the second day of training. He says it will involve the swing and clitoral stimulation with a toy, but no penetration."

Another long pause followed before he answered. "I trust Baron, but question whether you would you be able to use the footage in the film."

"I believe so. I will be wearing clothing to cover the important parts, and if it's shot properly, the action can be alluded to instead of shown."

"Call Holloway to confirm it. If he gives you the green light, Baron has my permission to proceed with the scene."

"Thank you, Sir." Brie paused before asking, "I would also like permission to speak with Ms. Clark privately."

"In regards to what?" he asked, sounding slightly annoyed.

"She wouldn't say because Baron was present at the time."

"You already know how I feel about Samantha, but if you'd rather not speak to her, you can tell her I would not allow it."

"To be honest, Sir, I'm curious to find out why she wants to talk, but I can't help thinking about Rytsar's concern."

"I highly doubt Samantha means you harm."

Again, she noted the irritation in his voice and wondered at the cause. "You're right, Sir. Thank you."

"Let me know how the conversation goes. Is there

anything else?"

He was trying to end the phone call, but she wasn't ready to let him go, so she asked, "Do you mind if I read you my journal entry from yesterday?"

Her request was met with silence, but to her relief he finally said, "Please do."

Brie read her emotional entry, choking on her tears several times as she read it to him. She waited to hear his response, hoping he would comfort her. Instead, she heard detachment in his voice when he confessed, "I was unable to write anything last night. I don't even remember how Lilly and I made it back to the hotel."

Goosebumps rose on her skin knowing Sir wasn't engaged with her. She was certain something was fundamentally wrong with him. "Please talk to me, Sir."

But he did not allow any further conversation, stating, "There's nothing to talk about. Start your day, Brie."

"I want to fly out to you."

"I left you with a duty to perform. Give Nosaka my regards," he ordered before hanging up.

She headed to the shower, needing to eliminate the cold chill that had settled over her. Afterwards she sought out Master Anderson, seeking his wisdom as a long-time friend of Sir.

Even though it was still early, Brie knocked lightly on his bedroom door. She heard nothing and was about to return to her room when the door opened. Master Anderson stood before her in nothing but his pajama bottoms.

When he saw the look on her face, he insisted that she come in, sitting her on his bed. "What's going on?"

Brie looked around, suddenly distracted. Unlike Sir's bedroom back home, there was nothing here that hinted at the BDSM lifestyle. She noticed family photos on the dresser but was too far away to see the faces of his kin. There was a feeling of intimacy being in his bedroom, as if another layer of the man was being peeled away.

"What's this about?" he asked as he sat down beside her. "I assume you must have spoken to Thane."

She nodded sadly. "You mentioned that Sir and I might be tested, and based on my conversation this morning, I'm afraid you're right. Something's wrong with Sir."

"Tell me what happened."

"I guess Lilly claimed that his mother opened her eyes, and she's convinced the Beast is recovering. Naturally the idea of that has Sir in a tailspin."

"I can only imagine…" Master Anderson muttered.

"But even more disturbing is the fact that Sir went out drinking with his sister last night and totally blacked out. That doesn't sound like Sir at all."

Master Anderson's eyes narrowed. "I'll see if I can't talk to him myself. It could be that he doesn't want to burden you with his problems after what happened to Tono."

"I'd be grateful to hear if he shares anything more with you, Master Anderson."

He growled under his breath. "Something is definitely wrong."

"I know." Brie's bottom lip trembled as she fought back her tears.

Master Anderson held out his arms to her and she

settled into them, soaking up his strength and comfort. He squeezed her tight, chuckling softly. "You are a tiny thing to carry so much weight on your shoulders. Would you like me to make you some more soup?"

She shook her head, a giggle escaping at the suggestion, even though she was upset. "I can handle whatever comes our way as long as I know *what* it is that I'm facing."

Lifting her bodily from the bed, Master Anderson put her down facing the door. "Get yourself ready to head to the hospital. I'll speak to Thane today and let you know what I learn."

Brie left his room feeling more confident with Master Anderson on the case. She felt certain he could get Sir to confess what was really going on.

"Good morning, Tono."

He looked up from his arm, where the nurse was drawing blood, and smiled at Brie. "Every new morning is a good morning."

She nodded in agreement. "How are you feeling today?"

"Actually worse than yesterday."

Brie frowned. "I'm sorry to hear that."

Tono shrugged with a grimace. "It's to be expected."

"Well, if that's the case, I hate to think how Todd is doing today."

"I'm going to walk to his room so I can see for myself."

"But you just had surgery!" she protested, not willing to have him sacrifice his health further.

Flora, the nurse, explained as she finished taking the last vial of blood, "Miss Bennett, it would be best if Mr. Nosaka starts walking today. It aids significantly in recovery."

Brie frowned at Tono, still concerned. "But you're already in so much pain…"

"And yet I must walk."

Brie sighed in frustration, lamenting, "I wish I could take some of the pain—that I could help somehow."

"You can. Once Miss Flora is done, take me for a stroll. Based on how I feel today, I have a suspicion that Mr. Wallace is in serious need of company."

Flora glanced up with a look of concern on her face at the mention of Faelan, but quickly looked back down, continuing her work.

Tono told Brie, "And that's all the motivation I need to get on my feet."

Brie watched helplessly as Flora helped Tono to stand. Although he grimaced in pain several times, the Asian Dom never made a sound, but she noticed his white-knuckled grip on the IV pole.

Tono took a couple of deep breaths before asking, "Would you help me, Brie?"

She hurried over, offering her arm as support, but cringed when she heard his sharp intake of breath as he took his first step. Tono wobbled momentarily from the pain, but straightened his back and willfully took another.

Red Phoenix

"Excellent!" Flora praised from behind him. "With that kind of determination, you'll be walking out the hospital doors in no time."

He gave her a slight nod. "I'm certain that under your exceptional care, my recovery will be doubly quick."

Tono took it slowly, halting several times to rest and regain his composure, but not giving up until he was standing in front of Faelan's hospital room. It was no surprise to Brie that Todd's parents were standing outside it, looking bereft.

Mrs. Wallace looked at Tono in shock. "How? How are you walking so soon after surgery?"

"It's a requirement if I am to heal."

She shook her head, tears falling down her wrinkled cheeks. "My boy is in no shape to walk. He seems even worse today than yesterday."

"That is why Mr. Nosaka came to speak to him," Brie said, putting her hand on the woman's frail shoulder, instinctively wanting to comfort her. "He knows the pain your son is suffering and can help him to fight through it."

Brie hadn't been prepared to see Faelan in the same condition he'd been in on her first visit. His eyes were closed and he was breathing in short, shallow gasps.

"Mr. Wallace," Tono called.

When he got no response, Brie begged, "Faelan, please open your eyes."

His eyelids fluttered open, but when he saw who was standing before him, he closed them again, growling as he scratched weakly at his arm. "The itching won't stop."

"I'm sure you've been told that once the kidney

88

starts functioning fully, the itching should cease."

Faelan opened his tortured blue eyes and stared at Brie. "It's driving me crazy, Brie. I can't make it stop."

"There is a solution," Tono informed him.

Faelan's gaze rested back on Tono, his tone desperate. "What?"

"Get out of the bed and start moving."

Faelan's nose crinkled into a sneer. "Are you out of your fucking mind, Nosaka? I can barely move, much less walk." He scratched angrily at his chest, snarling more loudly.

"Trust me, the pain of moving should take your mind off the itching. It will also speed the healing process."

Faelan huffed in resentment. "You may have donated your kidney, but you have no idea how much I'm suffering right now."

Tono sat down slowly, sucking in his breath as he did so. Once he'd settled into the chair, he looked at Faelan and smiled. "I agree. I do not know the level of your suffering."

Faelan stared at him, the anger in his eyes slowly transforming into guilt. "You almost died."

Tono nodded. "I stopped breathing, it's true. However, I was fully present. I saw the doctors working to revive my body and I felt the presence of Brie with me. It was a remarkable experience."

Brie turned to him, stunned to hear he'd had an out-of-body experience. And yet…it gave her considerable comfort too. Even in death, they'd been connected.

"Why do you do that?" Faelan complained. "Why do

you put a positive spin on everything?"

Tono raised an eyebrow. "It's how I have chosen to lead my life. How have you chosen to lead yours?"

Faelan looked away, unable to meet Tono's candid stare.

"You've been given a rare opportunity, Mr. Wallace. A second chance ripe with possibilities. What you decide to do with it is totally up to you. You are in control."

"You make it sound so easy, Nosaka, but you have no idea how hard I've had it."

"And you have no idea about me," Tono stated firmly. "Still, you can choose to be a positive force in the world or a negative one. I see no point in wasting my life being negative."

Faelan looked at Brie and said in an accusatory tone, "I suppose you subscribe to the same philosophy?"

"It comes naturally to me."

He rolled his eyes. "Well, it doesn't for this man."

Tono struggled to stand, accepting Brie's help when she offered it. Once he was on his feet, he straightened his back with great effort. "It's as easy as that. I choose to stand, even though it hurts. I accept the assistance of others because it eases the journey."

He held out his hand to Faelan. "Stand with me, Mr. Wallace."

"There's no way I can walk," he retorted.

"I'm only asking you to stand. Each obstacle you overcome will make you stronger."

Inspired, Faelan attempted to swing his legs over the edge of the bed after Brie lowered the side rail. He grunted in pain and frustration after several attempts, then lay still. When Brie tried to help, he slapped her hands away irritably.

"Get away, I can do this." After resting for several minutes he tried again, but the pain proved too much. "I can't," he finally cried, laying his head back in defeat.

"Why didn't you take Brie's hand?" Tono asked.

"I'm a man, damn it, not a mouse."

"You look like a mouse to me."

Faelan's nostrils flared in anger. He gritted his teeth as he lifted himself again, letting Brie help him to swing his legs over the edge of the bed. He reluctantly took the hand she offered as he pushed himself off. The jolt when his feet made contact with the ground caused him to grunt in pain, but he slowly straightened his back and glared at Tono, eye to eye.

The Asian Dom bowed his head in acknowledgement. "A good effort. The next few weeks will forge your character in ways you cannot foresee, and will solidify why you were spared those many years ago."

Tono had purposely exposed Faelan's greatest fear— the burden of surviving, which he had carried all his adult life. The look of vulnerability on Faelan's face when he stared at Tono nearly did Brie in.

"You believe that, Nosaka?"

"I *know* it for a fact. You were meant for great things, Todd Wallace, and this was the path you were destined to take in order to prepare for it."

When Brie saw Faelan wobble slightly on his feet, she took his arm and helped him back onto the bed. He continued to stare at Tono, as if he were afraid to believe him.

"You can endure pain, and you can do the same with disappointment, because both will hone your spirit. In some ways they are our greatest allies, even though we resent their company."

"Is that what life is to you, Nosaka? A constant struggle?" Faelan asked, shaking his head. "What's the point of going on if we're only meant to suffer?"

"I don't feel that way at all. I'm simply sharing my philosophy on living a satisfying life. I invite the lessons of pain and disappointment so that I will not dwell on them. Without resentment, I am free to enjoy the many facets this life has to offer." He looked at Brie. "Including deep and abiding friendships."

Brie looked at Tono, overcome by a feeling of love and gratitude. Faelan noted the expression on her face.

"Are you truly happy, blossom?"

She met his gaze and smiled. "Yes, I am."

Faelan tilted his head slightly as he studied her. "That must be why I found you attractive when we met. I never understood my obsession with you until now."

She gave him a questioning look. "I'm not quite sure how to take that."

"You are a positive force in the world."

She blushed under the intensity of his magnetic blue eyes and murmured, "Thank you."

Faelan growled unexpectedly as he started scratching again. "God, I hate this constant itching. It's going to be the death of me."

"Think of it as purposeful torture." Tono suggested. "You are being tested to prove which is more powerful—the discomfort, or your will."

Faelan breathed in deeply, forcing himself to stop scratching. After a few seconds he snarled, his body twitching in discomfort. "It'll require everything I have to fight against it."

Brie encouraged him, "Then let it take over. *Don't* fight it. I know it goes against your nature, but by submitting to the sensation—mentally allowing it—you'll tap in to a different kind of strength… At least, that has been my experience as a submissive."

"Sage advice," Tono agreed.

"I suppose if that fails," Faelan snorted angrily, "I'll try standing again, 'cause that hurts like a motherfucker."

Tono chuckled, then groaned in pain. "On that note, I will return to my own bed, but I don't plan on remaining there long." Tono grasped his IV pole and started towards the door.

Faelan called out, "Nosaka."

Tono turned slowly to face him.

"I appreciate it." Although he was obviously uncomfortable expressing himself, Faelan continued, "The kidney, the risk you took… This second chance—I won't let you down."

"I know your character, Mr. Wallace, and never questioned your success."

Faelan surprised Brie by putting his hands together and bowing his head to Tono.

Tono let go of the pole and returned the bow, a look of mutual respect on his face.

Brie felt lighter in spirit as she followed Tono out of the room, sincerely impressed by both men. Tono had the ability to strike at the heart of a problem, but in a way that empowered the individual, while Faelan remained young and stubborn, but showed an inner strength few possessed—now it was laced with a newfound humility that would carry him even farther.

She walked alongside the Kinbaku Master as he made the arduous trek back to his room. Brie stared at him in wonder as they walked, blurting, "You saved a life—literally. There aren't many people who can make that claim, Tono."

"To have that kind of opportunity is rare," he agreed, smiling even though he was panting with effort from the walk.

"Todd is lucky to have you in his life," she said, wrapping her arm around him in support, "but not half as lucky as me."

Baron's Sultry Session

B rie was surprised to come across Ms. Clark just outside the hospital when she was leaving. "What are you doing here?"

"I came to pay my respects. Why so shocked, Miss Bennett?"

"I suppose I'm not used to seeing you outside the school setting, Ms. Clark," Brie muttered, feeling completely unprepared for a confrontation with her.

The Domme put her fingertips together, highlighting her long, blood-red nails. "I wanted to inform you that I will be present when you film with Baron."

"That's not necessary," Brie assured her, feeling her hackles rise at the suggestion.

"Nonsense. You need someone to film the tight shots, don't you? I'm the best option you've got if you want it to pass Mr. Holloway's exacting standards."

"You have experience shooting film?" Brie asked her in disbelief.

Ms. Clark's eyes twinkled with unsettling merriment. "There's so little you know about me, Miss Bennett. If you would prefer someone else, I'll respect your wishes. However, I guarantee you'll compromise the shoot if you do." Ms. Clark gave her a nod and walked into the hospital without allowing Brie a chance to respond.

Unfortunately, Ms. Clark's assertion proved to be right. Brie was unable to find anyone comfortable enough with the camera to take over the shoot for her. She lamented the fact to Master Anderson that night.

"You should be grateful. It's rare for Samantha to offer help of that nature."

"Well, it doesn't feel like an honor to me. It feels like she's spying on me because Sir's not around. Speaking of Sir, were you able to reach him today?"

Master Anderson shook his head. "I left several messages on Lilly's phone and eventually ended up calling the hotel. Although I speak very little Chinese, I established that he was out for the day, as was Lilly."

Brie frowned.

"Until we hear differently, let's assume that whatever is happening has his full attention. I'm sure he'll call later when he has the time and inclination."

Brie grudgingly took his advice, but found it difficult to concentrate as she drove to the Denver Academy. She arrived an hour early, not thrilled about having to scene with Baron in front of her former trainer. She certain the Domme would be looking for flaws to point out to her later.

She had convinced herself that Ms. Clark didn't care for the idea of her being alone with Baron, even though Sir had given his permission. The thought of that provoked Brie to no end, but there was little she could do. Mr. Holloway had made it clear in her last meeting that she needed different angles and plenty of close-ups capturing facial expressions in each scene. Brie was afraid the lack of those elements had been the reason Holloway nixed Marquis' compelling performance. With so little time left, she couldn't afford to make the same mistake twice.

She placed Tono's flower in her hair and calmly waited for the Domme. When she heard the clicking of heels out in the hallway, Brie lifted her chin. She greeted Ms. Clark with a smile when the formidable woman entered the theater.

"Miss Bennett, it's fortunate we finally have a chance to speak alone."

"I'm sure you won't mind if I set up while we talk," Brie answered, wanting to establish that the film was her primary focus.

"We're both professionals here," Ms. Clark replied coolly, but Brie didn't miss the hint of annoyance lurking behind her tone.

It might have thrown Brie off in her earlier days, but she took a deep breath and set to work placing her reflectors. "What do you want to talk about, Ms. Clark?"

Her answer took Brie completely by surprise. "I want to speak to you about Lea."

Brie stopped what she was doing and stared at the Domme.

Is Ms. Clark about to confess her love?

"What about Lea?"

"I'm sure she's mentioned her feelings for me."

Brie nodded.

"Although I'm fond of the girl, it's recently become an issue."

Brie suddenly felt ill. "What do you mean, an *issue*?"

"As you're aware, Master Anderson is going to head the school in LA and Baron plans to join him, but I've gotten the impression that Lea plans to stay for my sake."

Feeling the need to protect Lea, Brie kept her answer vague. "She hasn't decided yet. I know she likes Denver, and her friend Autumn lives here."

Ms. Clark narrowed her eyes. "Miss Bennett, don't be coy with me. Lea has declared her love on several occasions."

Brie stared at her numbly, feeling certain her best friend was about to get her heart broken by the Domme.

"As I said, I…care about Lea," Ms. Clark stated, a red hue coloring her cheeks. Maybe Brie had misread the situation. "Because of that, I need you to do me a favor."

"Go on."

"Since you are such good friends with Lea, I was hoping you could convince her to return to LA when Master Anderson leaves."

Brie's jaw dropped. "But you just said—"

"Lea is an extraordinary person, but she's still young. I want to see her take full advantage of her potential while she remains free and unattached." There was a hint of regret in her voice when she added, "I've wasted too many years chasing ghosts. Lea should not suffer for it."

"So you love Lea?" Brie asked hesitantly.

The Domme shot Brie a look that let her know she had overstepped her bounds by asking. However, Ms. Clark surprised her by responding to her question a few moments later. "It's the reason I'm letting her go. She wouldn't leave if she knew my true feelings—you and I both know that."

For the first time, Brie felt empathy for the woman.

"You need to make a strong case for Lea to return to LA. It's best if she feels she made the decision to leave. It'll comfort her if she has moments of doubt later on."

"What about you?" Brie asked, realizing this would be the second time Ms. Clark had lost out on love.

"I'll be taking charge of the Dominant Training at the Academy. I need to focus on my skills rather than relationships."

The Domme's candidness left Brie mute. She returned to setting up her equipment. "I'll do what I can, but you know Lea has a mind of her own. She's held out hope you would collar her."

Ms. Clark surprised Brie by coming up behind her, so close that she could feel the woman's warm breath on her neck. "I'm depending on you to release her from that dream, Miss Bennett."

Brie didn't move, her heart suddenly racing. She turned to face the Domme and found herself staring at Ms. Clark's sensuous red lips.

"I'll…do my best." It was unsettling having those bright-red lips so close to hers. Why on Earth did she have the urge to kiss them? Brie shook her head and scooted away. This wasn't the first time she'd felt an uncharacteristic stirring for her former trainer.

What was it about the woman that inspired such an instinctual—albeit unwanted—attraction? She found herself blushing and turned away, hoping Ms. Clark hadn't noticed.

"Succeed, Miss Bennett, or I will be forced to hurt her, and I don't want it to end like that between us."

Brie could better understand her friend's obsession with the Mistress now that she knew Lea's affections were returned, but she wondered if it was possible to break her of such a powerful attraction—especially if there was any chance Lea suspected Ms. Clark's true feelings.

It seemed like an impossible task, but for Lea's sake, she would try.

Baron entered the theater, a playful smile on his lips as he asked in his deep, baritone voice, "Are you ready for me, kitten?"

Brie felt familiar chills as memories of their first encounter together flooded her mind. "Baron!"

Ms. Clark picked up the camera, pretending to look over the equipment as she composed herself. Brie caught the Domme staring at her intensely on several occasions as Brie talked to the Dom. She wondered if Ms. Clark regretted being so open with her. She'd certainly exposed a side of herself Brie had never seen before.

While Baron waited, Brie changed into simple black lingerie that showed skin but did not bare any intimate parts. She covered up in a silk robe before double-checking her equipment. Brie was definitely curious how he was going to play out the scene this time around.

Back when she'd first known Baron, he had frightened Brie because he reminded her of the violence she'd experienced as a child in grade school. Yet he had been so gentle that night, he'd been able to make a difficult lesson one she still looked back on with fondness.

Before they began, Baron explained, "I want you to think back on how you felt the second night we scened together. Let *those* feelings play out as we scene today. I'm striving to evoke the same emotions a new sub experiences when punished for the first time under the caring hands of a Master."

"I've never forgotten that lesson, Baron," Brie admitted. "It spurs me daily not to disappoint Sir."

Ms. Clark focused the camera on Brie and replied snidely, "And yet you still do, Miss Bennett. Maybe a second lesson *is* necessary."

Baron shook his head at the Domme. "Don't insult my kitten, even in jest."

Brie loved Baron for his protective nature!

After going over the details of the scene with Ms. Clark, Brie slipped off her robe, shedding her director's persona as she bowed at Baron's feet.

He rifled through his tool bag, retrieving an item before ordering her to stand before him. Brie let out an audible gasp when she looked up, caught off guard by the dark leather hood he was wearing.

Of course… Baron had worn a similar mask for that second session, and just like that night, it made the dark Dom seem dangerous and foreboding. She instinctively lowered her eyes.

"Look at me," Baron commanded.

Brie gazed up into his hazel eyes and was reminded again of their calming effect.

He handed her a tiny vial. "Rub five drops of this on

your clit before you join me." He left her to her task as he made his way onto the stage and waited.

Brie dutifully poured a few drops from the vial onto her fingertips and slipped them under her panties, covering her clit with the oily liquid. She did it a second time to apply all five drops her Dom had commanded.

She already knew the effect it would have, and was not surprised when heat started building between her legs. There was no doubt that Baron wanted to make this simple lesson a challenge for her.

She wiped her hands on a towel before joining him on the stage. As she approached the masked Dom, she felt familiar fears from her past take hold, and she willingly embraced them.

She needed to be scared.

Thinking back to that second day of training, she'd had no real connections with Sir, Marquis or even Tono at that point—there had only been the dark Dom, the stage and her own desire to explore her submissive nature.

She ascended the stairs with that in mind, meeting Baron as an inexperienced sub unsure of herself on her second day at the Center. When she reached him, Baron gave the order, "Turn and face the camera, kitten."

Brie turned away from him, looking at the camera with an expression she hoped conveyed both anticipation and fear. In truth, her heart was beating rapidly, just as it had that night.

Ms. Clark held up her fingers and counted down before hitting the record button. Baron took the cue and wrapped one arm around Brie's torso, highlighting the contrast of their skin tones. He placed his other hand over her heart and chuckled. "It's beating fast…"

Brie nodded.

"Have you ever tried a sex swing before?"

"No, Baron," she answered, as she had during her initial session with him.

"Good," he replied in a deep, soothing tone. "I enjoy introducing subs to new devices."

From above, the equipment began its descent. Brie watched, her eyes growing wider when the swing stopped descending level with her.

She laughed nervously when Baron swept her off her feet. He looked down at her with that black leather mask covering half his face. Although she had long since come to trust him, Brie purposely tapped into dark memories of her childhood—Darius, the boy who had tortured her daily—and the fear became very real for her.

Darius had tainted her innocence and stolen a part of herself she would never get back…

"Trust me, kitten."

Brie was grateful for Baron's reminder. "I trust you," she said aloud for the camera.

She relaxed in his arms as he placed her in the swing, helping her to put her feet in the stirrups. The swing comfortably supported her body as she lay suspended above the stage. Brie had forgotten how freeing a swing could be, and that it had a slight Kinbaku feel to it.

Since pleasuring him orally was not part of the scene this time, Baron had planned a different challenge for her. He leaned down and took Brie's face in his hands. "Kiss me."

When she lifted her head to kiss him, he pulled the swing closer so that her lips were only centimeters from his. The heat between her legs heightened her desire, and she ached for the simple contact—but Baron was in control.

Just before their lips met, he pushed her away. Brie giggled in surprise as she slowly swung away from him.

"I said kiss me," he teased in a low, chocolatey voice that sent shivers down her spine.

Brie tilted her head back this time and he let their lips brush for the briefest of moments before pushing her away again. It was a playful game of cat and mouse.

Baron drove her wild with their *almost* kisses as her pussy continued to burn with building desire. The anticipation he created using simple denial was deliciously effective, and had her whole body trembling with need.

"Do you feel the heat?" he growled seductively, staring at her mound.

Brie moaned softly in response.

He moved away from the swing, stating, "Now it's time I test your level of obedience, kitten."

She lay there, swaying gently, knowing he was intent on making her fail his new test. Although she'd come quickly on the first night, Brie was an experienced sub now. For the film's sake, she would eventually give in, but this time she was determined it would be on her *own* terms.

Baron returned with a confident smirk on his kissable lips. She saw that he held a portable version of what looked like a Magic Wand. He stood between her open legs and turned it on. "I plan to torture you with pleasure."

Brie took a deep breath, realizing he wasn't going to

let her pretend for the camera. This was meant to be a worthy challenge for an experienced sub. She knew she was at a disadvantage because of the addictively helpless feeling the sex swing evoked. Brie was unable to resist when he placed the vibrator on her lace-covered mound, and began moving it slowly up and down the length of her pussy.

Already hot and swollen from the generous amount of oil she'd applied, Brie threw her head back, more determined than ever to fight off the sensual vibration—but to no avail. In less than a minute, she cried out as her first climax hit.

Baron chuckled. "I'll let you have the first one for free. Now you have to wait for permission to orgasm."

Brie was mortified by her utter lack of control and smiled sheepishly up at him. "Yes, Baron."

The experienced Dom had correctly gauged her overconfidence and what was needed to strip it away. With renewed determination, Brie braced herself as he pressed the vibrator against her sensitive clit.

"Look at me, kitten."

Brie lifted her head to gaze at Baron. Those gentle hazel eyes behind the leather mask drew her in with their lust. She was caught like a rabbit in the hypnotic gaze of a predator, unable to resist what was about to happen. Baron licked his lips as he skillfully employed the vibrator, making her thighs shake as she tried to ward off the next orgasm.

She groaned, struggling to resist the pull of those magnetic eyes as he turned the vibration up. Then he changed the angle of the wand and all was lost. Baron's smile spread—he knew she was close.

"Noooooooooo!" Brie panted as her body orgasmed again.

Baron tsked as he turned off the vibrator. "Now you must be punished for failing to obey a direct command."

He left her swaying in the swing, alone on the stage, waiting for punishment. It was embarrassing that she hadn't lasted any longer than the first time, but she couldn't help admiring Baron's skill at playing her so well.

Baron walked back onstage holding a large flogger in his hand. Although she normally loved the touch of the instrument, when used for punishment it took on a whole different feel.

"I'm sorry, Baron."

"What did you do wrong, kitten?"

"I came without your permission."

"As a responsible Dom, it is my duty and privilege to punish you for your disobedience. Lean back and lift your legs higher."

She longed to close her eyes and take her punishment silently, but she knew Baron would not allow it. Instead, she kept her eyes on him and reluctantly lifted her legs to give him free access to her ass.

Originally, Baron had only lashed her once with the flogger, but this time he gave her five solid strokes. She whimpered, but took his punishment willingly. When he left the stage again, she recalled the ache she'd felt the first time, knowing she had disappointed Baron. She connected with those feelings now, letting the tears fall.

When she finally heard his footsteps on the stairs again, Brie wiped her eyes.

"Are you ready to obey me?"

"I *want* to obey you, Baron."

"Then focus on me."

Baron had the small wand clutched in one hand and rope in the other. He placed the vibrator against her clit and tied it securely, using creative rope work so that it remained snug against her pussy giving her no chance of escaping it.

He smiled at her as he turned it on. "A challenge worthy of a good sub."

Brie jumped in the swing and then giggled when she felt the vibration, unsure how long she could outlast the constant stimulation.

The dark Dom moved up to her head and commanded with a smirk, "Kiss me."

This time he did not push her away when she lifted her head and their lips met. Brie was grateful for the connection, but soon understood the danger of it when his tongue entered her mouth. Her pussy began pulsing again, needing release.

Brie moaned, but was determined not to fail this new challenge. Baron was ruthless as he plundered her mouth while the vibrator he'd secured teased her relentlessly. Even though she squirmed and moaned in desperate need of climax, she refused to come.

Eventually, Baron took pity on her and ordered her to orgasm.

Brie closed her eyes, letting the vibration consume all her senses. Her body twitched in the swing, releasing her sexual tension in rhythmic waves as they kissed.

She opened her eyes afterwards and purred, "Thank you, Baron."

"My pleasure, kitten."

Come to Me

B rie felt really good about the shoot with Baron. She'd gone over the footage that very night and was extremely pleased by the shots Ms. Clark had been able to capture. The raw connection and struggle that had defined her original session with Baron had translated well in the new scene, yet the creative camera shots kept it tasteful and artistic.

Brie was in the middle of editing it when she heard her cell phone ring. She'd left a message for Lea earlier and knew the conversation was going to be a tricky one, so she let it go to voicemail, promising herself she'd call her friend back as soon as she was finished. She was determined that Lea was *not* going to end up with a broken heart.

Once the rough edit was complete, Brie gave herself a mental pep-talk before retrieving her phone from her purse. She wanted to scream when she saw that the missed call had actually been from Sir. His calls normally had a particular ringtone that she responded to immediately, but he'd had to call her from Lilly's cell.

Brie hit play and put the phone to her ear. She closed her eyes when she heard Sir's voice, ragged with emotion as if he'd been grieving.

He only said three words. "Come to me…"

She burst into tears and tried to call him back. Although she dialed the number multiple times, he never answered. Brie shivered, overcome with cold reality.

Sir needs me.

She left her bedroom, desperate for company, but Master Anderson was at the Academy heading the submissive training for the evening. She went out into his backyard and sat down in the exact spot Tono had taken on the morning of his surgery. Brie looked out over the Denver skyline, taking a deep breath to quell the rising fear inside her as the same thought kept echoing in her head: *Sir needs me…*

Brie knew Tono would be able to handle if she left, but she was deeply concerned about Faelan. Would he give up if she suddenly disappeared?

Closing her eyes, she slowed her breathing down even further. There was a solution. She just had to discover it. When it finally came to her, she felt a prickly sensation course through her body.

It was perfect—for everyone.

Brie pushed herself off the ground and hurried back to her room. She contacted Mr. Gallant, although the hour was late—too nervous to approach Captain with her idea until she'd run it by her former teacher. Although Mr. Gallant was agreeable to her plan, he was unsure if Captain would feel the same and suggested she call him straight away.

Brie dutifully called Captain next. She worried that he was already asleep when he didn't answer, but she hung up and tried again, knowing time was of the essence. Her second attempt met with success, although he sounded annoyed. "Explain yourself."

"Captain, I'm sorry to wake you but I need to ask your advice and a favor, if you're agreeable."

He listened patiently as she explained the situation with Faelan and her need for a substitute. "I've talked to Mr. Gallant, but he said only you would know if she's ready."

Captain took a long time to answer. "I would never have considered such an idea, but I understand the reason for your request. Before I say anything further, I need to talk to Miss Wilson."

"Of course," Brie agreed. "Due to the urgency of the situation, I'm going to go ahead and purchase her tickets, whether she uses them or not. Please stress to Mary that her wellbeing comes first."

"Rest assured, Miss Bennett, my loyalties lie with Miss Wilson. I will only agree to what's in her best interests."

"Good," Brie said, grateful for his frankness. "If Mary *does* agree to come, send me a text tomorrow and I will meet her at the airport."

"Either way, I will call you, Miss Bennett."

"Thank you, Captain." An overwhelming sense of gratitude for the kind man caused Brie to choke up. "No matter what you decide, I will never forget your willingness to help."

"Think nothing of it. Finish what you must do, and get some rest. You won't be any good to your Master if you are dead on your feet."

"Thank you. I'll do my best to sleep," she assured him, although she knew she was too wound up to rest.

Brie booked the flight for Mary and then called Autumn. To her relief, her friend was still up and answered quickly. "I'm actually surprised you're still awake, girl."

"I was watching anime on my computer," Autumn confessed. "It's kind of an obsession of mine."

"I love anime too, so your secret's safe with me. However, I do have a favor to ask."

"Sure, Brie. Ask away."

"I have to leave for China as soon as possible, but Tono still has weeks of recovery ahead. He'll be staying at Master Anderson's once he's released from the hospital, but he still needs someone to take him to doctor appointments and look after him. I'd ask Lea, but she's in the middle of training, with no one to take her place. I know it's a lot to ask, Autumn, but is there any way you could help out?"

Without hesitation, she answered, "I'd be happy to. In fact, if Tono wants to, he can stay at my place. I have a guest room that's just gathering dust, and I'm sure my boss would have no problem with me working from home for the next few weeks."

Brie let out an inner sigh of relief. "I can't tell you how happy you just made me!"

"Actually, it's you who's doing me a favor," Autumn asserted. "I don't know if I would have gotten up the nerve to talk to him, and now I have the perfect excuse to talk to him twenty-four seven."

"That's music to my ears."

"So I'll talk to my boss in the morning and stop by the hospital tomorrow to see how Ren Nosaka wants to handle it."

"Awesome. You've just taken a huge weight off my shoulders."

"No problem, Brie. Hey, if you need anything else, give me a call. I mean it."

"I could just hug you right now!"

"And I could just hug you back, little missy."

After Brie hung up with Autumn, she was haunted by Sir's desperate plea. It spurred her to start packing even though she could barely keep her eyes open.

I'm coming, Sir…

Captain called Brie at the break of dawn to let her know that Mary had agreed to come. "I not only believe that Miss Wilson is ready, but I suspect she will also benefit from the task. I wasn't sure after speaking with you, but she and I had a long conversation. I'm releasing her from her collar with full confidence."

"That's wonderful, Captain! Of all the people Mr. Wallace could have as support, Mary is the only one he truly needs. I've been a pale replacement."

"You were what was needed at the time, Miss Bennett."

"You are very kind to say that." Her debt to him was so great, she felt the need to add, "I promise to thank you and Candy properly for everything the next time I see you."

"No need," he assured her. "Watching Miss Wilson grow into a more fully actualized person has been a rare gift for us both."

Brie was touched by the respect and admiration he held for Mary. She couldn't wait to see for herself just how much Mary had changed.

Brie was on pins and needles while she stood waiting at the airport. She literally squealed when she saw Mary emerge from the crowd. Brie scooted around the barrier to meet her, squeezing the breath out of Mary in her enthusiasm.

"You're here!"

"Yes, Stinky Cheese, I'm here," she said with an amused look on her face, as they started walking towards baggage claim.

"Who would have guessed the Three Musketeers would all end up in Denver?"

"Can't say it was ever a dream of mine."

Brie giggled, nudging Mary while they waited for the luggage. "Bet you can't wait to see Todd again, huh?"

Mary frowned. "Let's get one thing straight, here. I'm really pissed at you."

"Why?"

"You never said a damn word about what was going on with Faelan—not one fucking word."

"I was told not to," Brie answered defensively.

"So? I'm your friend, bitch. You should have told me."

"I wanted to tell you, but Sir said it was Todd's right to keep it from you. And after how you treated him at the commune…"

"It didn't give you the right to play God, damn it."

"I didn't play God, Mary. I only did what Todd asked."

Mary pulled her luggage off the carousel in a huff. "You're damn lucky he didn't die. I would never have forgiven you. Ever."

"And I never would have forgiven you for treating him like crap, so we're equal on that point."

Tears pooled in Mary's eyes and she swiped them away angrily.

"Look, I'm sorry it hurt you, Mary. However, I still stand by my decision."

Mary pursed her lips. "Fuck you, Brie."

Brie snickered. "Funny, that's just what Todd said when he saw me."

Mary's demeanor changed once they were in the car. "Shit… I wasn't sure I'd ever see him again. I'm nervous about it." She rolled her eyes. "I feel so stupid right now."

"I'll share something that should ease your mind. His mother told me that Todd calls out your name in his sleep."

"He does? Hell…the poor boy is worse off than I thought."

"He's really struggling to recover from the surgery, but now that you're here I wouldn't be surprised if he starts to walk."

Mary's smile suddenly disappeared. "You're telling me Faelan can't walk?"

"Yeah, the surgery really took a toll on him. But now that you're here—" Brie could tell that Mary was thrown off by the unexpected news, and patted her on the arm, confident everything would work out once Mary and Faelan were together again.

Her confidence slipped when Mary stopped at the entrance of the hospital, looking ready to bolt. Brie remembered feeling the same way, and grabbed her hand, pulling her inside. "The look on Todd's face is going to be priceless."

When they reached the room, she swung the door wide open and shouted, "Ta-da!"

Faelan rolled his eyes as he turned to face Brie, then froze as if he'd seen a ghost when he spied Mary.

They seemed both seemed frozen in time as they stared at each other, neither speaking.

Brie giggled, surprised by the odd reaction. "It's true, Todd. Your eyes are *not* deceiving you. It's Mary, here in the flesh."

The two continued to stare, ignoring Brie.

"It's good to see you again, Mary," Faelan said, finally breaking the ice.

Mary only nodded, looking more than ever like she was ready to bolt.

Brie shut the door to block Mary's escape and pushed her towards the bed. "I have to leave for China, so Mary has graciously agreed to take over for me."

Faelan tilted his head, gazing intently at Mary. "How are you?"

Mary snorted sarcastically. "Better than you."

He answered with a charming smirk. "Well, that wouldn't be hard, now, would it?"

Mary's smile seemed forced, and she took a step back from him. Brie saw the look of pain flash in Faelan's eyes.

"Where have you been? Brie told me you left the commune."

"I've been staying with Captain. He took me in."

Faelan stared at Mary in disbelief. "Were you wearing Captain's collar?"

She shrugged. "Temporarily."

"But you told me you would never wear a collar."

Mary raised her eyebrow, saying in a defiant tone, "Truth is, I would only wear a collar for one man."

"Who? Captain?" he spat.

She snarled angrily. "You're a fucking idiot, Faelan."

"And you're a cruel, heartless bitch."

Mary turned to Brie and shouted, "I shouldn't be here. This is your fault!" She ran out of the room, a flurry of curses flying from her lips.

Brie reluctantly faced Faelan and his accusatory glare. She explained, "The answer to your question was simple. Mary would only wear a collar for one man—you."

He shook his head, not believing her.

"Captain agreed to take Mary on to help her work through her past. She did it so she could have a real chance with you."

Faelan stared at the open door, a look of sympathy on his face.

"But I have no idea why she acted so strangely when she saw you..." Brie admitted.

"I know why."

She looked at him sadly. "I'm sorry. I've made a mistake bringing her here."

"No reason to be sorry," he answered, letting out a heavy sigh. "Bring Mary back this afternoon. I have something I need to say to her."

Brie was desperate for them to meet up again, hoping the two could resolve their differences when it was obvious they loved each other. "I'll make sure she comes."

She left to find Mary, but didn't come across her until she went outside and spied her sitting next to a water fountain. "What's going on, woman? What happened in there?"

"This was a mistake, Brie. A *colossal* mistake."

"But I don't get it. You love Todd and he loves you. How can this be a mistake?"

"You're as big an idiot as Faelan. I hope to hell that ticket you got me is exchangeable, because I'm flying back to LA this afternoon."

"Oh no, you're not! You're not pushing him away again. I don't know what your problem is, but you'd better get your act together real quick or you're going to lose the only man who's ever loved you."

"Don't tell me what to do, bitch!"

A group of orderlies walking into the building stopped due to the loud commotion. Brie waved them on. "Just a friendly spat. We're fine here."

She turned back to Mary once the orderlies had entered the building. "I'm going to fucking kill you if you break his heart again. But…if that's really what you intend to do, then you'll do it face to face. You don't get to play the coward this time."

Mary's glare could have melted steel. "God, I hate you!"

"Believe me, right now, I hate you too," Brie snarled.

"Just go! Leave me the fuck alone."

"Fine," she spat, "because some of us actually care about people, and I need to see Tono right now."

Brie marched into the hospital, so livid she couldn't see straight. Mary hadn't changed at all! How disappointed would Captain be when he found out all his sacrifice and hard work had been for nothing?

Brie escaped into Tono's room and shared with him everything that had transpired—from Sir's disturbing phone message down to Mary's rejection of Faelan.

Naturally, Tono struck at the heart of the issue. "Sir Davis comes first. You've done all you can here." Brie smiled weakly, grateful for his wisdom and encouragement. She noted the glint in his eye when he added, "Asking Miss Autumn to look after me was a stroke of genius."

She chuckled. "I'll admit I thought so too."

"Be confident in the fact that we all will be fine, including Mr. Wallace."

Brie's smile crumbled. "Tono, I can't stand it if Todd gets hurt again. It's the last thing he needs right now. I'll never forgive myself if it ends badly for him."

"I suspect there's more going on than we know, but whatever happens is fated. The fact that Captain agreed to release her should ease any concerns you have on that matter."

Brie looked at him tenderly. "You've always known how to speak to my heart."

He placed his hand on her chest, above the heart.

"We speak the same language, you and I."

Brie took hold of his hand and lifted it to her cheek, gazing into his chocolate-brown eyes. "Tono, I—"

Mary burst into the room and stopped short. "Whoa, I didn't realize what I was walking into. Don't mind me, Rope Freak, I didn't see a thing…" She made an about-face and exited the room.

Brie let out an exasperated sigh.

"Go talk to her."

"Yes, I'd better. Knowing how Mary's mind works, I can only imagine what she's thinking right now."

"Safe travels, Brie. Know that my thoughts will be with you and Sir Davis."

"I appreciate that more than you know, Tono." Before she left, she bowed low to him, holding back tears as she walked out of the room.

With help from the nursing staff, Brie found Mary in the waiting room, banging on the candy dispenser and screeching, "The hell you're going to steal my money!"

"Stop, already," Brie said, grabbing her hands. "I'll buy whatever you want downstairs. Come on, before they throw us both out."

Mary gave the machine a resounding kick before consenting to leave. "Fucking deny *me* chocolate!"

Brie noticed the nervous glances of several older visitors there waiting, and quickly ushered Mary out.

"I need to head out to get something for Master Anderson before I leave for China tomorrow," she explained. "So I'll just leave you here in the cafeteria, where you can eat as much chocolate cake as you want."

"Can't I join you?"

Brie was surprised by Mary's request, "Do I have a choice?"

"Not really."

Brie took it as a good sign, until they got into the car and Mary asked, "So tell me, what was going on back there with Nosaka?"

"Nothing."

"*Nothing...* Okay, 'cause I swear I saw you gazing all lovey-dovey into each other's eyes. It makes me wonder if that's how you 'cared' for Faelan."

Brie slammed on the brakes and pulled to the side of the road. "Don't even go there."

Mary shrugged. "Hey, I only call it like I see it."

"Tono died on the table during surgery, Mary. I bet you didn't know that. Well, I still haven't gotten over the shock of it."

"Look, I don't care if you're two-timing Sir—I won't tell. But you'd better not be pulling that shit with Faelan."

"What would it matter if I was? I asked you to come to Denver to care for him, but you're planning to dump him instead? I don't get you at all!"

Mary glared at her. "Let it go, Brie... Get your fucking errand done so I can go back and get this over with." She looked visibly shaken and turned away to hide it.

Brie was at a loss, but remembered Tono's assertion that there were things she didn't know about Mary—and might never know. Pulling back onto the road, she continued on her mission.

"What the hell is this place?" Mary grumbled when Brie parked the car in an old neighborhood north of Denver.

"A no-kill animal shelter. I owe Master Anderson," Brie answered, without explaining further.

Brie headed straight into the large home that had been converted into a shelter for dogs and cats, leaving Mary behind. She stopped just inside to watch a glassed-walled room full of tumbling puppies. She figured Mary couldn't resist such adorableness, and smiled to herself when Blonde Nemesis walked through the door and stood beside her.

"Aren't they the cutest?" Brie asked, giggling when one of the pups nipped its own tail and started running in circles.

"They may be cute to look at, but they're a pain in the ass to care for," Mary answered.

"Puppies are a lot of work… Oh, my gosh, did you see that? The little Golden just fell into the water bowl." Brie giggled.

"Get whatever you came for so we can get the hell out of here."

Mary pretended she didn't enjoy the puppy's antics, but Brie knew better. As she walked away to talk to the staff, she looked back and noted that Mary chose not to return to the car, staying to watch the adorable puppies instead.

Animals are good for the soul, Brie thought, and it made her that much more excited about her gift.

She spent nearly an hour observing and playing with many of the tiny creatures, wanting to make sure she picked the right one for the sexy Dom, being in no hurry to return to the hospital with Blonde Nemesis.

When she was convinced she'd found *the* one, Brie talked to the owner personally to set up delivery for her special gift. She walked out grinning like an idiot.

"Don't tell me you spent all that time in there for no apparent reason," Mary complained when Brie showed up empty-handed.

"Actually, I found exactly what I was looking for and am having it delivered to Master Anderson tomorrow."

"You'd better pray he doesn't kill you."

"I'm sure he won't. I got *exactly* what Master Anderson needs, I'm sure of it."

"Says the girl who fucked with my life."

"How did I fuck with your life? All I've ever done is try to support you. Please explain what I did wrong here. I'd really like to know."

"I never would have met Faelan if it weren't for you."

"And how was meeting him a bad thing?"

Mary's countenance changed. She shook her head and looked away, unwilling to look Brie in the eye.

"Talk to me, Mary. I want to understand."

Her voice was barely audible when she confided, "I finally give my heart to a guy…and he's going to die on me."

Brie put her hand on Mary's shoulder. "He isn't going to die."

Mary jerked away from her, turning on Brie, her eyes flashing with anger. "I saw him, bitch! Don't lie to me about that. You brought me here to watch him die."

Brie was stunned and just stared at her.

"So here's what's going to happen. You're taking me back to the hospital. I'll tell him goodbye and then I'm out of here—and you'd better hope to God I never come across you again."

Heartbreak

It was disturbing that Mary seemed serene as they drove back to the hospital, as if the task ahead meant nothing to her. It pissed Brie off.

Faelan needed support, and here Mary was intent on stabbing the poor guy in the heart when he needed her most—because she loved him.

"You'd better be kind," Brie warned as they entered the hospital.

"I'll be quick and to the point."

Brie groaned inwardly when she saw Faelan's parents standing outside his room, their faces glowing with excitement. Mrs. Wallace immediately walked up to Mary.

"You must be the girl. You're even more beautiful than I imagined."

Mary stood there, a look of panic on her face.

Mr. Wallace held out his hand to Mary. "What a pleasure to meet you, Miss Wilson. Although my son is close-mouthed about his personal life, it's easy to tell how much he cares for you."

Brie had to nudge Mary to take his hand.

Mary laughed nervously as she shook it, then looked back at Brie, a frozen smile on her lips.

Oh, hell, this was going to be so much worse than Brie had imagined.

Better to get it over with now—like ripping off a Band-Aid, she decided. "Mr. and Mrs. Wallace, Mary and I would like a chance to talk to Todd privately. I hope you don't mind."

Mrs. Wallace beamed with delight. "Of course not. He's expecting you."

Brie opened the door for Mary, but the girl stopped abruptly as soon as she entered the room, causing Brie to walk into her. "What the heck, Mary?" she complained, and then she saw the reason why...

Faelan stood before them, dressed in a suit, with his hand gripping the IV pole.

"What the—?" Mary gasped.

Brie noticed the white-knuckled grip he had on the IV pole, and understood the sheer effort he was making for Mary.

"Mary Wilson," Faelan stated, "you are mine."

Mary shook her head slowly, opening her mouth to speak.

Don't do it... Brie silently begged.

"Faelan, I—"

"I know you're scared, Mary," he interrupted. "I could tell it when you came in this morning. You probably thought you were looking at a dead man, but you're wrong. I'm not going anywhere."

Tears filled Mary's eyes.

"Tono Nosaka donated his kidney so that I could have this second chance."

"I don't…"

"Bow at my feet," he commanded. "It's either now or never, Mary. Make your choice."

Brie could see the inner battle Mary was fighting. The risk of loving him only to lose him was more than she could bear.

With great effort, Faelan took a step towards her and commanded again, "Bow to me, Mary."

Brie held her breath as Mary slowly approached Faelan, her eyes locked on his. She paused for a moment before gracefully lowering herself to the floor, kneeling before him. As an added gesture of obedience, she lowered her head until her forehead touched his feet.

Faelan undid the belt of his dress pants. "Look at me," he ordered. With painful determination, he looped the belt around Mary's neck, pulling it tight.

Mary gazed up at him with an expression Brie had never seen on her beautiful face—a look of pure joy.

"You are mine. From this day forward, you answer only to me."

"Yes, Faelan."

"Stand now and kiss your Master."

He tugged on the belt when she stood, bringing her lips hard against his. While they kissed, Faelan let go of the pole to caress her cheek. "When I get out of this hospital, I will get you a proper collar."

Mary smiled. "I don't care."

He brushed her bottom lip with his finger. "But I do. I want the world to know you are my cherished submissive."

Mary kissed Faelan again, with such passion that Brie lowered her eyes. When she started towards the door to give the couple privacy, Faelan called out to Brie.

"Don't leave just yet."

Mary turned to face Brie, but her loving gaze remained locked on Faelan.

"You have been a true friend in every sense of the word, blossom. I thank you for your diligence."

Brie smiled, tears coming to her eyes. She thought back to the man who had stood so confidently before her, expecting to receive her collar on Graduation Night. She would never have guessed how things would turn out. "It's been my pleasure."

He tugged on the belt, forcing Mary to kiss him again. Brie took his cue and quietly exited. There was just one more task to take care of before she could return to Sir's side.

Lea did not have much time to spare before heading to work at the Academy, but she agreed to meet, knowing Brie was headed to China in the morning.

"Okay, okay…we have to start this on a positive note," Lea stated when Brie opened the door to let her in. "What do you call a Chinese billionaire?"

"You're kidding me. I haven't even invited you inside yet."

Lea grinned. "Come on, Brie. What do you call a

Claim Me

Chinese billionaire?"

Brie rolled her eyes. "I have no idea."

"Cha-Ching."

"No, no, no…that was terrible!"

"Did you hear what happened on the opening day at the newest Chinese zoo?"

"I'm shutting the door now," Brie said, pretending to close it on her.

Lea stuck her foot out to block it. "It was Pandamonium!"

Brie laughed in spite of herself. "Barely redeemed yourself with that second one. I guess you can come in."

Master Anderson was finishing up his meal in the kitchen. "Don't be late, Ms. Taylor. You have a big scene to perform tonight."

"Don't worry, Headmaster. As much as I love me some Brie, work always comes first."

"I won't keep her, I promise," Brie assured him.

"See that you don't. Baron would look awfully silly trying to play the part of Lea in front of the training Dominants. I'm not sure he would ever forgive you." He pointed to a plate on the counter and smiled. "By the way, I made you brownies."

"Oh, thank you, Master Anderson!" Brie squealed, as both she and Lea descended on the plate.

"Have fun, ladies," he said, tipping an imaginary cowboy hat before leaving them.

"Isn't Master Anderson the best?" Brie purred, taking a huge bite of a warm brownie.

"Yes…oh yes…" Lea moaned in ecstasy, sounding freakishly similar to when she was having sex. "I'm sure

127

gonna miss that man."

Brie jumped on the comment, a natural transition to the reason she'd called Lea over. "You don't have to miss him…"

Lea smiled. "I know."

"Have you seriously considered moving back to LA?"

Lea took another bite of brownie and finished chewing before answering her. "Sure, I've thought about it. I mean, LA *is* awesome, but I have my reasons for staying here."

"If it's because of Autumn, you may want to rethink that. Who knows what's going to happen with Tono now that she's caring for him for the next few weeks? I've definitely seen some sparks fly between them."

Lea sighed. "Yeah, I've noticed that myself. I'm happy for them, don't get me wrong, but whenever people hook up, friends seem to get the short end of the stick."

"It's a natural process, I suppose."

"You know, with Baron and Master Anderson moving to LA, that leaves Mistress Clark all alone in Denver. It might be the best chance I ever get."

Brie's heart started racing. She was terrified she would say the wrong thing and screw it up. "I know how you feel about Ms. Clark, but have you ever wondered why nothing's happened between you? I mean, you did tell her how you felt, right?"

"Yeah, I've told her a few times, but you have to understand that Mistress Clark isn't one to jump into relationships quickly—not after Rytsar."

It seemed hopeless. Lea was never going to give up

on Ms. Clark. Brie put her brownie down and exhaled. "I can't lie—the idea of having you come back to LA thrills me to death. I've missed you so much, girlfriend."

"I've missed you too, Brie. You know that!" Lea leaned over and gave Brie a hug as she stole another brownie off the plate.

"Don't you miss the big city, Lea? There's nothing quite like Los Angeles. And the ocean…remember lying on the beach and listening to the waves come in?"

Lea took a bite and purred. "Oh, I *do* miss tanning on the beach. And all those hunks in swimming trunks…"

"You know, if Autumn and Tono hook up, they might end up in LA. He has a loyal following there. And as far as Ms. Clark…" Brie stepped carefully, formulating her next words. "You don't want to be that girl who pacifies a lonely heart."

Lea stated defiantly, "I love her, Brie."

Brie put her arms around Lea. "I know you do. I've never doubted it. Ms. Clark must know that too, which makes me question why she hasn't pursued the relationship. Damn it, Lea, you deserve a lover who will pursue you with dogged determination."

"She's hurt, Brie. It's not easy for her."

"Sir was hurt, but he couldn't let me go when I decided to walk away."

Lea's eyes lit up. "That's it! I'll tell everyone I'm headed to LA. When Mistress Clark realizes what she's losing, she's bound to make her move."

Brie frowned. "But what if she doesn't?"

Lea popped the rest of the brownie into her mouth.

After swallowing, she shrugged and said, "Then I suppose it wasn't meant to be."

But Brie didn't miss the glint in her eye. "It's a crazy plan, Lea."

She smiled. "It's the crazy ones that usually work."

"So if the worst happens and Ms. Clark doesn't realize what an incredible catch you are, will you stay in LA?"

"Of course, but don't get your hopes up, 'cause I see a bright, shiny collar in my future."

She knew Lea's heart was going to be broken, no matter what she did. Her only consolation was that she could be there for Lea when it all came crashing down.

Brie tossed and turned that night, but eventually fell asleep secure in the knowledge she would soon be in Sir's arms.

"Brie, I want to try something new," he told her in a husky voice.

She trembled, loving the idea of exploring something new with her Master, especially when it was something he desired.

"I'm all yours, Master."

"This will challenge you in ways you've never experienced."

She was even more excited and purred, "I look forward to it."

"It demands your trust and complete cooperation."

"Of course, Master. You have both, without question."

He smiled seductively as he explained, "I plan to fist you tonight."

She gasped, her loins contracting in fear.

"Is your heart racing now, téa? Are you still willing?"

"I'm not sure…"

"I've heard it is a singular experience," he growled lustfully in her ear.

"Yes, Master," she answered, trying to recover from the shock of his request. The word 'singular' had different connotations—both good *and* bad.

"Will you submit to me?"

The act of fisting frightened her, but still…the idea of being completely filled in that way had its own dangerous allure.

"If it pleases you, Master," she finally consented.

His look of approval made it worth facing her fears. "I'm glad to hear it, my little sub. I've watched it performed on numerous occasions, but have never experienced it myself."

That fact alone made Brie all the more willing to submit to his uncommon desire. To be his first in *anything* was a cherished gift.

"I promise not to take you past the point of breaking, but I *will* bend you tonight."

Brie moaned softly. To be taken to the edge by her Master was an intoxicating experience.

He laid out the lubricant, Hitachi Wand and a digital camera before placing a towel under her buttocks. "I expect you will cover this bed with your sweet come multiple times this session."

Brie bit her lip, suddenly hungry for what he was about to do.

She watched with nervous fascination as he covered his hand with the lubricant before massaging her tight opening. It reminded her of the same process he used when he relaxed her sphincter before fucking her deep in the ass.

He was gentle but firm as he stretched her vaginal muscles. "That's it," he praised, "open yourself to me…"

Brie tilted her head back, giving in to his loving but demanding touch while he kissed and nuzzled her breasts with his lips. The thought of being completely filled by him in a way she'd never experienced before had her moaning fearfully in anticipation.

He continued to massage her inner muscles, making sure they were loose and ready for his invasion. When he shifted off the bed to change position, she felt a moment of panic.

He looked at her knowingly. "You need to relax, téa." He pulled her to the edge of the bed and leaned down, kissing her inner thigh. "Trust your Master."

Brie let out a gasp, but spread her legs wider in submission to his will.

"Concentrate on letting me in—allow me to push through your resistance."

"Yes, Master," she answered breathlessly.

He started with three fingers, easing them into her as he described what he was doing. "First, we start out slowly to acclimate your body for what's to come."

Brie took deep breaths as he began thrusting them

inside her, helping to relax her further.

"And now I add a fourth finger."

Brie held her breath, then moaned as he started rotating his hand back and forth, further massaging her muscles as he slowly pushed all four fingers inside her.

She could barely breathe, the ache of his invasion taking over all thought.

"Good girl. Now, we're going to open that tight little pussy even more."

Master took his time, in no rush. He seemed to enjoy the process as he watched her resistant body slowly submit to his will.

"You might be frightened, but I can tell your body enjoys the unique challenge."

Brie licked her lips and nodded, moaning louder as he bit the flesh of her thigh.

"And now all five…"

He added more lubricant before adding his thumb, and he continued the twisting motion, forcing himself deeper inside.

Her young body opposed the unnatural invasion. To aid her, he turned on the Hitachi and pressed it against her pussy. With her clit stretched so tight, it didn't take long for her to climax. The moment her pussy began pulsing in release, his knuckles breached her opening.

Brie cried out in surprise, the ache of being filled beyond capacity almost too much.

Master turned off the Hitachi and placed it on the bed beside her. He waited several moments, allowing her to grow used to the new sensation, before continuing his conquest.

Brie made small mewing sounds as he persisted. Her body was being taken to its absolute limit…and that was when she felt the tingling start.

He leaned over and kissed her belly. "That's it, let go and fly for me."

Once he was wrist-deep with his hand curled up inside her, he started lightly thrusting. The intoxicating pressure on her G-spot was intense.

He smiled up at her from between her legs. "This is only the beginning."

She lifted her head and looked down to see Master's manly arm buried inside her. It was surreal and strangely erotic. She could feel every movement he made, no matter how slight.

Brie moaned, lying back down and throwing her head back when he began twisting his hand again.

"This will be an orgasm you will never forget," he murmured as he began thrusting his fist.

All of Brie's resistance disappeared as he forcibly stimulated her G-spot. The concentrated thrusts had her screaming as she released a gush of watery come.

"I'm not done yet," he warned her seductively, nibbling her quivering thigh.

Brie tensed as he settled back down between her legs. "I'm going to make you orgasm even harder."

The twisting motion started up again, loosening her before he started pumping his fist. Brie let out a long, primal cry as she began to shake uncontrollably, her whole body readying for the intense climax.

"Ohhh…my—" She stopped mid-scream as she gushed in release, coming long and hard.

He pulled his hand out slowly, reveling in the amount of liquid passion he'd been able to inspire from her. "That was a thing of beauty," he said, in a low voice ripe with lust.

Immediately following her powerful orgasm, Brie started shivering. He gathered her in his arms, pressing his hard cock against her thigh as he gently stroked her long, brown curls. "I am well pleased, wife."

Brie woke up with a smile on her face. The intensity of the dream had her panties soaking wet, but it was the feeling of intimacy that lingered in her mind.

It comforted her to know that today she would be in her Master's arms.

Cold Reception

B rie was still packing last-minute items when Master Anderson entered the guest room. "I have something for you."

He handed her a small mason jar of homemade soup. "Just in case you have need, young Brie."

Brie hugged the jar to her chest. "I hope to partake of your soup for no other reason than to enjoy its taste."

"That would please me," he said, smiling kindly. He then handed her a fistful of foreign bills. "I stopped by the bank yesterday and got some money exchanged for you—just in case."

"Thank you for looking out for me, Master Anderson."

"Thane entrusted me with your care, and I take the job seriously."

Brie took the money and slipped it into her purse, then carefully wrapped the jar in her clothing to protect it, placing it snugly against Sir's preserves. "At least I'm guaranteed not to starve while I'm in China."

Master Anderson put his hand on her shoulder. "No

matter what happens, don't lose sight of how much you're worth to Thane."

She was about to reply when the doorbell rang.

"Who could that be this early in the morning?" Master Anderson griped as he left to answer the door.

Brie snuck a peek from her room when he unlocked the door and opened it.

"Mr. Brad Anderson?"

"Yes. What's this about?"

"I have a delivery for you."

"Sorry, you must be mistaken. I haven't ordered anything," Master Anderson stated, starting to close the door.

"I was told this is a gift."

"Fine," he muttered, as if it was an inconvenience. "Where do I sign?"

The courier handed Master Anderson a cardboard box with handles and tipped his hat. "Have a pleasant day, sir."

Master Anderson stared at the box for a moment, then called out to the man, "Wait! Why does this box have holes in it?"

Brie had to stifle her giggle as he cautiously set the box on the coffee table and sat down. He pulled out the note attached and read it aloud.

To Master Anderson
May you find your joy and delight in this box.

He looked warily at the cardboard box again, mumbling to himself, "What the hell…" After lifting the lid, he chuckled as a tiny orange tabby enthusiastically jumped out of the box but overshot it, meowing pitifully as it tumbled off the table. Luckily, Master Anderson had quick reflexes and caught the tiny thing in his large hands before it hit the floor.

"Brie!" he roared.

She left the safety of the room, approaching him slowly, unsure whether he liked her gift.

"Did you do this?" he asked in an accusatory tone.

She twisted nervously where she stood. "Maybe…"

"A kitten?"

"I know you have a thing for redheads, and she was a cute little redhead who needed a good man."

The kitten attempted to climb up Master Anderson's muscular arm as Brie was talking. He gave up trying to control the furball and let it crawl up his arm to his shoulder, where it stood fearlessly, surveying the new landscape from its high vantage point.

"The last thing I need is an animal to care for," Master Anderson complained as he gently rubbed under the tiny creature's chin.

"I couldn't stand the thought of you coming home to an empty house anymore, Master Anderson. Besides, kittens make excellent chick magnets."

"Did you forget I'm moving in two months?"

"She'll make the move much more interesting for you. Trust me."

The kitten rubbed up against Master Anderson's handsome chin, purring loudly.

"Oh!" Brie cooed, putting her hands to her heart. "You two look so cute together."

Master Anderson picked up the tiny kitten and

looked it in the eyes. It let out a sweet little mew, and that was all it took—he was hooked. "Fine, I'll keep her, but be assured I will do a far better job caring for *her* than Thane did with my innocent herb garden."

Brie burst out laughing. "Well, that's a relief."

He passed the kitten to her. "Hold on to the little thing while I get your luggage into the truck. No reason she can't take the ride with us."

"What are you going to call her, Master Anderson?"

He looked at the tabby with an amused expression. "I haven't decided yet. I want to get to know her first, so I can give her a title befitting her spunky personality."

While he was carrying the luggage to the car, Brie kissed the kitten's tiny pink nose. "Yep, you don't know what a lucky little pussy you are."

When Brie stepped off the plane in Chengdu, she was hit by culture shock as she made her way through the busy airport. There were not many foreigners, and few people, if any, seemed to speak English. Since she had not been able to reach Sir before she'd left, there was no one there to greet her. She was completely on her own, which was a real challenge, since she knew very little Chinese.

Luckily, both she and Sir had tracking devices on their phones. It allowed them to keep tabs on each other while traveling, and proved vitally important to her now. Knowing that his missing phone was still lost at the hotel, she was able to find the exact location.

Once she had all her luggage and had finally managed to hail a cab, she showed the driver the GPS map on her phone. He shook his head, indicating that he didn't understand. She tried to pronounce the name of the hotel, but try as she might, the man could not understand her. Brie could tell he was getting frustrated and was afraid he would kick her out of his cab.

In a last-ditch effort, she googled the translation for the name of the hotel and showed him the Chinese characters. The man smiled, nodding his approval as he hit the gas. Although she was afraid the translation might be off, she grew more confident that they were headed in the right direction once the dot on her phone began to move.

Brie thought how terrifying it would be to get lost in this giant city of fourteen million people without knowing the language. She fervently prayed that Sir would be at the hotel when she arrived.

The drive took almost an hour and there were several heart-stopping moments. The streets were full of bicycles, motorbikes, pedestrians and buses, as well as regular cars and taxis. It took much weaving and braking to avoid hitting the different modes of transportation gathered on the same roadways, and the crazy intersections seemed like accidents waiting to happen. To Brie's relief, they arrived at the hotel unscathed despite (or possibly because of) her cabbie's haphazard driving.

The driver handed Brie her luggage and eagerly took the yuan Master Anderson had given her.

Thank you, Master Anderson!

Brie entered the hotel and walked up to the counter. "Sir Thane Davis?" she asked, hoping his name would ring a bell. The clerk said something in Chinese, so Brie said it again more slowly, pointing at the different room keys hanging behind the woman.

The clerk smiled and repeated Sir's name with her thick accent. Brie nodded enthusiastically, thrilled the woman understood. She was surprised when the woman left her post to personally escort Brie to the room.

The clerk knocked on the door and called out his name, but it was not Sir who answered. Instead Lilly stood there, looking as surprised as Brie. The clerk seemed unhappy, looking at both women as if she was afraid she'd done something wrong by showing Brie to the room.

To alleviate the woman's fears, she held out her hand to Lilly. "It's good to see a familiar face."

Lilly accepted the handshake, but failed to invite Brie in.

The front desk clerk was satisfied, however, and left them to return to her job.

"Is this Thane's hotel room?" Brie asked, surprised to find her there.

"Yes. I'm waiting for him to return from his daily jog before we visit Mother again."

"Good," Brie answered, brushing past her to enter Sir's room. She put down her luggage and collapsed in a nearby chair, sighing loudly. "It's been a long flight and I'm totally exhausted, but if I take a quick shower to freshen up, I can join you two."

When Lilly didn't respond, Brie asked, "You don't have a problem if I freshen up, do you?"

"Of course not," Lilly answered, but she sounded less than pleased.

When Lilly made no move to leave, Brie asked bluntly, "Do you mind giving me a little privacy? I promise not to take long."

Lilly seemed reluctant to leave Sir's room, but made her way out.

Brie shut the door behind her and headed into the tiny bathroom. Realizing she had little time, she quickly undressed and sponged herself, reapplying her makeup and fixing her hair. Before she dressed in new clothes, she spritzed herself with perfume and felt adequately refreshed.

Brie knelt at the door waiting for him. It was only a few minutes later when she heard him slipping the key into the door. She looked down, smiling to herself as it swung open, anticipating their reunion.

Sir entered the room and shut the door, stating only, "You came."

She looked up and her heart skipped a beat. "I...I did, Sir." He had a haunted, cruel look in his eyes that was unsettling to her soul.

What's happened to him?

Rather than the normal protocol of releasing Brie to serve him, Sir stayed where he was. "I met with Lilly in the lobby. She let me know you were here."

Brie wondered why Lilly had felt the need to tell him and spoil her surprise. She looked at his troubled face and asked, "Aren't you happy to see me, Sir?"

There was a light knock on the door.

"Excuse me," he said curtly. Sir answered it, telling Lilly, "Give me a minute. I'll come get you when I'm ready to head out."

He shut the door again and stared at Brie. The cold

look in his eyes reminded of her of the song "Demons" that he'd sung to her back in Tokyo, and his warning: *"When I shared that I have my demons, it was not simply idle talk, Brie. I am my mother's son."*

Brie could feel his hostility increasing. She was afraid she was about to meet his demons head on, but she held her kneeling pose as he approached, even though she felt like cowering.

In one solid motion, he lifted her from the ground and threw her over his shoulder, carrying her into the bathroom. There he stripped out of his jogging sweats and ripped her out of her clothes, pushing her against the shower wall. He turned on the hot water and let it cascade over them both.

Sir grabbed her hips so violently that she cried out. Instead of taking her, he wrapped his arms around her, holding Brie tightly against him—so tightly that she struggled to breathe. But she did not resist his restrictive embrace—she clung to him.

After several minutes, he began to shake as silent sobs wracked his body. Her own tears fell, her heart breaking for him.

Sir did not let go until the water became ice cold and Brie was shivering in his arms.

He shut off the shower and grabbed a towel, drying her in silence before taking care of himself. His expression remained just as tormented, but there were no telltale signs that he had been crying.

"We will leave when you're ready," he stated gruffly, exiting the bathroom.

Brie looked in the mirror, frightened by the change in him. With shaking hands, she wiped away her running mascara and applied her makeup for a second time. Brie slipped into her clothes and styled her hair simply.

She rejoined Sir, her hair still wet, hoping he would talk to her before they met up with Lilly again. It disturbed her that he would not look her in the eye.

"Sir…" she said, moving towards him.

He stopped her in her tracks with his accusatory tone. "What was the reason for the delay?" When she opened her mouth to answer, he snapped, "Never mind. Hand me your journal."

Brie immediately dug through her luggage and handed it to him. She wanted to explain, but stood silently, feeling guilty of a crime she was unaware she'd committed.

Sir sat down, not inviting her to join him as he starting flipping through her journal. Brie watched his expression carefully, hoping to see compassion. To her dismay, his face remained impassive, even though Brie had poured out her heart to him on every page.

It pained her to see him so cold and uncaring.

After he'd finished, Sir closed the book. "I have many questions for you, but not now. I have an appointment with the Beast. You are to remain here until I get back."

"But Si—"

He put up his hand to stop her protest. "Go to sleep. You've had a long day of travel. That's an order, téa."

Brie dutifully took off her clothes as he watched, and laid them in a pile on the nightstand before slipping under the covers of his bed.

She watched in disbelief as he walked out the door, leaving her alone in the hotel room while he joined Lilly.

What the hell is going on?

Brie felt certain Lilly was the cause of the disconnect with Sir. But the question she couldn't answer was why. What possible motive could Lilly have to do such a terrible thing?

As much as Sir wouldn't want to hear it, she knew it was time to voice her concerns about his sister, but Brie also understood that she'd have to tread lightly. Lilly was family and, in the short time he'd known her, Sir had grown to care about the girl.

Even though it was about to get ugly, as his submissive and future wife, Brie understood it was her duty.

Condors, Sir.

She eventually gave in to her exhaustion, falling into a fitful slumber. She dreamed of snakes and kittens, a wedding dress and black pearls…

Brie woke with a start. It took a moment to realize she was in Sir's hotel room. Just when her heart was slowing down, an unpleasant masculine scent assaulted her senses and then she heard movement.

Someone else was in the room.

Before she could scream, a strong hand wrapped around her throat pinning her to the bed. Brie struggled for her life, but her cries were muffled as her assailant squeezed her windpipe. His grip was hard and unforgiving as he strangled the breath out of her.

As she became lightheaded, her spirited thrashing quickly became feeble movements. Once she stopped fighting, recognition slowly dawned—*Master's touch.*

Even though his scent did not match because he was wearing the shirt of another man, it was Sir who held her by the throat.

Sir released the pressure of his grip but his hand remained tight around her neck. He growled ominously, "Don't make a sound." Sir ripped the blankets away, exposing her naked body.

He was playing out the scene she had written in her journal, but there was another element to it—a dangerous one that frightened Brie. She instinctively cried out, "Please don't hurt me."

Still keeping in character, he leaned down and whispered in her ear, "I won't unless you force me to."

Was it a threat or an invitation to play?

Sir's hands were unusually rough as he caressed her body, bruising and clawing at her in his raging lust. Brie whimpered under his touch, both turned on and frightened by his harsh treatment. He seemed like a man possessed.

Sir flipped her over and buried her face in the pillow as he rubbed his hard shaft between the valley of her asscheeks. He panted over her. "No lube this time."

Brie's frightened whimpers were muffled by the pillow as Sir positioned himself. She braced for his hard cock to thrust deep into her unprepared ass, knowing she had been the one to invite this scene.

She waited for his painful entry, but Sir loosened his grip and pulled away. His ragged breathing slowly returned to normal. "I thought I wanted this...but I don't."

Brie turned her head to look back at him. "Why?" she asked hesitantly, unsure if he was rejecting the scene—or her.

He stared at Brie, his expression unreadable. Then his eyes softened as he slid his hand over the curve of her ass. "I need to make love to you, Brie."

His unexpected answer melted her heart.

Sir gently turned Brie over and lay on top of her, smothering her with his large frame. He propped himself on his elbows and held her face in his hands as he gazed into her eyes. He said nothing, but Brie became entranced by his silent language.

Eventually, tears ran down her cheeks as she whispered, "I love you."

"I'm lost."

"We'll find the way back," she assured him, lifting her head and kissing him on the lips.

Sir nuzzled her neck. "This moment is the only thing that's real to me…my anchor in the storm."

"I will always be your safe haven, Sir," Brie vowed, trailing feather-light kisses down his neck.

Sir's impassioned groan reverberated deep in his chest. "Since I cannot make love to you with my cock…" She closed her eyes as Sir moved lower, tenderly kissing her thighs before concentrating on her pussy. In a world of kinky sex, with constant physical and mental challenges, she cherished such loving attention equally as much.

Brie ran her hands through his thick brown hair as his tongue and fingers made love to her for hours. It was his escape from the world, his stolen moment from the mounting pressure around him.

His lovemaking wasn't about how many orgasms he could elicit or how high he could make her fly—it was about expressing his love using only his touch and tongue.

Betrayal

It was obvious to Brie that Lilly was unhappy Sir had left her to visit their mother alone, because he received a scribbled note as soon as she returned from the hospital.

Thane, must talk.

Meet me in my room.

Lilly

Sir invited Brie to join him, the tension returning to his face. "Mother's situation has put a strain on our relationship, but I trust we can move beyond it after this is over."

After hearing his confession, Brie was surprised when Lilly opened the door with an inviting smile. That all changed when her eyes drifted down and focused on Sir's arm around Brie's waist. The light seemed to leave Lilly's face as her hands dropped to her sides, and she drifted over to the bed, not even bothering to invite them in.

It appeared that seeing Brie had triggered something dark in Lilly. The girl became silent and unresponsive even when Sir questioned her.

"Lilly, what's happened? Is it Mother? Talk to me."

The girl just sat on the bed with a blank stare on her face, as if she were a million miles away.

Sir shook his head, looking at Brie in confusion. "I can't explain it. I've never seen her like this before."

After a few minutes, Lilly seemed to come back to life. She nodded as if she'd made a decision, looking at Sir with deep sadness. In a hushed voice, she asked, "Are you going to tell Brie what happened that night?"

"What are you talking about?" he asked, sounding genuinely concerned.

"I've forgiven you, but will she?"

"I have no clue what you mean."

Lilly slowly shook her head, tearing up as she spoke. "I know you didn't intend to hurt me, Thane. I know it was the drink."

"What exactly are you accusing me of?" Sir demanded.

"Don't make me say it, Thane. Don't make me relive that moment." Brie could see that Lilly was visibly shaking, and wondered about the cause.

Brie looked questioningly at Sir.

Sir met her gaze. "I have no idea what she's talking about, Brie."

Lilly seemed genuinely distraught and looked on the verge of panic. "I forgave you, Thane. Please let it go…"

His nostrils flared in disgust. "You will not throw around veiled accusations, Lilly."

"Brie," Lilly cried piteously, "he must have been thinking of you when he grabbed me and forced himself…" She struggled to speak through her tears. "He…he…" She shook her head, breaking down in heart-wrenching sobs that pulled at Brie's heartstrings.

Brie looked back at Sir, the icy realization of what Lilly was accusing him of wrapping itself around her heart.

Sir's gaze remained fixed on Brie. "Even though I can't remember what happened that night, I could never do what she's insinuating. Never."

The look of agony on Lilly's face came from a place so deep it could not have been faked, but Sir…Sir could never hurt a woman that way, much less his own *sister*. The idea was too revolting to even contemplate.

"I don't know what kind of game you're playing, Lilly, but you are most definitely a carbon copy of your mother," Sir said with abhorrence, unmoved by Lilly's copious tears.

"How can you say that, Thane?" she sobbed. "You're the monster here, not me! Damn it, I forgave you. I forgave you that very night, when you broke down after realizing what you'd done."

Sir shook his head, but he had the look of an animal finding itself trapped. "Do you have any proof?"

Lilly cried, "I don't need proof! I remember what happened."

"You had as much to drink as I did…*sister*," he stated coldly.

"I know what happened, Thane."

"Then it comes down to your word against mine. I

know myself well, and without any evidence proving otherwise, I stand by my assertion that nothing happened between us."

"But it did!" Lilly whimpered, covering her face with her hands as she sank to the floor.

Brie craved to comfort her, instinctively responding to her pain, but she didn't make a move. To do so would be a betrayal of Sir if Lilly was lying.

So she stood anchored to her spot, unable to think.

"Brie, I wouldn't do that to a woman, no matter how drunk I was. You know that."

"Normally you wouldn't…" Brie agreed, trailing off as her throat closed up, an image of him with Lilly coming into her mind.

"Don't go there," he warned. "Don't allow what she's said to filter through your thoughts. She's lying, Brie. There's no other explanation."

Lilly looked up at him, her eyes red and swollen. "Even now, I forgive you. I know you didn't mean it."

The response struck Brie as odd. If Sir had really done the horrendous thing she was implying, there was no way Lilly could still forgive him after he'd just accused her of lying about it. No woman would let a man get away with that. It made Brie wonder if this was all an act to garner her sympathy so she would take Lilly's side against Sir's.

If so, what possible benefit would Lilly gain by this vile ruse? She'd just alienated Sir, her only sibling, and she'd never shown any interest in Brie until now.

None of it made sense.

"I don't know what I think," Brie muttered, looking

down at Lilly crumpled on the floor. The girl looked emotionally shattered.

"You have to believe me, Brie," Sir asserted. "I didn't... I wouldn't hurt her."

Brie couldn't leave Lilly lying there weeping, her pain too raw and real to be ignored. She lifted the girl to her feet and helped her into bed, covering her with a blanket. As they were leaving the room, Lilly called out to Sir with a look of regret. "I know you didn't mean to."

Sir snarled angrily. "Stop. Whatever game you're playing, just stop."

Brie was stunned. If Sir were guilty, his reaction to Lilly was unforgiveable. But if Lilly were lying—the betrayal to Sir was of horrific proportions.

Either possibility was unbelievably terrible.

They left Lilly's room, but when Sir reached out for Brie, she unconsciously stepped away, an unwanted image of Sir violating Lilly crowding her mind. "I have to get out of here," she cried. "I need time alone."

The look of hurt in Sir's eyes cut Brie to the quick, but it didn't stop her from running out of the hotel.

Brie walked the crowded streets of Chengdu, oblivious to the people around her. It terrified her that in one fell swoop, everything she'd believed in had been shaken to its foundation. Sir was an honorable man. Brie knew he would never do such a thing...and yet he had admitted to her on the phone that he had no recollection of that night, after liberally ingesting a local brew.

Was it possible that it had made him momentarily insane—unstable enough to hurt his own sister?

Brie couldn't get over the fact that Lilly had looked

genuinely traumatized. Something terrible must have happened to her. Still, the girl kept insisting she'd forgiven Sir. Why? And why would she continue to stay with Sir if he'd hurt her like that?

There *had* to be something more—something Lilly was hiding.

Yet visions of what Lilly had accused Sir of flooded Brie's mind, and once the tears started, they wouldn't stop. People began to stare. Out of desperation, Brie sought escape, finding an isolated wooden bench. Once she sat down, she held her head in both hands and sobbed uncontrollably, oblivious to everything and everyone.

Breathe, Brie, breathe… she reminded herself.

Eventually a strange but welcome calm took hold, and her heartrate slowed as her breaths became deep and soul-satisfying. Once the panic fled, clarity took over.

Sir would never do such a thing.

With shaking hands, she pushed herself up and wiped away her tears. It wasn't until then that she realized she was hopelessly lost. She hadn't brought her phone and couldn't remember the Chinese name for the hotel.

A fresh sense of panic took over as she glanced around, unsure from which direction she'd come. That was when her eyes landed on Sir. He stood a little more than a block away, ever her protector, even when she was questioning his integrity.

Without hesitation, she started running towards him, but before she reached Sir she stopped, suddenly feeling ashamed.

"Come to me, Brie."

She melted into his forgiving embrace and immediately apologized. "It was wrong of me to leave."

"No," he insisted. "While it was foolish to walk the streets of an unfamiliar city alone, I respect your need to process. You and I are not that different."

Brie looked up at him. "I know you never could…"

"No," he assured her.

"But why would Lilly do such a thing? It doesn't make any sense."

Sir shook his head. He seemed gutted when he answered her. "I was an idiot to believe she was any different."

Brie hugged him tighter. "I'm sorry I encouraged you to trust her."

"I have only myself to blame," Sir closed his eyes, a look of agony on his face. "… and now I understand what I must do."

He did not explain as he took Brie's hand and guided her through the streets, leading her back to the hotel. It felt to Brie as if he were facing a firing squad, but instead of losing his life he was going to lose the last living connection to his mother. Now Sir would never know closure or peace.

Once they reached the hotel, Sir headed directly to Lilly's room. She immediately answered when he knocked. Although her eyes were still bloodshot from crying, she stepped to the side and invited him in as if she was relieved to see him.

"We can talk this out, Thane. Despite what happened, I can't bear losing you."

Sir was not swayed by her heartfelt plea.

"I came to tell you that I'm going to issue the order to stop all life-support. There's no point pretending she's going to recover after the results of the latest scan."

"Don't, Thane… Don't punish Mother for this."

"It's not an act of punishment."

"But she opened her eyes. I saw it! Are you trying to get back at me for daring to talk to Brie about what happened between us?"

His voice was as cold as ice. "You can stop with the act. I never hurt you."

Her laughter was tinged with hysteria. "Brie, he claims he wouldn't hurt anyone, but he's set on killing his own mother." She screamed at Sir, "You cold-hearted bastard!"

"The only reason I entertained your false hope regarding the Beast was that I cared about your emotional needs. That is no longer the case."

"Don't say that. You still care about me—I'm your fucking sister for God's sake!"

"I have no sister."

The panic in her voice rose to a fever-pitch. "No… You can't abandon me like that, and I'm sure as hell not letting you kill Mother! You're fucking with the wrong person, Thane!" Lilly grabbed her purse and rushed out of the room.

Sir's eyes narrowed as he watched her go. He shut the door and ordered, "Look for the phone."

It was a shock to Brie how cunning Sir was. The two siblings were dangerously adept at manipulating each other.

She rifled through the drawers while Sir tore through Lilly's luggage with no luck. Sir scanned the room. "Leave nothing unturned—it's got to be here."

He finally struck gold when he overturned the mattress. The cell phone had been hidden between it and the box spring, stuffed clear to the center where it could not be found.

"I *knew* it," he growled furiously, holding up the phone.

Finding his cell was important on many levels. Not only did it prove Lilly's malicious intent, but just as critical to Sir, it had all his business contacts, information and messages.

"What a fool I was," he growled in disgust, slipping it into his pocket, "and I played right into her hands."

"I wish I hadn't encouraged you to ignore your cautious nature."

Sir shook his head. "You only told me what I wanted to hear. I needed to believe that Lilly was different, and now I'm paying the price for it."

"Not everyone is untrustworthy, Sir. You shouldn't have to question the loyalty of family."

"I forgot one fundamental rule—only bad comes from *anything* associated with my mother."

Brie wrapped her arms around him. "I disagree, Sir. You're proof of that."

Sir kissed the top of her head before directing her towards the door. "It's essential we distance ourselves from Lilly and everything to do with her."

"So we're not going to the hospital?" Brie asked in surprise.

"No. We'll be headed back to LA on the next available flight. I need to meet with Thompson to discuss how to proceed from here."

"What about your mother, Sir?"

"The Beast can rot for all I care!"

The harshness of his attitude was understandable, but it still shocked her. Such hatred could only hurt Sir in the end.

He saw her look of concern. "I will deal with her later, Brie. Right now I need to leave, or I'm liable to kill the Beast's daughter."

Sir took the hotel notepad on the desk and scribbled a quick message. He handed it to Brie and asked her to sign it, before leaving it on the disheveled bed for Lilly to find.

The phone has been located. Go crawl back to the hole you came from.

Further contact is prohibited.

Sincerely, Thane C. Davis and Brianna R. Bennett

On the plane ride home, Sir put his roomy first-class seat back in a full recline position and had Brie snuggle on top of him. He covered her with a blanket and held her, saying nothing. Those twelve hours were some of the most emotionally intimate she'd experienced with Sir, even though no words were exchanged.

When they finally landed, Sir whispered in her ear, "My safe haven."

"Always, Sir. Condors forever."

"Do you think I should get that tattooed on my ass?"

She smiled, giggling when she answered, "Only if it pleases you, Sir."

Sir spent his first week back locked in meetings with his lawyer, while Brie finished editing her film for Holloway's presentation. Although it was only a rough edit, she was determined to impress the man with her sequel.

Unfortunately, Mr. Holloway was in a foul mood when she finally had the chance to meet with him. If Brie had a choice, she would have cancelled the meeting right then and there.

As it was, she was forced to weather out the storm when he opened the meeting with, "Miss Bennett, I hope to hell it's good. I'm not in the mood for amateur hour."

"You'll be impressed," she replied evenly, handing him the DVD. He slipped it into the player and sat back, an unpleasant scowl on his face.

"Would you like me to come back another time?" Brie suggested before her film started, hoping he would jump on the offer.

"Hell, no. I'm behind enough as it is."

Brie kept her disappointment to herself, knowing there was a very real chance Mr. Holloway could pull the project, making all her hard work mean nothing. She took a deep breath, trying to calm her racing heart.

The intro began with a dark screen and some heavy bass. He paused the film and frowned. "What's this crap?"

"It's called dubstep, Mr. Holloway. It's popular among young people."

"Pick something more classic, damn it. Our target audience is much broader, Miss Bennett."

She nodded, mentally noting where she could add dubstep farther into the film as she wrote down his suggestion. He was right, of course—this documentary *was* meant to be multi-generational. "Got it."

He huffed, growling to himself, "Why I have to point out the obvious is beyond me."

Brie hated falling short of his expectations, but suspected that anyone who had the misfortune of crossing paths with him today was guaranteed to suffer similar humiliation.

She noticed his keen interest whenever Mary came onto the screen. This wasn't the first time he'd shown interest in her, and Brie was curious why. Was it simply due to her good looks, or did she and the producer have some kind of personal connection Brie didn't know about?

Whatever the case, Holloway seemed disgusted when the documentary ended. "I specifically asked for more scenes with Miss Wilson. Where the hell are they?"

"They're all there, Mr. Holloway. There were some unforeseen issues at the commune, which limited her screen time."

He leaned forward, snarling, "And I bet those *issues* would make great film, wouldn't they, Miss Bennett?"

"No."

"Yet again you disappoint me. You're not a great film-maker, Miss Bennett. You don't have the instincts for it." He leaned forward and added harshly, "You're so concerned about people's *feelings* that you sabotage your own damn work."

Brie felt sick. It was clear that Mr. Holloway hated the film...and even worse, he was right about her. Her concern for Mary and Faelan were more important than the success of this documentary. "I'm sorry to disappoint you, Mr. Holloway."

"It's not just me who's disappointed. Surely you must be disgusted by this amateurish attempt. Such a shame your parents wasted their hard-earned retirement putting the likes of you through college."

Had it been a year ago, Brie would have been crushed by Mr. Holloway's words—but not anymore. She was confident in her abilities and wasn't willing to back down. "I have a good handle on what the viewers want to see, and this second documentary has it. Wouldn't you agree that Rytsar Durov's scene is a powerful piece of film?"

He raised his eyebrow as he thought back on it. "With the recent publicity concerning him, that might play out in our favor—but it's not enough."

"You didn't care for my scene with Baron?"

A slight smirk greeted her question, but he quickly squashed it.

His unconscious reaction let her know that her film hit closer to the mark than he wanted to let on. Brie was certain that her work was not the huge disaster he was claiming it to be. The challenge was getting him to admit it without pissing him off.

"I thought the session with Ms. Clark playing with

her two subs was entertaining to watch."

He nodded. "The Domme is majestic on screen."

"I also believe the audience will go crazy for Tono Nosaka's modern version of Kinbaku."

Mr. Holloway took out a cigar and lit it, taking in a long drag before releasing the smoke slowly from his lips. "It has merit."

"Am I wrong in assuming that the issue you have with my film boils down to it not having enough drama?"

"No," he stated firmly, leaning towards her. "Not more drama, Miss Bennett. I asked for more of Miss Wilson. I couldn't have made it clearer—and yet you defy me." He pointed his cigar at her. "*That* is what I have an issue with."

Brie understood that the fate of her film was in jeopardy, and gently defended herself. "Defy is a strong word, Mr. Holloway. I *had* planned to get additional shots centering on Miss Wilson, but extenuating circumstances prevented it."

"As the producer, I'm not interested in excuses. Where is she now?"

"Mary is staying in Denver at the moment," Brie answered, not offering any specifics.

Mr. Holloway answered with a condescending smile, "Then I suggest you get on a plane right *now* and film Miss Wilson, like I asked."

Brie knew better than to argue with the man in his current state, so she swallowed her pride and stood up. "I'll take what you've said into consideration."

"No. You will do exactly what I say or I'll shitcan the

film."

It took everything in her not to respond. Instead of jeopardizing the film further, Brie simply nodded and started towards the door, but she couldn't help looking back and asking, "What is your interest in Miss Wilson, anyway?"

The surly man glared at her. "Out!"

Brie smiled. Whatever strange hold Mary had over Mr. Holloway, it was enough to keep her documentary alive—for now.

Brie laughed to herself as she exited the building, pleased by how much she'd grown. Before Sir and the Training Center, a heated confrontation like that would have completely derailed her, but now she actually felt energized by it. There was a thrill in being challenged on work she was passionate about.

This was a different kind of confidence. For Brie it wasn't about fighting to save herself, it was about fighting for the project and all the people who could benefit from the film. Little did Mr. Holloway suspect he had unleashed the dragon inside her, and woe befall any man who got in her way.

The Limo Ride

B rie did not take Mr. Holloway's advice about running back to Denver. Instead, she started rearranging the scenes in the film, having been inspired by their meeting. She knew Mary and Faelan needed time alone, and frankly, so did she and Sir.

Sir was extremely busy with his business and their wedding plans, but surprisingly, rather than spend his nights working, which had been his norm, he made the choice to put away his computer every evening and revel in his submissive instead.

Each night Sir sat, drinking his martini, as he admired a new pose he'd requested from her. It was like a game between them—she was his canvas and he was the artist. It had the feel of objectification, except for the fact she was the center of attention.

It reminded Brie of nude models who posed for hours as the painter captured the image, except that Sir painted his picture with words rather than brush strokes, describing what he saw as he leisurely sipped his drink.

Sir often played the song 'Cinema' by Benny Benassi

before they began the evening's entertainment. He said it expressed how he felt perfectly and every time Brie heard it, she was humbled and fell even more in love with him.

Tonight's pose had her naked on the tantra chair. She was lying on it, facing away from him but looking back over her shoulder. He had draped white silk around her, then adjusted it strategically so it exposed most of her back and just a hint of her ass.

"I like it when you are facing away from me, téa. Your coy expression as you look back at me moves your Master."

She smiled, a slight blush rising to her cheeks.

"But tonight's pose is especially erotic. I must applaud myself. Having the beauty that is your ass barely peeking out from the white silk… I could literally stare at you for hours and never tire of it."

She grinned. "How long has it been tonight?"

He looked at his watch and raised an eyebrow, admitting, "Already two hours and ten minutes. There's something alluring about having you displayed but not being able to partake of you that has my libido soaring."

"I feel the same, Master. I just want to turn around and open my legs to you."

He tsked. "Such a naughty girl." He pressed down on his slacks, adjusting his hardening cock. Sometimes Sir allowed her to play with herself to completion. On other days, he'd let her suffer.

Tonight was one of those nights when they were suffering together. Instead of driving her crazy, it seemed to draw her closer to him. Sir talked about the day, sharing moments he normally glossed over.

Rather than working hard on projects or having

mind-blowing sex together, they were spending time communicating about the little things, which led into broader topics and impassioned discussions about life, politics and the future of society. The entire time, Brie stayed in her pose and Sir watched her from his vantage point.

On occasion, he commanded her to pleasure him with her mouth at the end of the evening. In those rare instances, Brie swore he gazed down at her with a new level of admiration that had nothing to do with her skills as a submissive.

Brie received a text in the afternoon, and naturally assumed Sir was giving instructions for her next pose, but she was in for a surprise when she read:

Limo will pick you up at 7:00. Pearls a must. No undergarments.

She should have been excited, but her two experiences with limousines had both ended in disaster. It was hard to forget, but ever the optimist, she was willing to try again with Sir.

Brie smiled as she picked up the red velvet box that held the black pearls he'd given her for Christmas. Sir had created such incredible memories, despite his aversion to the holiday. She trusted that he would do the same tonight, changing the dread she felt about fancy limousines.

She chose a form-fitting black dress with a high neckline, long sleeves and a short, flouncy skirt that would focus all his attention on her legs. Brie took the pearls from their box and slid them across her lips, imagining where else those pearls might end up that night.

Putting the long strand around her neck, she slipped it under her dress at the back—a little tease for Sir.

Brie was meticulous as she applied her makeup and styled her hair. She wore it up to show off her long neck and added a few inviting curls to encourage him to nibble her throat.

Fifteen minutes before seven, she headed downstairs and found the limousine already waiting for her. She giggled nervously as the driver opened the door, but was surprised that Sir was not inside to greet her.

Brie found a note waiting for her on the leather seat instead.

Tonight we break the curse of the limo.

She kissed the ink of the note, loving his beautiful handwriting. It added a thrill to the adventure knowing he was waiting somewhere else for her to arrive.

Brie stared out of the window as the limousine made its way to the coast. The driver dropped her off at a private beach and instructed her to follow the sandy trail to her destination. He handed her a flashlight. "In case you get lost in the dark."

Brie thanked him before setting off, ready for the adventure to begin.

Without the moonlight to guide her, she found her

little flashlight invaluable as she navigated the thick vegetation out to the beach. When she saw a fire burning, she turned off her light and followed its romantic glow.

Brie was surprised that Sir was not waiting for her as she approached the fire pit, but she found a blanket with a picnic basket and a black sash. She spied another note and picked it up.

Take off your shoes, put on the blindfold.
Kneel towards the ocean and await your Master.

Shivers of anticipation coursed through Brie as she followed his instructions. She knelt on the blanket, the black sash secured tightly, and listened for his approach, but the smell of the ocean and hypnotic sound of the waves overtook her senses and she jumped when she felt his touch.

He chuckled warmly. "Did I scare you?"

"Surprised is more the word."

Sir paused for a moment, then asked, "Did you bring the pearls?"

"Of course."

He swept his hand over the material of her dress, finding the pearls she had hidden underneath. "Ah…" Each pearl tickled her skin as he slowly pulled the long strand out from under her dress. He caressed her hard nipples and commented, "I see your body remembers the pleasure of pearls."

"I have never forgotten," she purred.

Sir looped the strand several times before placing it over her head and tying a knot, so that layers of pearls rested tight against her throat.

A collar of pearls, she mused.

"Tonight you will try different aphrodisiacs and tell me which one turns you on the most, téa," he explained.

She grinned. "Sounds arousing, Master."

"The first has been an old standby for centuries." Brie listened as he opened the basket, then Sir growled huskily, commanding, "Open."

She opened her mouth to take in his treat and quickly regretted it as the salty sliminess of a raw oyster filled her mouth.

"Swallow."

With pure determination, she gagged the nasty thing down and opened her mouth again.

"Not a fan?" he asked.

She shuddered. "No. Nothing sexy about that, Master."

"Maybe this is more to your liking…"

She smelled its sweet scent before he brought it to her lips. *Strawberry…* Brie purred as the skin of the fruit broke between her teeth and its sweet juices washed over her tongue. "Oh, yes. This definitely does it for me."

He kissed her juice-covered lips after he fed the last of it to her. "So sweet."

Sir acquired a new item from the basket and explained, "Like the oyster, this has a *long* history of increasing desire."

Brie closed her mouth, now suddenly wary. She'd read once that balut, a fertilized duck egg, was considered an ancient aphrodisiac. After the oyster, she couldn't stomach the thought. "Please, Sir. It's not balut, is it? Please say it isn't."

His amused laughter was not promising. "Open, téa."

"Please don't make me swallow it if it is, Master."

"You will swallow everything I give you."

She opened her mouth to please him, but she could not stop from whimpering as she did so.

"Wider, téa. Stick out your tongue."

With trepidation, she did as he asked. The seconds dragged by as she waited, her innocent tongue defenselessly exposed to the mysterious aphrodisiac he was offering.

Brie cried out the moment the first drop made contact with her tongue, then giggled as sweet honey covered it. The complex flavors of the golden liquid teased her mouth, delighting her taste buds. Sir dribbled some onto her bottom lip so that it slowly dripped down to her chin, then he moved in and seductively licked it off.

Brie moaned in pure pleasure.

"I take it honey agrees with you?"

"Very much, Master." She sought out his lips again, kissing Sir deeply as she shared what was left of the honey.

He broke the kiss, mumbling to himself, "And you thought I was going to feed you balut…"

She felt his warm breath against her ear when he commanded again, "Open."

This time she willingly offered her mouth to him. The texture of the next food was creamy and smooth, although it was not sweet like the honey. "I didn't realize avocados were considered an aphrodisiac."

He growled into her ear. "Oh, but they are… Avocados are the only fruits that look like a testicle hanging from the tree and female genitalia when they're halved and pitted. Certain religions even banned them to protect their parishioners from sinful thoughts."

Sir placed another piece of it in her mouth. Brie appreciated the seductive feel of the flesh and its sinful creaminess.

"Your thoughts?" he asked.

"I have new respect for the naughtiness of the fruit, Master."

"Now for one that is a personal favorite."

Brie leaned closer to him, excited to know what he enjoyed most.

"Tilt your head up and part those pretty lips."

She moaned when she felt his warm lips on hers as he kissed her with wine in his mouth. She remembered the distinctive flavor of berries and vanilla, and it took her straight back to that day on the island when he'd 'kidnapped' her.

"Your father's wine," she said when he broke the kiss. "Definitely a powerful aphrodisiac."

"Brunello di Montalcino *is* a powerful force," he agreed. Sir left a trail of light nibbles on her neck before murmuring into her ear, "And to think one day I will be celebrating our child's rite of passage with it."

Brie's heart fluttered at the thought.

Our child…

Sir spoiled Brie with several long kisses, imparting more of the red wine and stoking the flames of her desire.

"I need you," she whispered.

Sir lightly caressed the pearls around Brie's neck.

"Patience, téa. We still have one left."

He collected it from the basket, telling her to open her mouth. "Women swear by this," he said in a low, sultry voice.

Sir placed a small morsel in her mouth, and she closed her lips around it as the decadently rich taste flooded her mouth. "Chocolate…"

"Does it turn you on, téa? Does it make you want to throw all caution to the wind and give in to your desire?"

Brie moaned as she felt his teeth graze her neck just above the pearls before he bit down.

"I'm burning with desire," she groaned.

"Then I think it's time to christen these black pearls." Her breath quickened as he untied the blindfold and let her watch as he carefully loosened the knot, removing the pearls from around her neck.

Sir lifted her dress over her head, leaving her naked before him. He then began to undress himself, his hard cock announcing the level of his arousal. He lay down beside Brie, holding the long strand of pearls. "Pearls are said to represent purity and harmony." He interlaced the fingers of his right hand with the fingers of her left. "Both attributes speak to your character. The purity of your love sustains me and the harmony of your spirit heals me."

Sir slowly wrapped the necklace around their wrists once and slipped one end through the opposite loop, pulling it tight. He then continued binding her to him, using the necklace like rope. When he reached the end, he laced the pearls back through the binding, securing it tightly.

"I have bound us together for a reason, téa."

She looked at their wrists joined by pearls, charmed by his creativity. "Why, Master?"

"I plan to show you how quickly a goddess becomes a slut."

Brie's loins contracted in pleasure as he placed her free hand on his rigid cock. "Your challenge is to make me come before you do."

She leaned closer and growled in his ear, "I *like* this challenge, Master."

"Whoever wins gets to decide where we will honeymoon."

"Anywhere?"

"Anywhere your little heart desires—provided you win, of course."

Brie frowned, realizing his strategy. "Did you just stack the odds in your favor by feeding me aphrodisiacs?"

Sir winked at her.

"You're playing dirty."

"It's about to get a whole lot dirtier, princess." Sir grabbed her throat with his unbound hand and started nibbling on her ear.

She felt a trickle of wetness between her legs, her body reacting favorably to his dominance. Determined to win, she started stroking his cock.

Sir held his bound wrist above her head, effectively pinning her left arm there as he moved out of reach, leaving a trail of kisses from her throat down to her breasts.

"Not fair," she cried as his tongue rimmed the outline of her areola, before he took her entire nipple into his mouth and started sucking. "Really not fair..." she moaned.

Brie reached out blindly with her right hand, stretching to find his cock. To his credit, Sir did not move once she found it. She wrapped her fingers around his hard shaft. Apparently he liked this game as well…

Maybe a little too much, she thought gleefully, when she felt the wetness of his pre-come dripping from his cock.

The natural lube made pleasuring him easier, and she soon found her rhythm as she stroked his length in slow, twisting motions.

Sir groaned, enjoying her attention. He removed his hand from her throat and began to caress her wet clit, giving as good as he got.

Brie arched her back, trying hard not to succumb to the delicious flood of heat he was creating. When he slipped his finger inside and found her swollen G-spot, she knew she was in trouble.

With a tighter hold, she pumped his shaft, hoping to break him before he broke her, but hearing Sir breathe heavily was such a turn-on… Her pussy started to pulse and she struggled to get away, but being bound to Sir made it impossible.

"Please…" she cried.

"You want to come?" he growled huskily in her ear.

"No…oooohhhhh," she moaned when Sir swirled his finger over the swollen spot.

Out of desperation, she changed the tempo of her stroking, slowing down rather than speeding up, concentrating all her attention on the head of his shaft.

When he stiffened against her, she felt victory was near. That was when his lips sought out her neck and he whispered, "And she comes…my goddess, my slut," as he bit down, sending chills rocketing straight to her groin.

Brie tensed as the first wave of her orgasm rolled over her against her will. She threw her head back, crying in frustration, "Nooo..." but it felt so good that soon she was moaning, "Yes...oh, yes..."

Before she'd finished climaxing, Sir joined her, his whole body shuddering as the warm liquid of his release covered her.

"That was so hot," she sighed as she looked up at the stars.

"And I won," he added with a grin.

"Not by enough to count."

He turned his head, raising his eyebrow at her. "Close only counts in horseshoes, babygirl."

"Cheater."

"Winner."

She laughed and sought out his warm body as the cool night breeze played with the sweat on her skin. She lightly kissed the 't' on his chest. "Where will the honeymoon be?"

"As with the wedding, it shall remain my secret."

She giggled, feeling too content to care. She held up their interlaced hands and gazed at them thoughtfully. "I know it will be amazing."

"I hope to take your breath away."

"You already do, Sir."

Sir leaned over and kissed her before undoing their pearl bond. He gathered her into his arms and they lay there, listening to the soothing sound of the ocean as the fire crackled beside them.

"This is enough," she declared.

White Russian

Brie woke up to the sound of two male voices in the kitchen. She quickly donned her silk robe and made her way out of the bedroom. She immediately recognized the deep tones of the Russian's laughter.

"Rytsar! What the heck are you doing here?"

"*Radost moya*," he said, his arms outstretched.

Brie looked at Sir as she hugged the burly man, shaking her head in surprise.

"Rytsar has come to escort you to Denver before you meet me in China," Sir explained.

She was stunned by his statement. "Why?"

Sir's smile faded. "I need to go to New York with Thompson. There are a few items that must be ironed out."

"With Lilly? Then I should go with you."

He shook his head. "Thompson will act as my liaison, so there will be no face-to-face contact with the girl. You, on the other hand, need to get that last bit of footage for your film."

"But I've decided not to—"

"No, Brie. To defy Mr. Holloway would be a grave mistake. Wallace and Miss Wilson know the reason you are coming. I leave it up to you to work out the details of the shoot."

Brie frowned. "Sir, I don't want to be separated from you again. Not when it's so close to the wedding."

"I'm here to act as your Master's stand-in," Rytsar declared. "You will not miss him."

Brie giggled. "While I'm grateful, Rytsar," she looked at Sir, "I want to be with you."

"And you will be—for a lifetime. It's unfortunate that this extra step is necessary to end the Beast's life."

Brie walked over to Sir, wrapping her arms around his waist. "At least you won't be alone when it's time."

"Although she is already dead, I will be grateful to have both of you beside me when she breathes her last."

"You are doing the right thing, *moy droog*," Rytsar assured Sir, slapping him on the back. "Since I have known you, she has haunted your life. It is time."

Sir laughed uncomfortably. "I'm unsure whether I can handle the loss."

Rytsar's tone was sober when he answered, "You will be surprised how much you miss the weight on your shoulders initially, but trust me, *moy droog*, you grow used to it."

Sir nodded. "I look forward to that day, old friend."

"Are you sure Lilly won't fight you over this?" Brie asked.

Sir's voice became ominous. "She will have no choice. Thompson and I are seeing to that. Once the Beast is gone, all familial ties will be severed."

"And you will finally be free," Rytsar stated.

"A new life," Sir agreed, kissing Brie on the top of the head.

She looked up and smiled. "As man and wife."

"With a kinky white Russian," Rytsar added, grabbing her ass in his strong hands.

"Hands off, old friend. We are practicing abstinence."

Rytsar smiled knowingly, taking his hands from her ass and placing one on her tummy. "That can only mean one thing."

"Well, we're going to start trying, at least," Brie said, blushing.

Rytsar stared at Sir. "Thank you, *moy droog*."

"For what? This will be my child, not yours," Sir joked.

Rytsar shook his head and said solemnly, "For showing me what's possible."

Silence followed his statement.

Eventually Sir nodded. "You said yourself the defective should not accept a lesser life."

"*Da…*" He gazed at Brie wistfully, then smiled. "I amaze myself with my wisdom."

Brie discovered just how possessive Rytsar could be when they traveled to Denver. Although Master Anderson graciously offered his home to them, the Russian would have none of it. "When you are under my protection, no other man will care for you."

It wasn't a topic up for discussion, so Brie accepted it when they stayed at a hotel instead. She quickly learned, however, that it also meant she had to ask permission whenever it involved others—even a simple phone call to Mary.

She had just dialed the number and hadn't even said hello yet when he hung up the phone. "Who are you calling?"

"Mary! Why did you do that, Rytsar?" Brie protested.

"No calls without permission."

"But why? I'm not wearing your temporary collar."

"You are precious to me, *radost moya*. I must know where you are and who you are talking to at all times. I will not fail you or your Master while you are under my watch."

The passion in his voice touched Brie, so she did not question him again. "May I call Mary?"

"*Da*, but you must okay any meetings with me before you commit to others."

Brie gave him a chagrined look. "Fine."

"Fine what?" he asked in his sexy Russian accent.

"Fine, Rytsar."

"*Nyet*."

"Fine, Rytsar Durov."

"*Nyet*."

"What, then?"

"You may address me as Ruler of My Universe."

Brie giggled, but answered dutifully, "Fine, oh Ruler of My Universe."

"Better, but I could do without the giggling."

She broke out in a peal of laughter, shaking her head as she called Mary again.

Naturally, Rytsar insisted on being present during the filming, confiding to her, "I still do not trust Wolf Boy."

"Should I get a shotgun for you?" she teased.

"No," he answered, with a smug look on his face. "My 'nines should do nicely if he crosses the line."

Mary had informed Brie that Faelan was recovering well, considering where he'd started from, but that she was still concerned about the scene. "*You* are not worth his health, Brie."

"I agree. I wasn't even planning to ask, but Sir insisted. I've been thinking about it and I believe what I have in mind shouldn't put any strain on his body. Really, I have no idea why Mr. Holloway is so obsessed with you."

"Eh, it doesn't surprise me."

"Why? Do you know him?" Brie asked, hoping to sate her curiosity.

Mary laughed. "No."

"Oh, so you just naturally assume he's obsessed because of your charm and good looks."

"You know it, Stinky."

"Well, I think he must have a mental disorder, just like Todd."

"Odd…"

"What's odd?"

"You're asking me for a favor and yet you insult me."

"Hey, what are friends for?"

Mary scoffed. "I find friendship highly overrated."

"Says the girl with no friends…"

Brie met the two at the Denver Academy, with Rytsar glued to her side.

Faelan was *not* thrilled to have a fellow Dom observing him. As soon as he entered the room, he asserted his dominance over the Russian.

"You, over there," Faelan ordered, pointing Rytsar to a far-off corner. "You will not speak or offer direction while I'm scening today."

Rytsar snorted. "One inappropriate word or touch, and you will be crying to the moon, Wolf Boy."

"Why did you have to bring him?" Faelan complained to Brie.

"Rytsar is my escort, as per Sir's orders."

Faelan's blue eyes sparkled with amusement. "What? Is Davis back to worrying about me now?"

Rytsar growled under his breath and started towards Todd, who immediately backed away from Brie. "Calm down, old man. I have no need to fish elsewhere." Faelan turned to Mary, looping his finger around the ring of her new collar, pulling her close. "This sub suits my needs just fine."

Brie was impressed by how good Faelan looked. He moved stiffly, hinting at the pain he still suffered, but his color was good and his eyes were just as magnetic as ever. Faelan's recovery seemed like a miracle, and she felt certain Mary had everything to do with it.

She explained the scene to Faelan, "I want this scene to showcase a simple lesson many subs experience, while letting you basically just lie there without having to tax your body."

Mary teased, "Oh, I'll make sure he taxes something."

Faelan winked at her. "Tax it, baby."

Rytsar grunted in the corner, their silly banter too much for him, but Brie was thoroughly charmed by it.

"I don't want you undressing for this scene, Todd. Keep your shirt and tie on, as well as your pants. Women love a well-dressed man, and it will hide your recent scars from the camera. Oh, and do you mind calling her 'pet' for the scene?"

Faelan looked at Mary with a smirk.

Brie instructed Mary, "You will wear only your heels, bra and panties."

"Nice," Mary commented. "What do I get to address him as? Motherfucker?"

Brie laughed. "No, you get to call him by his title."

Mary sighed, but faced her man and asked, "May I strip, Faelan?"

"Of course, pet. I want you to show that scowling Russian over there what he's missing."

Rytsar kept his eyes locked on Faelan with a fierce look of distrust.

Watching Mary undress had a visible effect on Faelan. He loosened his tie and undid several of the buttons of his white shirt. His exposed chest would read well on the camera, along with his magnetic blue eyes. No doubt women would eat this scene up.

"Okay, Todd, you'll sit here in the leather chair. I'll be filming directly in front of you. Try to find a comfortable position, because you'll be staying in it for the entire shoot."

Brie felt wickedly clever. She hadn't liked feeling pressured by Mr. Holloway to get this last shot, so she'd created a scene meant to tease the producer—as well as the audience.

"Now, Mary, remember you're supposed to be new at this."

"Yeah, yeah…"

"Don't 'yeah, yeah' me. This is serious. I want you to come off as a believable novice."

"I got this, Brie."

"Do you have any questions for me?" Brie asked Faelan before they began shooting.

"Sure." His eyes sparkled mischievously. "How many times do you think I could make you come with just my tongue?"

Rytsar answered for her from where he stood, "None, because you would be picking up your teeth from the floor after I gave you a proper Russian hello."

Brie smiled at Rytsar as she positioned herself behind the camera. "Mr. Wallace, I believe Rytsar is trying to protect you from a sexual harassment lawsuit."

Faelan's laughter was cut short as he sat down. Brie noticed him grimacing with pain and figured it only served him right for baiting Rytsar like that.

"Mary, if you could open his shirt a little more…yes, that's it. Perfect."

"He fucking is," Mary agreed as she got down on her

knees between Faelan's legs. "How do I look?"

"The back of your head is pure perfection."

Mary glanced over her shoulder. "I *can't* believe you told me to spend extra time on my makeup."

Brie snickered to herself.

"Whenever you're ready," Faelan said. She nodded and started her silent countdown before hitting *record*.

Faelan began the scene by caressing Mary's hair.

"Undo my belt and unzip my pants, pet. I have a new lesson for you."

Mary looked down at his crotch and hesitated for a second before doing what he asked.

"Do you see how hard you make your Master?"

She nodded, her long mane of blonde curls moving alluringly up and down her back with the movement of her head.

"Open your lips and take it into your mouth."

Mary moved with a lack of confidence as she made an awkward attempt to free his cock from its confines and giggled softly from the effort. The sound of her innocent laughter was charming.

She took his shaft in one hand and stared at it for a second before slowly lowering her head.

Faelan sucked in his breath, indicating the moment her lips made contact with him. Brie felt the first stirrings of desire in her nether regions.

Crap, this might prove a harder shoot than I thought.

Soon Mary's head was bobbing up and down, but it wasn't enough. "Deeper," Faelan commanded gently.

She took it a little deeper, not really challenging herself. "Deeper," he ordered, his tone more demanding.

Mary lowered her head and made a choking sound, popping back up as if she were scared by the feeling.

"That was good, pet. Try that again, but don't pull away this time," Faelan encouraged.

Mary went back down on him, lowering her head until she started to gag.

"Good, keep it there. Get your throat used to the feel of my cock."

Mary only lasted a few seconds more before she lifted her head, pretending to gasp for air.

"Again," he told her.

Mary obediently went back down on him, but this time when she tried to pull away, Faelan pressed her head lower, "Deeper, pet. That's it…" He continued to hold her even as she struggled to breathe.

When he let go, she came up gasping for breath.

He wiped her mouth, looking down lustfully at her. "There we go—I want to see your mouth dribbling with more spit."

Mary moaned softly, indicating her excitement at trying to please him.

"Do you want to try again, pet?"

Brie really liked how Faelan was demanding more but still taking it slow with Mary—encouraging with his praise rather than forcing her to submit.

Mary nodded enthusiastically. This time she went much lower, taking most of him into her throat, but when he started to thrust she began sputtering and struggled to break free. This time Faelan held her down on his shaft, saying repeatedly in a soothing voice, "Take it, pet, take it…"

She coughed when he finally released her and wiped the water from her eyes.

"A challenge, yes?" he asked.

"Yes, Faelan, but I like it."

"Good, because this time I'm going to fuck your pretty face."

Mary took several deep breaths to ready herself before descending on his cock again. As she took him into her mouth, he fisted her hair, forcing his cock even deeper down her throat. It was actually a turn-on to watch Mary struggle as she instinctively pushed her hands against him as he thrust.

"Hands, pet," Faelan warned her.

Mary put her hands behind her back and continued to take his lustful face-fucking.

Brie had to give the woman kudos. She totally believed, based on Mary's performance, that this was her first time.

Mary moaned loudly when Faelan finally released her.

"You like that, don't you?" he growled, pulling her head back to look him in the eye.

"Yes," she whispered hoarsely.

"For being such a willing student, I will come in your mouth."

Mary stared into his eyes, neither of them saying anything for several moments, the connection evident during their intimate yet voiceless exchange.

"Are you ready?"

Brie felt her pussy react to Faelan's question and rolled her eyes, vowing never to let Mary know a towel would be necessary after the filming of their scene.

When Mary nodded, Faelan commanded firmly, "Open."

He took her head in both hands and forced her mouth up and down his shaft, grunting with pleasure. Mary moaned enthusiastically, her hair bouncing rhythmically on her back with each thrust. Finally Faelan's body stiffened, his hands gripping her head as he released his come deep in her throat.

"Swallow, pet."

Brie bit her lip, panning back to show Mary's beautiful body, her hands still behind her back in a perfect submissive pose as Faelan finished off inside her mouth.

Well done, Mary…

Once Brie was finished packing up her equipment, she went over to them with Rytsar standing protectively by her side. "That was amazing to watch. I totally believed you were inexperienced, woman. How did you pull it off so convincingly?"

"It was easy, Stinky Cheese. I just pretended I was you."

Brie looked at her in shock, then burst out laughing. "You're such an ass, Mary."

Brie spent the night in the company of her dearest friends. Autumn had invited her over to join Tono and Lea for dinner. Naturally, Rytsar joined her as well, acting as her charming yet intimidating bodyguard.

As soon as she entered Autumn's home, Brie was attacked by Lea. "Girl! How lucky am I? I didn't think I'd get to see you again until the wedding."

"Yeah, I can't believe you're going to be there with me. It's so far to travel, you know?" Brie answered, hoping to trick Lea into telling her the wedding destination.

"Nebraska's not that far from here."

Brie couldn't tell whether Lea was teasing her or not. "Right, Nebraska…"

A deep red blush crept from Lea's cheeks to her breasts, as if she had just realized she'd said too much. She made a funny face and blurted, "What's the difference between Nebraska and yogurt?" Lea didn't even wait for Brie to answer before giving away the punchline. "Yogurt has an active living culture."

"But that's not a joke, girl, because it's true," Brie replied, swatting Lea's butt. As they made their way into Autumn's kitchen, she was left wondering if she had just been played. There was no way her wedding would be in Nebraska—no way!

Brie was impressed by Autumn's cooking skills. The girl had truly outdone herself, having made four different kinds of pizza for them to try. The pies filled the kitchen with their heavenly aroma as the cheese bubbled under the broiler. Brie noted she'd made some of Tono's favorites.

The Asian Dom was the picture of health, and his soulful spirit seemed to take over the room. He stood up and bowed to Rytsar and then to her. "It is a pleasure to see you both again."

If he was surprised by the presence of the Russian Dom, he didn't show any indication of it, but Brie explained, "Rytsar Durov is taking me to China to meet with Sir."

Tono's expression saddened. "Has the time finally come?"

Brie nodded, unable to tell him all that had gone on during her first trip to China. She had no doubt that Tono could tell there had been terrible complications, but he only said, "I'm sorry for your Master, but I know you will be a great comfort to him."

His simple encouragement soothed her troubled spirit, and she bowed. "Thank you, Tono. I take great solace in that."

Autumn cried out as she pulled the last pan of sizzling-hot pizza from the oven and quickly placed it on the table, sticking two of her fingers in her mouth.

"Are you okay?" Tono asked, moving to get up.

She waved off his concern. "No, no… It's nothing, Ren. Please don't get up."

Brie didn't miss that Autumn was calling Tono by his first name. That was huge in the Japanese culture and spoke of a deeper level of friendship. It appeared that her caring for the Kinbaku Master after his surgery had progressed their relationship in a positive direction.

Autumn gave her a hug. "So glad you could come for a surprise visit, Brie."

"Yeah, it seems there's no rest for the wicked, but at least I get the perk of seeing you guys again. By the way, Autumn, I forgot to introduce you. This is my good friend—and part-time bodyguard—Rytsar Durov."

Autumn glanced apprehensively at the impressive Russian. "Are you really her bodyguard?"

"In spirit," he answered with a slight smirk. "It is a pleasure to meet you, Miss Autumn. Or as we would say in my country—Miss *Osen.*"

"Oh, I like the way that sounds, Mr. Durov."

"Most things sound better in Russian."

Autumn laughed, then asked shyly, a blush rising to her cheeks, "Can I tell you a joke? I've been saving this one for a while."

"Please," he answered.

Brie stifled a giggle, knowing Rytsar had no idea what he was in for.

Autumn seemed really nervous, but forged ahead anyway. "I'm really starting to dislike those stupid Russian dolls."

He tilted his head and asked, "Do you mean the *matryoshkas?*"

"Yeah…" She paused for a moment. "They just seem so full of themselves."

Rytsar threw back his head and laughed. Not just a polite, forced kind of laugh, but an all-out rolling thunder of a laugh. The entire kitchen rocked with it, and everyone soon followed.

That was one of the best Brie had heard—and who better to share that joke with than Rytsar?

Goodbye

T he plane ride to China was such an excruciatingly long one that encouraged either sleep or deep conversation.

It was something that Brie actually appreciated, since she was with Rytsar. Once the stewardesses finished fawning over the Russian Dom and had retired to their stations, Brie turned to him and asked, "What happened with the girl from America after she revealed your name? Has there been any fallout from it?"

He shook his head, an amused look on his face. "You Americans…"

"What?"

"So tenacious."

"Why? What did she do?"

"It's not her, it's your damn reporters. Every few weeks, a new one shows up at my door begging for an exclusive interview."

"So they know where you live now?" Brie asked with concern.

"It was only a matter of time, *radost moya*. Thankfully,

no serious professionals, just little girls sent from the entertainment side of your news. So strange, the fascination you Americans have with celebrities…"

Brie lowered her voice, "Have you heard from the Russian police?"

"*Nyet*. Although I'm getting too much attention, having young female reporters from America hound me weekly has only made me a target for jest."

Brie sat back in her chair, sighing with relief. "I'm glad to hear it, Rytsar. I've really been worried."

He confided, "I've been tempted to show a few of the obstinate ones my true interests when they flirt so outrageously, hoping to get an interview. However, I do not think they could handle it."

"I agree," Brie said, laughing. "Most girls think being tickled with a feather is kinky. They have no idea what they'd be in for with you."

Rytsar's expression changed when he shared, "The girl, Stephanie, did send me a letter. I have not answered it because it would only complicate matters, but I keep it with me." Rytsar pulled out his leather wallet and took out a folded note, handing it to Brie.

She unfolded the letter, noticing the perfect penmanship, and wondered how many times the girl had rewritten it, wanting it to be flawless.

Dear Rytsar Durov,

I have not been able to stop thinking about you and what you did for me.

It's hard being back home. I'm not the same

person. No one understands me. Only someone who was there could know how I feel.

I know it's stupid, but every day I listen for a knock on the door, hoping you are there to rescue me from this strange existence. I feel so alone. You told me I am a survivor and that has helped me on those days when nothing makes sense.

I feel so ungrateful, because you have done so much for me. How can one person ever truly repay another for saving their life? I would do anything, give anything to do just that for you. Please, Rytsar, tell me what I can do. It would make me so happy to fulfill the debt I owe you.

Sincerely, Stephanie

"She is on the edge, *radost moya*. This letter is like taking a peek into Tatianna's soul." He glanced at the letter, stating, "It hurts me to read it."

Brie wrapped her arms around him. His whole body was tense, the muscles of his arms shaking with unreleased emotion. "She'll be okay," she assured him.

"I have sent a counselor to her, one who has much experience with freed sex slaves, but I'm uncertain whether it will be enough."

"You have done more than most people would ever do, Rytsar. You have to trust she can recover from it."

He looked at her, all his defenses down. "Do you know what my given name is?"

"No. Sir never told me."

Rytsar smiled. "He is a trustworthy comrade."

The Russian's intense blue gaze caused her to momentarily stop breathing when he spoke. "When my mother passed, I refused to be called by the name she'd given me, preferring my title instead." He looked down at her tenderly. "I would like to hear it spoken from your lips."

"What is your given name?"

"Anton."

Brie placed her hand on his square jaw and smiled when she said it. "Anton."

Tears came to his eyes. "Thank you, *radost moya*."

Rytsar folded up the letter and placed it back in his wallet. He stared out the window, seemingly lost in a sea of past pain and regret.

Priceless one... Brie knew that was the meaning of his name and could appreciate the power it must have over him. His mother was gone—how or why was still a mystery to Brie, but she suspected it had everything to do with his father.

Don't give up, Stephanie, Brie called out in her head, sending positive thoughts to the girl he'd rescued. *People are counting on you to survive.*

Rytsar's demeanor changed once they landed in Chengdu. He stayed beside her, his hand gripping the back of her neck. It was a very possessive hold that let others know to stay away.

"It's okay, Rytsar," Brie said, looking up at him. "I've been here before. It's a safe city."

He shook his head. "*Nyet.* There are human traffickers looking for foreigners like you. You are *not* safe."

Brie quickly scanned the airport in shock, wondering as each person passed which one held evil intentions behind their stoic expression. It was a frightening thought that Brie had never considered.

She could not hold back her excitement, however, when she recognized a familiar face in the sea of Chinese. "May I?" she asked Rytsar.

He released his hold, and Brie ran straight for Sir, nearly tripping over herself in her haste.

"Slow down, babygirl."

Brie buried her head in his chest, sighing with relief.

"Did Durov treat you well?" Sir asked, sounding concerned.

"I was the model of decorum," Rytsar answered as he walked up.

"He was, Sir. I'm just thrilled to see you."

Sir shook Rytsar's hand. "Thank you for taking care of her. I've had enough to worry about."

"How did it go in New York?" Rytsar asked.

"It was worse than I imagined, but it's done. Time to face the last unpleasant task."

"*Moy droog*, keep your eye on the prize. You're to be married in a few days."

Sir looked down at Brie. "I hope it's everything you've dreamed of."

"If I'm marrying you, it will be."

He ruffled the top of her head. "Good, because I questioned the location, although I know it means a lot to your parents."

Brie shot a look at Rytsar, hoping to see a look of

amusement, but he just smiled sympathetically at Brie.

Oh, wow, I really am getting married in Nebraska…

She sighed, realizing it didn't matter. Although she had hoped for someplace exotic, as long as Sir was the groom, she could have her wedding in the middle of a garbage dump and still be happy.

"What are the plans for today?" Rytsar asked him.

"We go to the hotel and partake of your favorite beverage. Tomorrow I will face my demons."

Brie took Sir's hand in hers and squeezed it. A silent reminder that she would be with him every step of the way.

Brie hadn't seen Ruth since the meeting at Mr. Thompson's office, and was unprepared when she walked into the luxurious private hospital room. Sir had spared no expense keeping the woman comfortable, despite her condition.

But it wasn't the accommodations that threw Brie off, it was Ruth herself. It was as if time had stood still, just as Sir had described—like Sleeping Beauty in the fairy tale. Ruth looked as if she were resting peacefully, a slight smile on her pink lips. It was disturbing on so many levels.

Brie could finally sympathize with Lilly for believing Ruth was still alive, because it truly seemed she might wake up at any moment. No wonder Sir had struggled with this decision…

A woman walked in wearing a crisp white outfit. She stopped short when she saw them and hastily explained, "I am here to do Madame's daily exercises."

"It's not needed anymore," Sir told her.

The woman bowed her head and left the room.

Brie felt tears threatening when she saw the look on Sir's face. It was killing him inside to do this. She put her arm around him in support.

"I hate you," he said, his voice full of venom as he stared down at his mother. "I hate that you are making me do this. I want to slap that fucking smirk off your face."

Rytsar slapped Ruth's face hard, the sickening sound of it echoing in the room.

"Why did you do that?" Brie asked in horror.

Rytsar told Sir, "She's not here, *moy droog*. You're talking to a ghost."

Sir nodded.

"Even though she is gone, if you would find solace in beating her, I will shut the door and let you have at it."

Brie's jaw dropped at the suggestion, but she kept silent in case Sir was seriously considering it.

"Beating a dead body would bring me no peace."

"Fine, but I do recommend screaming at it. There is great satisfaction to be had in letting your rage out."

Again Sir nodded.

"Would you like us to stand outside the door?" Rytsar asked.

"Yes."

Brie willingly went with Rytsar, although she was surprised that Sir wanted her to leave.

Rytsar shut the door, standing in front of it with his arms crossed while Sir's impassioned ranting began. Although Brie could hear the pain and anger in his voice, she could not make out his words.

The Russian looked down at her. "Do not feel bad that he sent you out. There are things that should remain between them. Memories too terrible to be shared."

"Why? Did he share them with you?"

"No, *radost moya*, I speak from my own experience."

"I'm sorry, Rytsar."

"There is no need to be sorry. It's not your burden to carry."

Brie frowned as she stared at the closed door, wishing with all her heart that she could share some of the burden Sir still carried. His tirade went on for what seemed like hours, then the room became deathly silent.

As the silence stretched on, Brie braved cracking open the door and found Sir on his knees beside the bed.

"Sir?"

When he did not respond, Brie entered the room and approached him hesitantly.

"Sir, are you okay?"

He did not look up, but answered in a broken voice, "No."

Brie knelt beside him and slipped her hand into his. "I'm here for you."

Sir looked up and questioned her. "Why do I still care? Why do I have any empathy for this beast of a woman?"

"She was a good mother when you were young. She loved both you and your father once."

"I wish I could forget," he snarled. "I don't want to feel any love towards her."

"You may hate me for saying it, but I don't want you to forget. I believe it's important to hold on to what was good, because it shaped you into the man you are today."

"It was all a lie."

"I don't think it was, but even if it was, you had a good childhood—you said so yourself. Hold on to it and let *that* be the legacy your parents leave behind."

Sir stood up, and stared at Ruth for several minutes before he took her limp hand. "Momma…"

Brie felt tears well up at the sound of love in his voice when he said the simple name.

"There was a time I loved you. It is my reality, although I wish I could deny it. I loved the games you played with me when we waited for Father's return. You let me rescue you from pirates and we explored the deepest jungles of Africa together from the safety of our living room. Your enthusiasm and creativity was something I cherished as a boy." He paused, looking at her frighteningly beautiful face. "It's hard for me to reconcile there was ever a time I felt safe and loved in your arms."

Tears began to fall as Brie watched Sir gather his mother's limp body in his arms and hug her. "But I'm still here, Momma. The little boy you once loved—your little *tesoro*. There's no reason to be frightened. The end of your suffering is here. It's time for you to let go…"

He laid her gently back down and said to Brie, "Tell Rytsar to get the doctor."

She silently exited the room, so choked up with emotion she was barely able to speak when she passed on the information to Rytsar. She returned to Sir, holding his hand in silent solidarity as they waited.

All three of them stood together and watched as the doctor began removing the tubes, saving the respirator for last.

"Are you ready, Mr. Davis?"

Sir closed his eyes, letting out a long breath. When he opened them again, his tone was resolute. "Yes."

Rytsar put his hand on Sir's shoulder as Sir wrapped his arm around Brie.

Once the respirator was turned off, Ruth's body started jerking as it fought unsuccessfully to take another breath.

"Go in peace, Momma. I forgive you…"

Brie began sobbing silently as Ruth's struggles ceased and the heart monitor went flat. The doctor checked her over before pronouncing her dead.

It wasn't until then that Sir cried. Brie knew he was mourning the death of the young mother he remembered, but Brie cried for an entirely different reason. Her pain came from knowing that Ruth would never have the chance to undo the wrongs she had done.

When the nurses came in to care for the body, Sir wiped the remaining tears from his eyes and announced, "We're done here."

They walked out of the hospital without saying a word. Rytsar hailed a cab and they went directly to the airport. He said his goodbyes as soon as they entered the building.

"I'm sorry to leave so soon, but I must run if I am to make my flight."

He leaned down and gave Brie a crushing hug. "I will see you in a few days, *radost moya*. Save a dance for me."

He put his hand on Sir's shoulder and grasped it tightly. "It will take time to adjust, but the worst is over, *moy droog*. Concentrate on the wedding, and deal with the lingering effects later. They aren't going anywhere."

"Sound advice, old friend."

Sir gave him a hug that lasted longer than normal, causing several passing businessmen to stare. The two men slapped each other hard on the back before letting go.

It was difficult to watch Rytsar walking away—it felt like part of their strength was leaving with him.

"Come, Brie," Sir said, handing her a plane ticket. She looked down to see if they were heading to Nebraska and was shocked to see the word "Italy" written on her ticket. Sir explained, "I thought it was important that we see my grandparents before we get married."

"I think we all need that, Sir."

"I agree, babygirl." Sir placed his hand on the small of her back as he escorted her through the busy airport. The despondent look on his handsome face was enough to break a girl's heart.

La Famiglia

B rie was just as enchanted by the island as she had been the first time they'd taken the boat ride to Portoferraio. She could see the change in Sir as they drew closer to his father's hometown. He faced into the ocean breeze coming off the water, a look of expectation and exhilaration on his face.

She felt it too—a sense of coming home.

Sir smiled and squeezed her hand as the ferry approached the port and docked. "It's good to be back."

"It's been too long," she agreed.

The sky was a brilliant blue and the sun shone down on them with its gentle warmth as they walked the narrow streets towards his grandparents' home. Brie was captivated by the bright magenta flowers that graced the walls and fences of many of the buildings.

"What are these called? They're absolutely beautiful, Sir." She took a branch in her hand to smell it and quickly let go, surprised that the flowers had nasty thorns.

Sir laughed as he brought her fingers to his lips and

kissed them. "They're bougainvillea. Beautiful to look at but painful to cuddle."

She giggled, taking his arm as they continued their trek up the steep hill. "Have you ever considered living here, Sir?"

He stopped and looked towards the ocean. "Maybe when we're older and life has slowed down for us."

Brie snuggled against him. "Wouldn't it be lovely walking these streets as a happy old couple?"

He gazed down at her and smiled. "Yes, it would."

Sir led her to the apartment with the vivid red door Brie remembered well, and he knocked. From inside she heard the excited voices of numerous people. "It seems they're expecting us this time."

Sir's Aunt Fortuna, whom Brie had met on their first visit, opened the door wide and grabbed him. "Thane!" A flurry of Italian words followed, which obviously meant she was glad to see him. She ushered them inside, directing the two upstairs.

At the top of the stairs stood Sir's grandfather with his arms outstretched. "*Nipotino!*" There was excited chatter as other members of his family gathered around him, wanting to welcome Alonzo's son home.

Brie scooted to the side, watching the excitement, hoping someday she would be greeted with the same enthusiasm.

"Brianna," a gentle voice called behind her.

She turned to see Sir's grandmother grinning up at her. Brie bent down to give the frail woman a hug. Brie was surprised by the crushing strength of her embrace. She might be tiny and old, but the woman was *strong*—so much stronger than the last time they'd met.

"It is so good to see you again," Brie said. When she saw the look of confusion on the woman's weathered face, she said hesitantly in Italian, "*Buongiorno.*"

The old woman smiled and grabbed her cheeks, kissing her on the lips. "*Buongiorno.*" His grandmother then made her way through the crowd to greet her grandson.

It was beautiful to watch, this apartment full of people who were thrilled to be in the presence of Sir. Not because of his reputation and many talents, but simply because he was family.

Brie and Sir were taken up several flights of stairs, all the way to the roof, where tables had been set out for a meal. Brie and Sir were directed where to sit, and the men of the family sat down with them while the women disappeared back inside. They returned a few minutes later with platters upon platters of food.

When all the ladies had set down the food and taken their seats, silence ensued.

Brie looked at Sir and noticed that his head was bowed. She did the same and listened to the beautiful sounds of his grandfather's prayer. A hearty "Amen" followed from all, and everyone dug in. Unlike the dinner at Isabella's, Sir's family served themselves. It was much less formal and much more to her liking.

Although she could not follow much of the conversation, Brie kept hearing the word '*matrimonio*' thrown around. The word for wedding was being said with joy and excitement, but she noticed that Sir's grandmother was *not* happy. It showed in the woman's face and in her voice.

"What's going on with your grandmother, Sir?" Brie asked.

He sighed deeply. "We're at an impasse."

"What do you mean?"

"My grandmother wants us to get married in church. She's not happy about my decision to have a civil ceremony."

This was the first Brie had heard anything about the wedding, and she pressed. "Civil ceremony, Sir?"

"I see no point in getting married in a church when neither you nor I are believers. Hell, I'm still on the fence if there even is a God."

His grandmother started talking, the tone of her voice expressing her anger. Sir's grandfather started in, and then the entire family began adding their two cents. It seemed they were very passionate about having a church wedding.

His grandmother looked at Brie and said in disbelief, "No God?"

Brie didn't know how to respond but nodded her head. "I…believe there's a God."

"Church?" the grandmother asked plaintively.

Having never gone to church other than attending other people's weddings or funerals, Brie could only shake her head no.

His grandmother's eyes grew wide and she started back on lecturing Sir. He stood up, his eyes flashing with anger as he argued with the tiny woman. Brie was shocked to see Sir react in such a way to his grandmother.

What was supposed to be a joyous occasion seemed

to be causing nothing but a terrible rift between them.

"Sir," Brie said quietly. When he didn't respond, Brie said more loudly, touching his arm, "Sir."

He sat back down and took her hand in his. "What is it, Brie?"

"If it would make your grandmother happy, I wouldn't mind getting married in a church."

Sir sighed. "I appreciate the sentiment, babygirl, but you don't understand. We are not allowed to get married in my grandparents' church unless we are practicing Catholics."

Brie grinned, the tension in the air momentarily forgotten. "Does that mean we're getting married *here*—in Italy?"

He kissed her hand. "Yes, Brie, it does."

She broke out in a smile, looking over at his family, bursting with love for them. Without explanation, she got up and hugged each and every one, saving the last hug for Sir. "We're getting married in Italy!"

The family was unsure how to react to her joy in the midst of a heated argument. Sir explained. "They had no idea you didn't know."

Brie smiled at them all, throwing together Italian words she knew, trying to express her joy. "*Grande famiglia, ti amo.*" She hoped it meant "Big family, I love you," but their silence was disconcerting.

His grandfather stood up and put his arms out to her. Brie grinned as he enfolded her in his embrace. The conversation started up again, but with a much more loving tone. Brie looked over at Sir, her eyes brimming with happy tears.

After the meal, Sir sat down with his grandparents, pulling out some papers from his suitcase and handing a set to them and to Brie. He told her, "Read it over carefully. This is what will be said at the ceremony. There's nothing romantic about it, simply a dry list of what makes up a marriage. The government requires that it be recited in Italian, so I want you to read over the English version now so you understand what is being said."

His grandmother spat at the paper in disgust, handing it back to Sir, highly displeased.

Brie looked the paper over and was surprised that it sounded more like a list of rules than wedding vows. "Are there any other scripts we can choose from?"

"For our marriage to be legal, this is how it must be."

Brie looked through it again. There was only one point in the whole ceremony where she was expected to speak. "How do I say 'I do' in Italian, Sir?"

He smiled. "*Lo voglio.*"

All of the women in the room let out an audible, "Awww…"

Brie blushed, repeating it several times until she had the pronunciation right. "So that's all I need to do, just say 'I do' and we're married?"

"For a civil ceremony, yes."

She looked sympathetically at his grandmother, better understanding her displeasure. "Tell her it's the love of the couple, not the ceremony that matters."

Sir translated her words.

"How do I tell her it's okay?" Brie asked.

"*Va bene.*"

She smiled at the old woman and said with passion, "*Va bene.*"

His grandmother shook her head sadly, patting Brie on the hand.

"Well, that went well," Sir joked when they left hours later.

"I love the idea of getting married here, Sir. It's worth the discord with your family."

"We're not getting married here, Brie."

Brie turned to face him. "No?"

"No. I have something very special in mind."

"The island where you and your father used to treasure hunt?"

He chuckled loudly. "No—that would have been a challenge to pull off."

"Where, then?"

"You'll have to wait and see, Miss Bennett."

They strolled down the street towards the dock in silence.

"Sir, does your family know what happened to your mother?" Brie asked.

"No, and I don't plan to tell them. At least, not for now. She caused my father's family too much grief as it is, and I don't want it tainting our wedding in any way."

She took his hand. "I'm sorry you've had to carry that burden alone."

"I'm not alone, babygirl," he said, smiling down at

her.

Sir walked Brie to a small house on the beach. She was surprised to see it was full of people. "Your friends, Sir?"

He shook his head as he opened the door. "Not my friends—*our* friends."

"Surprise!" everyone shouted.

Brie looked at the group in shock, stunned to see her dearest friends. "I can't believe you're here!" she cried as she ran to hug Lea.

"I know—I never knew Nebraska looked a whole lot like Italy," Lea said with a snicker.

"You liar," she complained good-naturedly.

Brie looked over her shoulder at Tono, who was standing next to Autumn. "You guys are here too?"

"In the flesh," Tono replied. "Your fiancé insisted."

Brie turned to Sir. "I can't believe you did this."

"What's the point of a wedding if your family and friends aren't there to celebrate with you?"

"Brianna."

She heard her dad's voice and searched the room expectantly. "Mom, Dad!" she cried, running to them. "I can't believe this!"

"Your fiancé is an extravagant man," her father said, as her mother hugged Brie.

When her mother let go, Brie heard another familiar voice behind her.

"What am I, chopped liver?" Rytsar complained, picking her up and giving her a bear-hug. Brie struggled to breathe in his tight grip.

When he put her down, she laughed. "And I thought

you were headed back to Russia."

"I am, *radost moya*—after my layover in Italy."

"Could you stack the cigarettes for me, Miss Bennett?" Mr. Reynolds asked beside her.

"I haven't seen you and Judy in ages," Brie exclaimed, breaking out in delighted giggles as she hugged him.

"You two have been busy little beavers," Judy said, giving Brie a squeeze. "I'm sure we'll see more of each other once you settle down."

"I hear you're planning for a bun in the oven," Mr. Reynolds whispered.

Brie blushed, surprised that he knew. "Sir told you?"

"He'll make a fine father. I think he just needed a little reassurance from his Unc."

She looked over at Sir and nodded. "I agree, Unc."

Brie squeaked when strong hands covered her eyes.

"Guess who."

Not only did she recognize his voice, but he had a distinctive scent she'd become familiar with, having visited his home on several occasions. "Master Anderson!"

"How did you know?"

"I smelled you," she answered.

He sniffed his armpits and shrugged. "Dang, and I even showered today."

Brie laughed, and her smile widened even more when she saw Mary. She walked over to her and joked, "Long time no see."

"Bet you didn't expect to see me here, did you?"

"Nope. Not at all, but I'm thrilled."

"The doctors said Faelan can't travel for a while, but he insisted I come, and wanted me to give you this…" Mary surprised Brie by hugging her.

It made Brie all teary—the love of both Mary and Faelan being conveyed in the embrace. She dabbed her eyes afterwards. "Please let Todd know I deeply appreciate his sacrifice letting you come…as well as the heartfelt hug."

"I'll be sure to tell him."

Mary seemed to be glowing with an inner satisfaction, so much so, that Brie felt compelled to say, "I have to admit, woman, you're looking especially good—all domesticated and docile."

"You know how to cut a woman down," Mary complained, but then she smiled. "However, you're right. I do find myself enjoying the collared life."

Brie nodded in understanding.

She rejoined Sir, soaking in the joy of the moment. "I don't think I could be any happier, Sir."

He kissed the top of her head. "Good. That's what I was going for, Miss Bennett. Do you know what this is?" he asked, gesturing to the group.

She shook her head, smiling.

"This is our wedding party. Rytsar is my best man, Lea your maiden of honor, Anderson and Nosaka my groomsmen, Mary and Autumn your bridesmaids, your parents, and my uncle and aunt acting as my parents for the ceremony."

Brie looked them over with a sense of awe. They were an incredible collection of people, and each had significantly influenced their journey.

All the sadness surrounding Ruth's death and the tension caused by the civil ceremony melted away that evening as Brie and Sir celebrated their upcoming nuptials with their closest friends and family.

I Do

Brie and Sir left Isola d'Elba early the next day. He insisted that she wear a blindfold for the trip. She found it romantic and adored the BDSM feel as he led her around in broad daylight.

Whenever strangers asked why, Sir explained that he was surprising his soon-to-be bride, and they gushed with congratulations. It seemed everyone loved a wedding, even when they didn't know the bride and groom.

Sir had her stand on the deck of the ferry so she could feel the ocean breeze on her face. "As you know, one of my loves is the ocean," Sir told her.

Brie nodded. "It has a life of its own. I feel like I'm breathing in its energy."

"That's an excellent way to describe it. The ocean does give off an energy all its own." He kissed her on the shoulder and asked, "Would you like to know where you're getting married tomorrow?"

She laughed. "No, Sir. I'm not curious in the least."

"Fine."

When he said nothing more, she begged, "Please, Sir,

any little hint would be appreciated."

He chuckled, kissing her other shoulder. "My family has a long history here. Many generations, going back to the eleven-hundreds."

"I can't imagine having a family line with that kind of history," Brie confessed.

"It means I'm related to influential people who are honored to help out Alonzo's son."

"You have my curiosity piqued, Sir."

"Good—then I'll leave it at that."

Brie stuck out her bottom lip. "Such a cruel Master."

"I prefer to think of myself as a devoted fiancé."

Once the ferry had docked, Sir guided her down the long flight of stairs and off the boat, telling her the blindfold must remain.

"You're lucky I get off on this kind of thing, Sir."

He chuckled. "I do have method behind my madness, babygirl. I want to you to be fully aware of your surroundings. The smell, the temperature of the air, the sounds, even the feel of the ground beneath your feet—not only what you see. This land is a part of me, Brie, and I want you to be familiar with every aspect of it."

She did as he asked and took in everything, appreciating the language of the people as they walked by, the sound of the birds above her, the mechanical smell of the train station—everything. She was determined not to miss a single characteristic of his Italy.

After a lengthy train ride, Sir transferred Brie into a tiny convertible, which he drove way too fast once he got out of the metropolitan area. She could tell by his laughter that he was having fun as he whipped around the corners of the windy roads. She laughed along with him, loving the aromatic air and the quiet of the country roads once they left the bustling city behind.

When Sir finally pulled up to their destination he slammed on the brakes, causing a cloud of dust to swirl around them. "Do you have any idea where you are, Brie?"

She didn't answer him until she got out of the car, noting the freshness of the air after the dust had settled. It reminded her of the mountain air of Colorado, but there was an added sweetness to it. She listened to the chirping birds and the buzzing of bees nearby. She slipped off her shoes and felt ticklish grass between her toes and announced, "I think we're in hill country, but I don't know where exactly in Italy, Sir."

"Fair enough. Hold out your hand."

Sir walked her to a wall and placed her hand on it. "What do you think this is?"

She felt the rough surface. Believing they were in farming country, she guessed it was a simple building made of stone. "Is it an old barn?"

He laughed. "Definitely not a barn, but it's a reasonable guess."

Sir led her through an entryway and she felt the coolness of an enclosed room around her. There was a slight echo to it, hinting that it was large.

"You may take off your blindfold now."

Brie untied it and let the silk fall into her hands. She gasped when she saw the intricately painted scenes of rolling vineyards on the walls, with gold accents on the ceiling above. "What is this place?" she asked in awe.

"A castle owned by my great, great, great grandfather."

"We're getting married in a castle?"

"A castle in Tuscany," Sir answered, kissing her on the lips. "I wanted to wow you, babygirl."

"Consider me wowed…"

Sir pulled out two rings from his pocket. "Tomorrow, at the ceremony, we will be exchanging these rings. I wanted you to see yours before we do so."

Brie picked up the delicate ring, the entire band encrusted with diamonds. "It's beautiful, Sir."

"Look at the inscription inside."

She tilted the ring and saw an outline of a condor and the word *Mine* written on it. "It's perfect, Sir. Did you look at the engraving on yours?"

Sir shook his head, examining his wedding band closely. Brie had picked that particular ring because she liked the combination of black tungsten and white gold. It had a manly look befitting a Dom.

Sir read the inscription out loud, "Condors forever." He chuckled, charmed by the similarity. "Although we won't say vows for the civil ceremony, Brie, I want you to think about what you would say to me. Tell me with your eyes when we exchange these symbols of our commitment."

"That's so romantic, Sir."

He leaned down to kiss her, and the two remained locked in the embrace—lost in their own little world.

After a morning of feminine pampering, Brie was met by Lea, Mary and Autumn who'd come to collect her. They led her through the labyrinth of halls in the castle to an isolated room, where her mother was waiting for her with the wedding gown.

It looked even more beautiful than Brie remembered. Her mom held it up proudly for her to see, but Brie noticed an odd expression on her mother's face as she stared at the back of the gown.

"Did something happen to the dress?" Brie cried.

Her mother smiled. "Something most definitely happened to the dress. I have to assume your fiancé had something to do with it." She turned it around to show Brie.

The beautiful lace gown now had three long strands of white pearls set at the shoulders, the loops draping down the back. The addition artfully complemented the shape of the scooped back and added an extra element of sophistication.

"I can't believe he did that," Brie said as she ran her fingers over the pearls. "They have a special meaning to us," she explained to her mother.

"I must say Thane has excellent taste, sweetheart. Shall we see how it looks on you with the new embellishment?"

"Yes please." Brie's heart skipped a beat as her mother lifted the dress over her head with Lea's assistance. The silk of the lining slid down over her body, caressing her with its soft embrace as the lace train pooled behind her.

Brie turned her head to admire the added loops of

pearls caressing her back. Her mother was about to remove the cloth covering the full-length mirror, but Brie stopped her. "No, Mom! In Italy, the bride isn't allowed to see herself before the wedding."

"What fun is that?" Lea complained. "You should see how beautiful your ass looks in that dress. You're looking mighty fine, girlfriend."

"Actually, Brie, a bride *can* look in the mirror if she takes off one of her gloves," Mary informed her.

Brie rolled her eyes. "Ah…I'm not wearing any gloves, genius."

Mary had a superior look on her face when she fished out a long, thin box from her purse and handed it to Brie. "I happen to have a gift for you, although I am unsure now if you deserve it."

Brie smiled as she opened the box and took out two fingerless gloves made of delicate lace. "They're exquisite, Mary."

She shrugged. "I bought them just in case you wanted to play by the rules, but feel free to use them with Sir if you prefer."

Brie giggled as her mother turned a deep shade of red. Brie could only guess what she was imagining. The funny thing—whatever it was—she was probably right.

Lea slipped both gloves onto Brie's hands, stating, "Let's play by the rules, then. 'Cause you've got to see yourself in this dress."

She took off one glove and held it in her hand as her mother pulled away the cover from the mirror.

Brie was stunned by her own reflection. The princess neckline accentuated her full breasts, making a beautiful backdrop for the Italian lace that covered the entire dress. She turned to the side to admire the back of the gown. It was even more beautiful than she'd imagined. The strands of pearls accentuated her back and seemed to direct the eye downward to her shapely bottom, but Brie suspected it was really meant to draw the eye to the brand that barely showed. She knew with certainty that Sir's eyes would be riveted to that particular spot.

"Wait, the dress is too short," her mother lamented as she examined the hemline.

"Nope!" Lea announced, handing Brie a small silver box. "Your fiancé has something he wanted you to wear instead of heels."

Brie giggled with delight as she lifted the lid. Inside was a set of golden jewelry for her feet, accented with tiny pearls.

"He says he wants you barefoot for the wedding."

Barefoot and pregnant? Brie wondered, smiling to herself.

"What an odd request," her mother complained.

Lea helped Brie to take off her heels and stockings, replacing them with the jewelry that looped around her second toe and attached around her ankle. It made an enticing jingling sound when she moved her feet.

Brie knew it was slave jewelry and loved the symbolism behind his gift, even though she still wore her collar. On this most vanilla of ceremonies, Sir was reminding her that she was his beloved submissive.

"What girl gets married in bare feet?" her mother protested.

"I'm sure it's an ancient Italian custom, Mom."

Mary piped up, "No one will think it strange but us, and we're the only ones who know."

Her mother nodded. "I suppose you're right. The dress *will* cover her feet."

"It makes your feet look so darn adorable with your pink toenails, girlfriend," Lea squealed. "I could just kiss those cute little piggies."

"Probably what Sir plans to do tonight," Mary said, adding under her breath, "among other things."

Brie's mother blushed again and awkward silence ensued.

Luckily, there was a knock on the door and Sir's grandmother entered the dressing room. She took one look at Brie and tears came to her eyes.

Brie reached out to her. "*Nonna…*"

The old woman held a small silk pouch, which she handed to her. "*Qualcosa di blu.*"

Brie caught the word 'blue' and opened the pouch with excitement. Inside was a tiny antique stick-pin made of gold with a single blue crystal. Brie smiled at her, knowing it was meant as good luck. It seemed some traditions were universal.

Sir's grandmother took it from Brie with her frail hands, to pin it on her wedding dress. To Brie's surprise, she let out a small gasp while she was pinning it. Sir's grandmother touched the lace of the gown with a look of wonder. She called out excitedly, and called out again when no one came.

Aunt Fortuna ran into the room, looking upset. "What, *Nonna*? Why the big fuss?"

Sir's grandmother pointed to Brie's dress, speaking

excitedly.

Aunt Fortuna had the same look of amazement as she lovingly stroked the lace. She gazed up at Brie, shaking her head in disbelief. "Where did you get this?"

"I found the dress waiting for me at a little dress shop in Los Angeles."

Aunt Fortuna put her hand to her lips, looking like she was about to cry. "I made this lace, Brianna. The fact that this dress found you…that is *destino*."

Brie threw her arms around her. "Then I must thank you for helping to create my gown."

Sir's grandmother joined in on the hug. If there had been any misgivings before about the wedding, they all seemed to wash away in that moment.

Rytsar walked in on them, looking devastatingly handsome in his smoky gray suit with matching vest and light-gray tie. The refined Italian suit took Rytsar's rough, masculine charm to a higher level.

"Well, you certainly look handsome, Mr. Durov," Brie complimented.

A slow smile crept over his lips. "*Radost moya*, you are perfection."

Brie gave a little bow. "Thank you."

She noticed that all the women were staring at him, the younger ones in playful longing and the older ones in open admiration.

"Did you need something, Mr. Durov?" Brie's mother finally asked, breaking the spell he had created with his presence.

Rytsar snorted. "Your future husband wanted me to ask if you received his gift."

Brie lifted her gown to show off the slave jewelry gracing her feet. "Tell my future husband that I love his gift and will walk out to meet him wearing them proudly."

Rytsar looked down at her delicate feet decorated in gold and pearls, then gazed up at her. "I will inform him that they enhance the perfection that is you."

Brie blushed and looked away, embarrassed by his praise. Rytsar gave her a little bow and then did the same to the ladies in attendance before leaving the room.

"Such a fine Russian gentleman," Aunt Fortuna said, fanning herself. "He could teach me a thing or two in the bedroom…"

Mary smirked. "You have *no* idea."

Brie shook her head at Mary in warning. Aunt Fortuna did *not* need to know about Rytsar's uncommon tastes.

The sound of violins began, letting them know the ceremony was about to begin. Sir's grandmother and aunt gave Brie another hug before leaving the room.

Brie took the opportunity for one last look in the mirror, her stomach fluttering as she gazed at herself. The woman before her stood confident and proud in her gown of white lace. From her pink lips down to her pink toes hiding under the dress, she was the picture of femininity and elegance.

She knew Sir would be pleased when he saw his bride walking down the aisle. She touched the beautiful flowers Autumn had placed in her hair and thought of Tono. The love and confidence the Asian Dom had instilled were a permanent part of her now. She was the direct result of all of the Doms who had played a role in shaping her into who she was today.

Brie became teary-eyed at the thought, and hoped someday she would be able to properly thank all of them for this moment.

"Are you ready, Brianna?" her mother asked.

She smiled at her mother, dabbing her eyes, before putting her glove back on.

"For the best day of my life? Absolutely."

Her mother leaned in and whispered, "This may be the best day of your life for now, but I guarantee the day you bring new life into the world will top even this."

Brie's lip trembled and she had to fight back more tears, knowing her mother was referring to the day she'd been born. "I love you, Mom."

"You're so elegant and accomplished, Brianna. I couldn't be prouder."

Brie gave her a hug, bursting with overflowing love for her mother. She heard a click and saw that Autumn was taking a picture.

"You want to preserve moments like this," Autumn explained, sounding apologetic.

"Thank you," Brie told her, grateful to have these private moments recorded. "I don't want to forget anything about today."

"My pleasure, Brie. It's a joy to be part of such an important event."

There was a knock on the door and her father entered. He was dressed in the same stylish suit as Rytsar and looked like a completely different man because of it.

"Dad, you should wear suits more often."

He fussed with his tie. "I can't stand these monkey suits."

Her mother walked over and straightened his tie for him. "I wish you did, honey. You look absolutely dashing."

He grumbled, but gave her a kiss when she was done. "Thank you, dear."

Her father took a long look at Brie, shaking his head in gratified disbelief, looking every bit the proud papa.

"I've come here to collect the bride."

"Oh, my goodness, it's time!" Brie cried, throwing her arms around her father.

"Whoa, you're going to mess up your pretty hair," he cautioned.

"It's okay, Dad," Brie said, squeezing him tighter. She heard Autumn taking more pictures and was glad for it.

When her father let go, he looked at her mother and sighed deeply. "Are you ready for this, Marcy?"

She nodded, wiping away tears as she smiled at Brie.

Brie was anxious for the wedding to begin and asked Lea, "Where's the bouquet?"

Lea looked heart-stricken. "I don't have it, Brie! I've never seen it. Oh, heck, what does it even look like?"

"I don't know!" Brie whimpered. She scanned the dressing room while everyone else tore the room apart looking for the bridal bouquet.

"You wouldn't happen to be looking for a bouquet, would you?"

Brie knew that calming voice and looked up to see Tono. He looked swoon-worthy with his chocolate brown eyes, long bangs and sexy Italian suit.

"I was sent to inform you that a bouquet is waiting for you outside."

"That's highly unusual, isn't it? Do you want one of us to get it for you, honey?" her mom asked.

"That's not necessary," Tono assured Brie's mother. "It's being delivered personally."

"Thank you, Tono. That sounds lovely," Brie said, smiling at him.

Tono bowed his head slightly. "I must return to the groom and let him know the message has been delivered."

After he'd left, her father held out his arm. "I guess it's time, my little girl."

"Oh, man, I've got to get myself out there, girl-friend," Lea squeaked. She gave Brie a quick peck on the cheek before she left the room.

Mary came up next. "I always said you were a fool…"

Brie waited, ready for the worst.

"But you've done well, Brie."

Brie's jaw dropped.

Mary leaned in and whispered, "I really said that for your parents, Stinky Cheese. You're still an idiot in my book." She laughed as if she had shared a humorous joke with Brie as she followed behind Lea.

Brie loved Mary for it.

Her mother gave her one last kiss before leaving her to get in line.

Brie took a deep breath, looking at her dad. "This is really it."

"Want to run?"

She giggled. "Actually, I can't wait to tie the knot."

"Figuratively or literally?" he asked with a straight face.

Brie glanced at him. "Did you just make a joke?"

He looked ahead solemnly, refusing to answer.

"I can't believe you just made a joke," she said, smiling to herself.

They exited the room and followed the procession as they walked up a long flight of stone stairs. Brie noticed that every other step was decorated with lemons, greenery and baby's breath. She was so enchanted by the simple elegance that she didn't even notice who was waiting for her at the top.

"Hello."

Brie looked up to see Sir holding a bouquet in his hand.

The sight of him took her breath away. He wore a black suit, with a dark vest covered in a silvery vine pattern that matched the pattern of his bow tie. Sir was stylish perfection, all the way down to his polished Italian shoes. On his lapel he wore a single magenta flower that matched the ones in the bouquet he was holding out to her.

Sir smiled charmingly as he explained, "It's tradition in my family for the groom to present his bride with her flowers."

Brie took the stunning bouquet, admiring the white calla lilies and freesias with accents of greenery, baby's breath and the bright pink bougainvilleas she'd admired on Isola d'Elba.

She lifted the bouquet to her nose, taking in the sweet scent of freesias. "It's so beautiful."

"As are you, Brianna."

The sound of her full name rolling from Sir's lips was like a song. He walked away to take his position for the wedding, looking so unbelievably handsome that Brie wanted to cry.

The wedding party waited until the traditional wedding march began. Brie felt the tingling start. This had been fated from the moment she was born. Everything she'd experienced, everything that had transpired since—all of it had led to this point in time.

Brie held her head a little higher but kept it at a respectful angle, eager to walk down the aisle to meet her husband and Master.

"Ready, my little girl?"

"Yes, Daddy," she said with conviction as they took their first step to the rhythm of the song.

The courtyard was filled with people, far more than Brie would ever have imagined. She glanced around in surprise, recognizing many familiar faces she hadn't expected to see. It seemed Sir had invited most of the Training Center to join them for this momentous day.

Brie's eyes traveled to the end of the aisle, where she spotted Sir waiting under a simple wooden trellis covered in the same flowers as those in her bouquet. Beside him stood Rytsar, Master Anderson and Tono, and on the left stood Lea, Mary and Autumn—the girls looking stunning in their sleek magenta gowns that harmonized with the bougainvilleas in her bouquet.

Brie was so mesmerized by Sir's smile as she came

down the aisle that she could barely breathe.

Oh, Sir...

Her father released his hold and physically placed her hand in Sir's open palm, nodding to him before joining Brie's mother in the front row.

Brie looked up into Sir's eyes, stunned that she was actually standing beside him, about to take her wedding vows. Her smile faded as the importance of this moment suddenly hit her full-force.

Here, before all their family and even God himself, they were making the commitment of a lifetime. Although it had the same significance to her as the Collaring Ceremony, this union held more weight with the rest of the world.

The man who would marry them, the mayor of the local village, cleared his throat to get the attention of the crowd. He said something in Italian and half the guests sat down. Brie's American friends quickly followed.

Brie listened to the beautiful sound of the mayor's voice as he rolled off the legal requirements spelled out in a civil wedding. Although there was nothing romantic about what he was saying, everything sounded more romantic in Italian.

She knew the time was close when Sir looked into her eyes after the man paused. He smiled confidently at her and said loudly, "*Lo voglio.*"

Brie's heart fluttered.

The mayor then asked her the same question in Italian. With her heart racing, she said with passion, "*Lo voglio.*"

He then made a pronouncement, and the Italian

guests smiled and clapped. Brie looked out at her friends and family, wishing they could understand what had been said.

Rytsar handed Sir her ring.

Sir took Brie's hand in his, slipping the wedding band onto her finger. As he did so, he looked into her eyes, expressing his love for her.

Rytsar placed Sir's ring in her hand and winked at her before taking his place behind Sir. Brie's hand shook so badly that she had trouble putting the band on his finger, and she had to laugh at herself. She looked up at him when she was done, forgetting the silent vow she had meant to say with her eyes and simply mouthing the words, "Condors forever."

Brie assumed the ceremony was over, until she saw Marquis Gray take the place of the mayor with Sir's cousin, Benito, joining him.

"Now that the civil wedding is complete, we will continue with the exchange of traditional vows."

Brie heard her Americans friends voice their approval while Benito translated Marquis' words into Italian for Sir's family. She looked at Sir in surprise, before turning her attention back to Marquis.

Marquis Gray met her gaze with those dark, intense eyes, but there was a spark of pride behind them she hadn't seen before.

"We are gathered here today in the sight of God, and the presence of friends and loved ones, to join in one of life's greatest moments. Thane and Brianna have invited us to share in this celebration of their marriage—their wedding. We are here not to mark the start of a relationship, but to recognize a bond that already exists.

"This marriage is one expression of the many varieties of love. It is fitting at this time to speak briefly about the power love can have in our lives. We live in a world of joy and fear, searching for meaning in the seeming chaos of life. Yet we discover the truest guidelines to our quest when we realize love in all its magnitudes. Love is the eternal force of life. Love allows us to face fear and uncertainty with courage."

Marquis turned to Brie first. "Brianna Renee Bennett, will you have this man to be your husband, to live together in the covenant of marriage? Will you love him, comfort him, honor and obey him, in sickness and in health, forsaking all others as long as you both shall live?"

Brie stared deep into Sir's eyes as she answered proudly, "I will."

Marquis turned to Sir. "Thane Lorenzo Davis, will you have this woman to be your wife, to live together in the covenant of marriage? Will you love her, comfort her, honor and protect her, in sickness and in health, forsaking all others as long as you both shall live?"

Sir raised his eyebrow charmingly when he answered. "I will."

"The couple will now exchange personal vows."

Sir smiled, lifting Brie's hand to his lips and kissing the ring on her finger before speaking. "Brie, from the moment we met, I was mesmerized by you. I've never known a woman more loving, kind or stubborn than you."

There were several knowing chuckles from the

guests.

Sir glanced at them and grinned before returning his gaze to her. "I'm unsure whether these people know how truly extraordinary you are, but I do." He cupped her chin with his right hand. "This ring is a physical representation of my vow to you—my bride. With my body, I thee worship. With my heart, I thee cherish. All that I am, I give to thee. All that I have, I share with thee. From this day until forever done."

Brie had to fight the tears that threatened, and squeezed Sir's hand. She waited several moments before she spoke the words she'd wanted to tell him.

"Thane, you have shown me a whole new world I never knew existed. My love for you is boundless and my respect for you runs deep. Meeting you that fateful day in the shop altered the course of my life, *but* loving you has changed me. I look forward to growing old by your side as your lover, wife and best friend. Condors forever."

Sir's gaze held hers as Marquis spoke again.

"This is a moment of celebration, but let it also be a moment of dedication. The world does a fine job of reminding us of how fragile we are. People are fragile; relationships are fragile too. Every marriage needs the love and support of a network of friends and family.

"On this wedding day, I ask all of you to be friends of Thane and Brie as a couple. Be friends of their relationship and be there with them through the trials and triumphs ahead."

Marquis addressed Sir and Brie again. "May the flow of your love help brighten the fate of the Earth. May the strength of your love touch and bless us all, gracing our lives with its color and courage."

He looked out over the crowd and exclaimed proudly, "It is my pleasure to introduce to you...Mr. and Mrs. Thane Davis." Then he said to Sir, "You may kiss your bride."

Sir swept Brie into his arms, bending her backwards as he gave her a deep and passionate kiss, to the roaring applause of their family and friends.

It was a moment Brie would never forget.

The Dance

Brie couldn't take her eyes off her husband as they greeted their guests in the reception hall inside the castle. He seemed equally infatuated with Brie, and kept her close to him, his hand resting on the small of her back, lightly touching her brand.

Brie's mom was the first to come and congratulate them. "Such a touching ceremony, Brianna." She turned to Sir. "This has to be the most beautiful wedding I've ever seen."

Sir held out his left arm, still keeping hold of Brie as he gave her mother a hug. "Thank you, Mom."

Brie's mother looked proudly up at him. "It means so much that you call me that, Thane. Never stop."

Brie heard an undercurrent of emotion in Sir's voice when he told her, "It is an honor to be known as your son."

Brie's father held out his hand. "You know my thoughts on your extra-curricular activities, but as a husband to my little girl, I couldn't ask for a better man."

Sir shook his hand firmly. "That means a lot, sir."

Her father got an odd expression on his face. "Actually, I would prefer you called me Dad from now on."

Brie couldn't believe it.

Sir appeared equally shocked. "I did not expect such an honor. Thank you…Dad."

The word 'Dad' sounded so strange coming from Sir's lips, but it touched Brie greatly. Sir was part of her family now. A family with no other agenda than to see them happy together.

She threw her arms around her father. "You've made me so happy."

"I'm proud of you, my beautiful daughter."

Brie laid her head on his shoulder, soaking in the tenderness of the moment—making her feel like a child again.

Sir's grandmother was standing a distance away, but Brie could tell she was anxious to speak with them. She gave her father a kiss on the cheek before excusing herself.

Brie and Sir made their way over to his grandmother. Her eyes radiated youthful excitement as words tumbled from her mouth. Sir explained to Brie, "My *nonna* was very touched by the English version of the ceremony. She despised the civil ceremony, but was moved by what Marquis Gray shared, as well as our vows to each other."

Brie smiled at the old woman who was now her grandmother by marriage. "*Nonna*, it means the world to me that you were here to share in our happiness. I love your grandson very much."

She pinched Brie's cheeks hard in her zeal. "Joyful couple," she said in English, slapping Brie's cheeks afterwards. Although Brie's cheeks burned from the contact, she enjoyed the woman's enthusiasm.

"Yes, very joyful," she agreed, her smile widening.

Sir's grandfather walked up and gave her a quick kiss on the lips, his eyes twinkling mischievously. He spoke in Italian, letting Sir translate for him.

"*Nonno* says that I will make you happy."

The look in the old man's eye hinted at the fact that he meant more than simply as her spouse. Brie nodded, blushing as she answered, "Your grandson is a very generous man."

The old man nodded, then hugged Sir. Whatever his grandfather whispered in his ear left Sir teary-eyed. He quickly regained his composure, but gave his grandfather another hug.

"Mrs. Davis, may I be one of the first to congratulate you?"

Brie blushed, her heart thrilling at how her new name sounded when spoken with a Russian accent. She turned to him and nodded gracefully. "Thank you, Rytsar."

"I have been watching your husband closely, *radost moya*. The way he looks at you leads me to suspect I will be a *dyadya* very soon."

Brie let out a small gasp as she looked at Sir, imagining him taking her. The lust she felt was reflected in his eyes as they stared at each other.

"Possibly a *dyadya* to twins…" Rytsar stated, laughing as he walked away.

Sir pulled Brie to him. "It's true—I desire you, wife."

Brie felt butterflies on hearing Sir call her his wife. Such a simple thing, seemingly insignificant, but it thrilled her to the depths of her soul. She stood on tiptoes to kiss his cheek. "My husband…" she sighed contentedly. "I love calling you that."

"Soon you will be screaming it," he growled in her ear, grazing her brand with his finger before shaking the hand of the next person who approached them.

When Lea announced that dinner was being served, Sir escorted Brie to a long table where the entire wedding party already sat, waiting for them. The length of the table was decorated with simple white flowers and greenery lining the middle. It was simple in its elegance, like everything else.

As she sat down next to Sir, Brie took notice of the charming table setting. The linen napkins had been tied with sprigs of rosemary, and each person had their own tiny vial of olive oil and a small tulle bag with sugared almonds.

"Every single detail makes me smile, Sir."

Sir took her hand and kissed it tenderly. "I'm glad, wife."

Rytsar stood up, clinking his glass to get the attention of the guests. "Before we begin, I would like to propose a toast."

"Hear, hear," Lea said, smiling at Brie.

Rytsar turned to Sir. "This man has been my friend since college, but he is much more than just a comrade—he is my brother. There is no one in the world I trust more and no one else I would lay down my life for."

He looked at Brie. "I remember when he called me about a girl. *Moy droog* claimed she was something special and asked if I would come to America to meet her."

Brie blushed, remembering what had transpired during that first meeting…

"I had to agree with him. Brianna Bennett was indeed a rare find. I've never seen my comrade as content as he is now. The peasant has even been known to smile on occasion."

Several of the guests laughed.

Rytsar looked over the crowd, his tone and expression serious. "It is an honor to call Thane Davis my brother, and it is an honor to know his wife. I hope someday each of us will experience the kind of happiness these two share. It is tradition in my country for the first toast to be to the newlyweds' health, so I say with a full heart, *Dlya zdorov'ya molodozhenov.*"

Everyone raised their glasses, and Brie heard Sir's family shout, "*Salute degli sposi!*"

Lea stood up next, holding her glass out towards Brie.

"I met the lovely Miss Bennett over a joke about credit cards."

Brie giggled, remembering the lesson on obedience—one that Lea had failed miserably.

"This girl is like no one else I've ever met. Brie's fearless and strong, but she cares about people—I mean *really* cares about people—even those who are hard to love." Lea glanced over at Mary and winked. "She has the ability to bring people together. You just have to look around this room to see proof of that."

Lea looked at Brie with a wicked grin. "A little fact you may not know about my friend is that she's a sucker for a good joke. So in honor of that, I would like to tell one now."

"Oh, no…" Brie muttered under her breath.

"What do you call two spiders who just got married?" Lea giggled before she burst out, "Newlywebs!"

Loud groans erupted from the crowd.

"Okay, that was just the warm up—here's the real one. So a little girl was attending a wedding for the first time and whispered to her mother, 'Mommy, why is the bride dressed in white?' Her mother answered, 'Because white is the color of happiness, and today is the happiest day of her life.' The child thought about this for a moment and asked, 'So why is the groom wearing black?'"

This time her joke was met with chuckles from the men.

"But seriously, ladies, we know why Thane Davis is wearing black today. He's Italian and he knows the power of a good suit."

The women twittered in agreement.

"And just look at my girlfriend. Have you ever seen a more gorgeous bride? It's scary to think how good-looking their children will be. Am I right?"

Brie blushed as she glanced shyly at Sir.

"I can't wait to celebrate with them fifty years from now, when they're old and gray but still just as in love."

She held up her glass to them. "Here's to condor love, baby!"

Their friends shouted, "To condor love!" while the Italians answered with a hearty, "*Auguri!*"

Brie grinned as Sir intertwined his arm with hers so

they could drink from each other's glasses.

Just before dinner began, Master Anderson stood up. "If you don't mind, I would like to add my own toast before the festivities begin. Like Rytsar, Thane and I became friends in college. You wouldn't know it to look at him now, but he was a real nerd back then."

The group laughed, with Sir shaking his head, a smirk on his face.

After the laughter died down, he continued. "Thane Davis is a rock, the person I count on. He's a leader among his friends, but still humble enough to take advice from them. In Brie, he's truly found his one and only—his counterpart. The strength of the love they share inspires even an old cynic like me."

He held his glass high. "May you two enjoy a long and fruitful life together."

Sir's family shouted in unison, "*Per Cent'anni.*"

The meal began with a small bowl of *ribollita,* followed by a course of fresh vegetables and white beans, both favorites of Sir's. The main course consisted of the most delicate and delicious *gnocchi* Brie had ever tasted, and she moaned in pure bliss.

"I hope to hear more of that shortly," Sir mentioned in a casual voice before he turned to talk to Rytsar.

Brie let out a little squeak, suddenly anxious for the meal to be over.

After the final course, Sir stood and held out his hand. "Shall we?"

Brie took his hand and proudly walked beside him, barefoot under her dress, each step making a delightful jingling sound. It was exhilarating to feel the smooth tile beneath her feet—their little secret.

Sir led Brie over to the wedding cake, a tall, simple, white, layered cake decorated with pink bougainvilleas and greenery. Rather than a traditional cake topper, Brie noticed the silver base that held the cake was etched with filigree that had both their names and an artful likeness of condors on either side.

Once again, Sir had charmed her with his taste and attention to detail.

Her heart skipped a beat when he moved behind her and took hold of the knife. His closeness had her senses reeling, and she blushed as they pushed down the knife and cut into the cake.

Brie took the piece to feed him, feeling a little silly about the ritual, but when she put the cake to his lips and he took a bite, she found it incredibly sexy. Brie licked her lips in sexual frustration as he took another bite, finishing it off.

She parted her lips, taking the bite he offered, her eyes locked on his. When he leaned down and licked the frosting from her lips, her knees almost buckled. Sir took hold of her arm to steady her and smiled, knowing the effect he was having on her.

"Are we okay, Mrs. Davis?"

She nodded, completely entranced by the man.

Lea announced, "Single ladies, it's that time! Get yourselves out there and get ready to catch that bouquet."

Brie moved where Lea directed her and turned around, facing the wall. When Lea said they were ready, she threw the bouquet into the air, then whipped around to see who caught it.

There was a frenzy of activity, but it was the girl who didn't move a muscle who ended up catching it. Autumn blushed as she held up the bouquet, to the applause of the crowd.

Rytsar brought out a chair and instructed Brie to sit down. He then covered Sir's eyes with a blindfold before he was allowed to remove the lacy garter she wore.

Sir looked sexy-hot as he knelt down before her and reached out his hands. Brie giggled nervously when he made contact with her knees. Just that simple touch alone had her quivering inside.

Once he got his bearings, Sir's hands found their way underneath her dress. He gently caressed her bare leg as his hand traveled slowly up. Goosebumps rose on her skin as he got closer to his target.

When he finally touched it, Brie let out a soft moan only Sir could hear. He shook his head and murmured, "Naughty girl." Sir pulled off the garter and held it up in triumph as he untied the blindfold.

Lea instructed the single men to line up, and had to push several reluctant bachelors standing on the sidelines to join before she would let Sir throw it. Unlike the women, the men seemed scared of it, moving out of the way as it came down. It was Master Anderson who ended up catching her garter, much to his chagrin.

Brie clapped, thinking he was the perfect man for the honor.

He held it up with a charming grin as a herd of eligible women descended on him.

Sir watched the pandemonium with amusement. "I'd

say he doesn't have long."

"I agree, Sir," Brie giggled.

He turned to face her, a romantic look in his eyes. "Are you ready to dance with me as my wife?" he asked, holding out his hand to her.

The butterflies took over as she placed her hand in his. "I would be honored."

The area cleared as Sir guided her to the middle of the dance floor and waited. A solo violin began to play. Brie instantly recognized the sound of Alonzo's violin. Sir placed his hand on her waist and took her left hand in his, guiding her across the dance floor as his father joined them—the recording of his powerful performance filling the reception hall.

Tears came to Brie's eyes as they danced. "It's beautiful, Sir."

Sir twirled her around, then grasped her waist again, drawing her to him. "I knew he would want to be here with us today."

Brie lost herself in the moment, feeling as if she were floating on clouds as the sweet sound of his father's violin carried them along. When the melody ended, Sir led her over to Lea. Her friend slipped a delicate silk purse onto her wrist.

"What's this for?" Brie asked.

"Your gifts, silly" she replied. Lea held out a small envelope. "Although Ms. Clark couldn't attend, she wanted you to have this." Lea slipped it into Brie's pouch and gave her a quick kiss on the cheek before walking over to the crowd of ladies around Master Anderson and humbly requesting a dance.

Rytsar walked up to Brie with an envelope in his hand. "May I have the honor of this dance, Mrs. Davis?"

She looked at Sir, who explained, "It's tradition for the men to give a gift before they share a dance with the bride."

Brie nodded and turned back to Rytsar. "It would be a pleasure to dance with you, Rytsar Durov." She took his envelope and placed it in the pouch. "Thank you."

He whisked her away from Sir, grinning like the Cheshire Cat. "You make a beautiful bride, *radost moya*."

"And you make a fetching best man. I've noticed quite a number of young ladies vying for your attention this evening."

"It is my Russian charm. No one can resist it."

He twirled her several times, the jewelry on her feet making a pleasant sound.

"Ah, I love the sound of slave jewelry. I appreciate the way your Master thinks." Rytsar twirled her several more times before he ended the dance in the middle of the song.

"Why so short?" she asked, surprised when he handed her over to Marquis Gray.

Rytsar leaned in and whispered, "We promised your husband not to take too long. He is anxious to make me a *dyadya*."

Brie blushed as Marquis Gray presented her with a small silver envelope. "A gift for the bride," Marquis announced formally. She put it in her pouch, thanking him before taking his hand.

"The ceremony was exquisite, Marquis Gray," Brie gushed as they glided across the floor. "What you said at our wedding meant more to me than you'll ever know."

"It was a privilege to officiate the union of two people I deeply respect."

She smiled, touched by his praise. "I remember when you were not thrilled by my choice of Master."

"I never held it against you, Mrs. Davis. It was your Master I had issue with."

"Do you have issues with him now?" she asked, looking over at Sir, who was talking to her parents.

"He's proven himself worthy since then. I'm encouraged by the fact he dealt with his mother before you began this next part of your journey. It shows his level of commitment to this marriage—and you."

Brie's voice shook when she told him, "It was difficult, Marquis."

"I'm sure it was." He held her tight as he twirled her around so fast it left her breathless. Gazing deep into her eyes he told her, "You will be stronger for it. Hold on to that knowledge and enjoy your evening, Mrs. Davis. Many blessings to you and your husband."

Marquis led her over to Mr. Gallant, who was standing on the side waiting for her. Brie graciously accepted his gift before taking his hand to dance.

"Oh, Mr. Gallant, I can't tell you how pleased I am that you're here tonight."

"I'm grateful as well, Miss B—excuse me—Mrs. Davis. As a student you made an unusual choice on the night of the Collaring Ceremony, and you've continued to astound me with the direction your journey has taken. It is a joy and honor to know you."

She blushed. "The honor is mine. I still think back

on my training days and wish I could attend class with you again."

"I recall those sessions with great fondness."

Before he let her go, Brie leaned in to tell him, "Mr. Gallant, I want to thank you for what you did for Candy. Mary, Mr. Wallace and I will forever be in your debt."

He was startled by her declaration and asked, "How did you—?"

Brie pressed her finger to her lips, gliding gracefully over to Baron, who was smiling at her.

"Kitten…"

"What a lovely surprise," she said, grateful that he had come.

"I would not miss such a happy occasion."

With a devilish smile, Baron handed her a red envelope, then escorted her onto the dance floor. She stared up at him while they danced, captivated by his smile.

"Have you moved back to LA yet?"

"I have. Found a nice place in an established neighborhood. Good people, walking distance to most things, and best of all, I feel Adrianna's spirit there."

"That doesn't upset you?" she asked in surprise.

"No, kitten. It feels as if it's meant to be. That I have found my new home and do not have to lose her in the process."

"Then I'm glad for you, Baron, and even happier I'll be seeing more of you."

He hugged her before letting go. "I want you and Sir Davis to visit me when you get back. I have something I want to show you."

On that mysterious note, Baron handed her off to

Master Coen, who was waiting for her next.

"This is an honor, Headmaster."

Master Coen placed his envelope into Brie's hand before holding out his beefy arm to her. "I had to pay my respects to the girl who tore the trainers apart."

"What?" she asked, stumbling over her own feet, unsure she'd heard him correctly.

Master Coen explained, "I'm headed off to Australia, Ms. Clark is stationed in Denver, and your Master is out of the program altogether. Three of the original four are no longer part of the Training Center. We were a stable group until you and your film came along."

She smiled shyly. "I guess you were right to be concerned after all."

"You're certainly a catalyst for change, Mrs. Davis. I never would have guessed Thane would marry. I'm still stunned by it, in fact, and yet here we are."

"Yes, here we are…"

"I have no doubt you will continue to shock and surprise me." He swatted her once soundly on the ass before letting her go. "But don't stir up too much trouble while I'm gone. I expect you to visit me Down Under—both you and your husband."

Brie looked over at Sir and found him staring intently at her. It seemed he couldn't take his eyes off her. It didn't matter where he was in the room or who he was with, his gaze kept returning to her. It was magnetic in its pull, and she longed to join him.

"Mrs. Davis, may I have this dance?"

Brie turned to see Captain looking quite distinguished in his military uniform. He was even more striking with the handsome leather patch over his eye. "I'd be honored, Captain," she replied, putting his gift into her pouch.

She gladly took the hand he offered. "You look quite dashing tonight."

His chuckle was low and deep. "My pet seems to agree with you."

"Where is she?"

Captain nodded to Candy, who was talking with Mary.

"You must be proud of her."

"Which one? Both are exceptional women."

Brie grinned, charmed by his answer. "I would agree with you, Captain."

His moves were exacting and flawless as he danced, guiding her effortlessly across the dancefloor. She felt graceful and beautiful in his skillful hands. Brie looked up at him in admiration.

"I never knew what a fine dancer you were."

He kept his serious expression, but the edge of his lip rose in a half-smile.

Brie felt proud to be his partner and was disappointed when the song came to an end. He took her hand and kissed it formally, thanking her before leaving to return to Candy.

Sir's cousin Benito came up to her holding out his envelope. "*Bella donna*, may I have the honor?" Brie graciously took his gift and continued to dance as she partnered with the men from the Italian side of her new family. They dazzled her with their beautiful language as they swept her along. Brie was acutely aware of Sir's eyes on her, and wondered if he could hear the jingle of her dancing feet whenever she twirled past him.

She was taking a much needed water break when Tono walked up to her, a tender look in his eye. "Mrs. Davis."

"Yes, Tono?"

"Master Anderson regrets that he cannot dance with you tonight, but he asked me to give you this." Tono handed her a thick envelope.

Brie took it and looked across the room at Master Anderson, who was surrounded by a harem of women. He shrugged with his hands up, an expression of "What can I do?" on his face.

She threw him a kiss and waved, happy to see the sexy Dom preoccupied.

Tono addressed her again. "Although the evening is still young, Sir Davis has asked me to retrieve you."

"Retrieve me?"

"Your husband wishes to speak with you—privately."

Brie's heartrate shot up. She looked around for Sir but didn't see him. "Where is he?"

"You'll find him down the spiral staircase through there," Tono said, pointing to an entrance on the other side of the reception hall. "I should warn you that the stairs are steep."

Tono handed Brie an envelope marked with his signature orchid. "I am forsaking my dance so that you may go to him sooner."

His kindness melted her heart, and she longed to return the favor. "Tono, I would love it if you would dance with Autumn in my stead."

He smiled but informed her, "She's not comfortable on the dance floor."

"Tell her it was my solemn request."

Tono bowed his head, a smile gracing his lips. "I will tell her."

When he turned to leave, Brie called out, "Tono."

"Yes?"

She threw her arms around him, laying her head against his chest to listen to his heart. Brie sighed softly when she let go. "I just needed to hear that."

Tono kissed her on the forehead. "May the years ahead be everything you wish for, toriko."

Exchange of Souls

B rie walked down the steep flight of narrow stairs, wondering where they led. When she reached the bottom, she found a red carpet lined with candles leading into the dark underground hallway.

She followed the trail and found Sir waiting for her at the end of it.

"Wife."

Her stomach fluttered pleasurably.

"What is this place, Sir?"

"It's a dungeon."

She gasped, looking at the iron gate behind him.

"It's real, used to protect the castle's inhabitants in the past."

She stared at the gate in fascination.

"Would you like to see it?"

When she nodded, Sir moved aside and opened the gate wide so she could enter.

Inside was a single pole with iron cuffs attached. Two elaborate candelabras burned on either side, bringing warmth to the room. On the left side of the room hung several tools used for punishment.

Sir came up behind her, caressing her shoulder with his fingers. "Do you want to play?"

Goosebumps rose on her skin. "Yes."

With hungry hands, he caressed her body—touching skin, pearls and lace...exploring her dress with all his senses.

"What's this?" Sir asked, when he came across the small blue pin.

"*Nonna* gave that to me."

He took it off carefully and examined it with a slight smile on his lips.

"When I was a boy, she told me this pin was her most cherished object in the world." Sir looked at Brie with tenderness. "It was given to her by her mother, an heirloom that has been passed down for countless generations. *Nonna* claimed it guaranteed the lucky bride who received it a strong and lasting marriage. This is fiercely coveted by the women of her family."

Sir shook his head as he stared at it. "The fact that she gave it to you, a foreigner, is almost scandalous, Brie."

She touched the small pin reverently. "I believe the gift was really meant for you, Sir. Your grandmother wanted to ensure you had a long-lasting marriage, even though we weren't married in church."

Sir stared at it, his expression unreadable.

Brie whispered his name, and when he turned his head towards her, she kissed him.

Sir slipped the pin into his pocket and went back to his task, caressing her skin as he removed each piece of clothing. When only the slave jewelry decorating her feet was left, Sir told her to kneel.

Sir placed a leather crop in her mouth. "Wait for me, wife."

He gathered her clothes and shut the iron gate behind him. The clank of the metal sent shivers through her as she watched him disappear into the darkness.

Brie could hear the muffled laughter and music from above, and smiled with the crop clamped in her mouth. Her thoughts drifted back to Sir, the thrill of the unknown enhancing her excitement. While she waited for his return, Brie watched the wax of the red tapered candles dripping seductively down their length. She was curious whether he would use the candles tonight.

Her heart started racing when she heard his footsteps returning. Sir opened the gate and stood before her, taking the crop from her mouth. "First I romance you with a wedding, and now I take what's mine. How does that make you feel, my bride?"

"Wanted, husband."

"Good."

Sir ordered her to stand next to the wooden pole, then cuffed her wrists in the hard, uneven shackles. There was no doubt the unforgiving metal had effectively held prisoners for centuries.

"We will play before I make love to you. I desire your body to ache as badly for me as I ache for you."

She moaned softly as he lifted her chin and kissed her, parting her lips with his tongue. His kisses were demanding, communicating the lust he'd conveyed all evening.

Brie's body responded eagerly to it, longing to sate that desire.

Sir pulled away, looking admiringly at her breasts. "You look cold, my dear. Shall I warm you up?" He took the crop and began warming up her skin with it. He started out light and progressively increased the licks of the instrument, pinkening her chest and torso.

"Now that the skin is warmed up, let's concentrate on the nipples," he said alluringly. Sir took one of the red candles from the candelabra and held it just above her left nipple, letting the wax drip onto it.

She sucked in her breath, the heat of the candle contrasting sharply with her cool flesh.

"Do you want more?"

"Please," she begged.

Sir covered both nipples in the hot wax, letting it fall at different heights to control the heat on her skin. When her breasts were completely covered, he put the candle back and slowly took off his jacket and vest, rolling up the sleeves of his shirt.

Sir took the flogger hanging on the wall and hit the tool against his hand so Brie could hear the distinctive sound of the leather.

"Chest out," he commanded.

Brie arched her shoulders back, thrusting out her chest. She held her breath as she watched Sir warm up in front of her. The first stroke released bits of the wax as it hit the side of her breast. He stroked the other breast and another cascade of candle wax fell to the floor as her breasts bounced alluringly from the impact of the flogger.

"How beautiful is that?" he murmured to himself.

With precise control, he released all the wax from her skin while stimulating her breasts with every swing. Brie threw back her head back, begging him to hit her harder.

"Very well."

Each stroke of his flogger resonated through Brie, the weeks of longing magnifying the effect of his attention on her body now.

"Are we wet?" he asked as he slapped the tails lightly against her pussy. Brie cried out in pleasure, the jolt of it making her clit pulse with need. He slapped the flogger between her legs again, a little harder, and she moaned with passion.

Sir hung up the flogger and returned to Brie, kissing her on the lips as he felt the wetness between her legs.

His groan was low and inviting. All she wanted was to be taken, pinned against the pole, defenseless to stop his claiming of her.

"Please," she begged.

With rough hands, he twisted Brie around so that she faced the pole and pushed her up against it, the chains on the cuffs tightening their hold as they twisted above her head.

"Would you let me do anything to you, wife?"

"Yes…" she breathed.

She heard the dangerous crack of a bullwhip beside her head and cried out.

He growled behind her. "This bullwhip may be smaller, but it still carries a nasty bite."

Her breaths came in gasps as he made her wait for his pleasure. Brie closed her eyes and consciously slowed her breathing, wanting her body to relax for his play.

"Good girl."

The first lick of the whip against her buttock was light, teasing her with its caress. The second was a little harder and stinging.

"I want your pretty ass pink for me."

Brie opened her eyes and looked up at the roughly cut roof above her as he began the rain of strokes. She grunted softly with each strike, afraid others might hear her.

"Cry out, woman."

Brie nodded, realizing her mistake. Her Master wanted her to vocalize.

With the next blow of the whip across her butt, Brie let out a scream. Nothing changed above, the party too loud for people to hear her.

"That's better…" he encouraged.

Brie cried out again as the whip left its stinging mark. "More, please."

Sir's chuckle was low as he granted her wish, some lashes light, some hard, with an occasional crack of the whip next to her ear. It kept her on her toes, trembling as she waited for the next stroke.

When he finally stopped, she heard the bullwhip fall to the floor. "I don't want you flying so high that you'll miss the moment of our union."

Sir took his time to unroll his sleeves and put on his vest and jacket, letting her wait expectantly as she hung in her iron bonds.

When he was finished redressing, Sir came up behind her. He undid the cuffs with care, rubbing her wrists, kissing the inside of each before kneeling down to kiss the warm skin of her tender ass. He stood up again, turning her to face him before he swept her naked body into his arms.

Sir kissed her deeply then, claiming her mouth with his tongue. Brie moaned, her whole body on fire for him.

"And now the lovemaking begins."

He carried her out of the dungeon and down the candlelit hallway, stopping midway. She heard the echoes of the party still going full-steam above.

Brie snuggled against his chest, sighing with contentment.

"Few know that this castle has a secret passage," Sir stated, as he pushed against a portion of the stone wall with his shoulder. It moved, revealing a narrow passageway.

Brie was intrigued as he walked through the opening, still carrying her in his arms. Sir took her up a new flight of stairs, these with steps decorated with the wedding embellishments she'd seen earlier, but with the added charm of burning candles.

"Today has been a fairy tale come true, Sir."

"I'm not done yet, wife."

Her stomach did a little flip. Brie didn't think she would *ever* tire of hearing him call her by that title.

Massive double doors greeted them at the top of the stairs. Sir pushed his back against them and the doors slowly swung open, revealing an opulent bedchamber fit for a king. An impressive canopy bed immediately drew Brie's attention.

"Are you ready to make love with nothing between

us?" he asked huskily.

"I think I might combust from the pleasure of it."

"As long as you combust all over my cock, I'm fine with that."

Sir laid her on the massive bed and unfastened the slave jewelry from her feet, freeing her from it. "Listening to the jingle every time you took a step was a turn-on for me." He lifted her foot and kissed the tops of her painted toes as he looked ravenously into her eyes.

"It was alluring for me as well, Sir," she admitted.

He leaned forward, putting his finger to her lips. "Tonight we are simply husband and wife."

"Husband," she purred, loving the sound of it as it rolled off her tongue.

"I want you to put these on while I change," Sir said, gesturing to a set of white stockings and heels he'd laid out for her on the bed.

Brie begged, "Please don't change yet." She trailed her hands over the silver buttons of his vest and the chain of his grandfather's pocket watch. "You look so handsome; I just want to admire you a little longer."

"As you wish."

Instead of changing, Sir stood to watch as Brie put on the hose. She slipped them on sensually, smiling at him in an alluring manner as if she were doing a striptease. Then she stood and stepped into the six-inch heels.

"My favorite look for you, other than when you're bent over receiving my cock."

Brie had expected he would fling her onto the bed and ravish her, but he did not. Instead, Sir asked her to turn around. "Let me take in the beauty of my bride."

Brie slowly twirled for him, feeling the warmth of his gaze.

"Now come to me, wife. Let me touch you."

Brie walked to him, her steps long and graceful as she swayed her hips. She hoped the smile on her lips was equally irresistible.

When Sir touched her skin, she felt an electrical jolt, her body humming with a desperate need to connect. His hands, which had been rough with her before, were now gentle as he worshipped her with his caress.

Brie let out a long, impassioned moan as he stroked the brand on her back. "How is it that I find your body even more tempting than when I first took you? It's a mystery I plan to spend our lifetime exploring."

She cried out when she felt his warm lips on her neck and the light pressure of his teeth. Her body craved him like the air she breathed; it required satisfaction or she would die. "I'm burning with need, Thane."

"Undress me then."

Brie smiled as she started with his jacket, tiptoeing to slip it off his shoulders. She placed it on the back of a chair and went for his vest next, carefully unhooking his grandfather's pocket watch from the silver button before taking the vest off. She lovingly placed the timepiece on the desk and came back for the bowtie, grinning as she untied it and slipped it from his collar.

Brie held it in her teeth as she began unbuttoning the starched white shirt, each undone button exposing the handsome man underneath. She opened the shirt, tracing her finger over the brand on his chest.

Sir looked down at her, his gaze intense.

Brie smiled with the ribbon of the bowtie still in her mouth as she undid his cufflinks and pulled the shirt off his fine body. She put the items on the chair and returned to him, placing her hands on his toned chest. She slowly traveled downward, caressing his stomach muscles until she came into contact with his belt.

She looked up at him as she undid the belt buckle and slowly pulled it from the loops. She held it up and laughed sweetly. "And I remember when I used to be scared of your belts…"

Brie walked over to lay it on the chair and came back to him, walking with slow, graceful movements, knowing there was no reason to rush. She had waited too long not to savor this moment.

She sank to her knees and kissed each dress shoe before untying them. After slipping the shoes off, she removed his socks, purposely brushing his feet with her long hair and giggling when he wiggled them in response. She placed the socks inside the shoes and moved them to the side.

With trembling hands, she undid the button on Sir's pants and unzipped them, releasing his hard cock from its confines before sliding his clothing off.

Sir groaned in appreciation, causing Brie to gush with more wetness. "I'm on fire…" he whispered huskily when she took his shaft into her hand. It burned with the heat of needed release.

She placed her lips on the head of his shaft, but he groaned in protest. "Stop."

Brie looked up questioningly.

"I need to sink my cock into you. I have never wanted anything as badly as I want you now."

She purred, taking his hand as he helped her to her feet. Sir led her to the bed, picking her up and laying her on it.

Sir lay beside her in all his naked glory. Brie glanced down at his cock, framed by dark hair, and felt her loins contract. For the first time it was not just an instrument of pleasure. When he penetrated her this time, there was a chance his seed would find its mark.

She looked up at Sir, struggling to breathe. "Make love to me, husband."

He claimed her mouth as he moved between her legs, spreading her wide. She ached for the union, expecting he would thrust, but he stopped himself.

"No..." Sir said to himself, pulling back. "Just as I did when I took you as Master, I want you to remember this moment."

Sir moved down between her legs, licking her excitement. "God, you have never tasted so sweet..." His tongue began teasing her already sensitive clit.

She grabbed his head. "Please stop, I'll come too fast."

"I want you to come, wife. I want your body primed to receive my semen."

Brie threw her head back and moaned, her pussy already pulsing with an impending orgasm. Sir moved his head back and forth as his tongue danced over her clit, then the long licks began.

"Give in to it," he murmured passionately as he continued his slow, rhythmic licking.

Sir knew her body well, and soon her hips bucked as the climax took over. Sir tasted her watery come with obvious pleasure. Growling as he wiped his mouth, he crawled up from between her legs. "I can't get enough of you, woman."

He ran his fingers through her hair, looking deep into her eyes. "I love you, Brie. You are the breath of life to me."

"All I want is this moment—and you."

Sir positioned his cock against her wet opening, the head of his shaft almost scorching her with its heat. He looked her in the eyes as he slowly sank his hard shaft into her.

Brie wrapped her legs around him, wanting all of him, *needing* all of him.

Sir began slowly stroking her with his cock, rolling his hips to deepen the thrusts. She matched his rhythm, staring up at him with tears of joy. "Thane, I don't think there's anything sexier than making a baby."

Sir pressed his lips to hers, grabbing her ass cheeks as he forced himself deeper. "Two become one," he murmured as he came inside her, his cock throbbing with each release of his seed.

Brie cried out, the pleasure of it overwhelming on every level; the consummation of the marriage, the release of sexual tension, the intense connection and the primal act of procreation all rolled up into one monumental moment.

She held on to him fiercely, knowing his essence was inside her seeking to make new life. Brie closed her eyes in sheer ecstasy as her spirit melded with Sir's…

(Special Bonus)
16 Years Earlier
Master's POV

Thane had been studying hard for the last three weeks preparing for his semester exams. He knew if he could pass these courses with outstanding marks, he stood a good chance of being able to advance a full year. As far as he was concerned, the sooner he was out of college, the sooner he could start his adult life and forget the horrors of the past.

Financial independence was his primary goal—his only goal—and he'd do whatever it took to sever any and all ties from the Beast.

His singular focus was admired by his roommate, Brad Anderson, and as a special reward for Thane's scholarly diligence, he insisted on the two going out to enjoy a night on the town like good ol' college boys. "Life's so much more than books and endless tests, young grasshopper, but how can you know that when you spend your days stuck in this room? It's time to live a little."

"That is exactly what I *am* doing," Thane corrected Brad. "I'm going to graduate early through sheer will and effort so I can begin my life."

Brad shook his head. "But you're missing the whole point. This *is* your life—right now. You're a young man living on a campus of possibilities, my friend, and it's my solemn duty to open your eyes to what you've been missing."

Thane put his arm around his roommate in a fatherly manner. "And it's my duty to help you realize life is not all fun and games. What's the point of going to college and going into debt on tuition if you aren't going to seriously apply yourself every day you're here?"

Brad frowned, and the light seemed to leave the room. Thane half-regretted his words when he met Brad's harsh gaze. It looked as if the boy were about to explode in a ball of pent up anger. Instead, he lifted his chin up and howled with laughter. "You're one insulting little bastard, Thane Davis. No wonder you don't have any friends…"

Thane only shook his head at the insult. "As much as I appreciate your need to 'fix' me, I'm content to remain here in our room, focused on my school work. Go enjoy your night out with your college buddies."

"It that really how this is going down?" Brad asked.

"I'm afraid so."

"Then you leave me no other choice." His roommate left without any further explanation.

Thane settled down to start on a long session going over his Physics notes. He found the subject thoroughly fascinating and looked forward to taking a more advanced class in the fall.

Half an hour later, Brad burst back into the room followed by a stockier built Russian.

"Leave me alone, Durov," Thane protested, not in the mood for their games.

The Russian picked him up and started physically dragging him towards the door. "You're coming with me," he insisted, unceremoniously shoving Thane out into the hallway.

Thane straightened his clothes before turning to face him. "I have no interest in getting drunk tonight."

The Russian only laughed. "Trust me, comrade. I have something *far* more interesting in mind."

Thane looked at Brad. "Do you have any idea what he's talking about?"

Brad shrugged. "Not a clue, but if Durov's involved, you can be sure trouble isn't far behind. I'm game if you are."

"I will only offer this opportunity once, *moy droog*. After tonight, it will be closed to you forever," Durov said. The Russian's serious tone surprised Thane.

"What kind of opportunity?"

"A chance to visit a private club I frequent. It will change your life, but I warn you it is not for the faint of heart."

Thane had to admit he was interested. However, if he was expected to sacrifice a full night of study, he needed further details before agreeing.

The Russian flatly refused. "Either you trust me or you do not."

Trust was not something Thane gave easily, but he admired the burly Russian. While the young man certainly enjoyed his vodka and women, he excelled as a student without devoting hours with his nose planted in books.

"Why pass up this once-in-a-lifetime opportunity? Your Physics notes aren't going anywhere," Brad encouraged with a winsome grin.

Thane stared hard at Durov, glancing momentarily at the huge text book sitting on his desk beside his pile of notes. Thane couldn't explain why, but he was suddenly overcome with a sense of exhilaration he hadn't felt since he was a boy. "I have a feeling I will live to regret this…" he muttered.

The Russian raised an eyebrow, a wicked grin spreading across his face. "If truly living for the first time in your life is a problem for you, then yes, *moy droog,* you will regret this night."

Brad slapped Thane on the back. "Here's to having our minds expanded outside the realm of text books."

As the three were making their way out of the building, Thane suddenly stopped cold. "Your 'private club' wouldn't happen to be some kind of drug den, would it?"

Durov burst out in uproarious laughter, attracting the attention of passersby. "My drug of choice is naturally produced. Although it may be too harsh for the likes of you, peasant."

Thane laughed. "I'm not easily squeamish, although I can't speak for my roommate here."

Brad punched Thane in the arm in protest. "If you're calling me a sissy, I've got a bullwhip I'd like you to meet."

"It was actually your experience with the bullwhip that got you invited tonight," Durov informed Brad.

"Russian Cowboy Club, is it? Do you Ruskies ride steers for fun on the weekends?" Brad joked.

"I ride something, yes, and it often grunts and squeals with pain," Durov answered cryptically.

Thane studied the Russian, coming to the realization he didn't know Durov at all.

Brad frowned and said to Thane. "I don't know what kind of crazy shit you're getting us into."

"Me? You're the one who started this."

"Hey, Durov's your friend, not mine."

"You will both thank me once the evening is over. Trust me," Durov said in his thick Russian accent. Putting his arms around both of them, he added, "This is a solemn gift I give to you. Whether you choose to pursue it or not is up to you, but I guarantee you'll be changed by what you experience tonight." He grabbed their shoulders in a painful, vicelike grip before letting go—and laughed.

Foolish or not, Thane was intrigued and willingly followed the Russian as he took them to the shadier part of town, guiding them down dark alleys until he came to a small abandoned warehouse. He knocked on the door three times in quick succession.

Someone behind the door asked, "What's the one truth?"

To which Durov replied, "All is fair in passion and pain."

The door opened, and the man behind it gave Durov

a curt nod before staring harshly at Thane and Brad.

"These are my friends," Durov informed him. "I spoke to the Dungeon Master about them coming tonight."

The man did not acknowledge his reply, but opened the door wider so the two could pass as he growled under his breath, intimidating them with his hostile glare.

Durov seemed unconcerned about the man's lack of hospitality. Instead, he explained as they walked down the hallway, "Tonight, you will only observe." He added with a dangerous glint in his eye, "Keep your distance from the scenes."

Thane swore he heard a woman scream below him. "What the hell is going on, Durov? Are people being tortured in here?"

The Russian met the question with a roguish smile. "What some consider torture, others consider ecstasy."

As they walked down a long flight of metal stairs, the woman let out another tormented scream, but Thane clearly heard her cry afterwards, "Please Master, more! More…"

He put his hand out to stop Durov before the Russian opened the door. "I have an eerie feeling that I won't be able to look at you in the same light after this."

"*Da,*" Durov agreed with a mischievous smirk. "Tonight you will both be required to address me as *Rytsar.*"

"Isn't that Russian for the word knight?" Thane stated, rather than asked. "You can't be serious."

Durov's expression became grave, as did the tenor of his voice. "I assure you, I am."

Brad bumped shoulders with Thane. "Knight, asshole, it's all the same." He gave Durov a quick bow. "So be it...Rytsar Durov."

They heard a commotion on the other side of the door with several men cheering loudly as a lone girl cried out in pain after an extremely loud snap.

"What's happening to her?" Thane demanded.

"There is only one way to find out, *moy droog*."

The exhilaration Thane had felt earlier increased as he reached for the door handle.

Rytsar slapped his shoulder hard, proudly stating, "Welcome to my world..." as the creaking door slowly swung open.

"Rytsar!" a young woman shouted in greeting from deep within the room. The girl was bound naked on a pole set in the center of the large basement. It was obvious she was thrilled to see him, which seemed odd considering her body was covered in angry red marks as if she'd been brutalized.

Durov left his friends as he confidently strode over to the young woman, grabbing a fistful of hair and pulling her head back to kiss her roughly.

Brad and Thane remained rooted where they were, watching in stunned silence.

The large warehouse basement was dank—cold brick and cement flooring made up the room, strange contraptions lined the walls, with heavy chains hanging from the ceiling. The space was populated by severe looking men dressed in black leather and a preponderance of naked girls.

"What is this Duro—Rytsar?" Thane blurted, when the Russian returned to them.

He gestured to the massive room. "It's a BDSM dungeon, *moy droog*! Down here we fulfill our darkest fantasies with those who hunger for our brand of pain."

Thane watched in disbelief as a young woman was paraded into the room from another entrance, led by a leash by another female, and was ordered to strip in front of them.

Durov took over once the girl was naked, barking a command and she obediently placed her wrists in metal cuffs above her, not objecting when he secured the locks and jerked the chain to tighten it.

His tone became menacing as he muttered words in Russian while he circled the girl. The look of lust in her eyes was tainted with genuine fear. Thane understood he was about to witness something dark and perverted, and yet he could not turn away as his friend picked up an ominous looking multi-tailed whip and swung it in the air.

Such a device had no business touching, much less striking the girl, and yet Rytsar laughed seductively as he began lashing her with it. Her cries filled the dark dungeon as he let loose on her back.

The idea of purposely causing pain was a foreign concept to Thane, and it would have sickened him if it weren't for the devoted look the girl gave him every time he paused between volleys. Even as Rytsar delivered his demanding strikes, the girl begged for more, shuddering and moaning in pleasure by the time he was finished.

Thane never knew such sexual power was possible— delivering pleasure with pain.

He glanced over at Brad and could see he was equally

entranced by the concept. Rytsar released the girl from her bonds and gave her one last kiss before smacking her on the ass and ordering her to clean up.

He came striding over to Thane, a self-assured look on his face. "What do you think, *moy droog*?"

"I'm not quite sure what to thin—"

A woman's scream of pure terror interrupted his answer. Thane immediately turned to see a girl bound spread-eagle on a wooden table. The man attending her began whipping her pubic area.

Rytsar glanced her way and said dismissively, "The girl was being grossly disobedient and must pay the price for her willfulness."

When Thane moved to intervene, Rytsar stopped him short. "It is not your place."

"But he's hurting her!"

"Hurting her yes, but not harming her, comrade. There is a difference."

Brad growled in irritation. "I'm with Thane on this one. As witnesses to blatant abuse, we are *required* to stop it."

"Each girl here comes of her own accord, knowing full well what will happen. There is no need to feel sympathy for them. This is what they live for."

Thane shook his head as he watched welts rise on the girl's thighs. "Well, it looks harmful to me."

"It's consensual play between two adults, and is none of your business, *moy droog*," Rytsar asserted. "The girl has a safeword. Unless she calls it, he has her permission to punish her."

"It's not right…" Brad said, sighing heavily.

Rytsar grinned, shaking his head. "But it feels so right. I have played with submissives since my father first introduced me to BDSM when I was fifteen. I guarantee you, I understand women far better than either of you."

"And they like this stuff?" Brad asked incredulously.

Rytsar grinned. "Yes, they can't get enough of it. Imagine a girl laying down her will, allowing you to do whatever you wish to her body…"

"Well," Brad replied in a sarcastic tone, "if I had *my* way, I wouldn't be beating the girl unless it was with my substantial cock."

The Russian raised his eyebrow. "Think about it. Isn't there a part of you that would like to lick her body with your bullwhip, and watch her squirm in pleasure?"

Brad glanced around the room, staring at the girls in various states of arousal, a new appreciation dawning in his eyes as he considered Rytsar's words.

Durov put his arm around Thane. "The power exchange between two souls is intoxicating, *moy droog*. It is like a drug—nothing compares."

"I couldn't whip a girl," Thane declared.

"Did I not say you could do *whatever* you wished with them? You are full of tension—I can see it in your face—and it's holding you back in your studies. The best way to break your stress is to release it on a willing partner. Trust me."

Thane smirked. "Is that how you maintain your high grades?"

"*Da*, I am stress-free thanks to the devotion of my subs, and I can think straight because of it—unlike you."

The girl from earlier had been untied and walked

over with her eyes focused on the ground as she bowed at Durov's feet. "How may I serve you, Rytsar?"

Durov looked at Thane and grinned. "This is a virgin Dom. Introduce him to our world."

The girl didn't miss a beat, looking up at Durov and answering confidently, "Yes, Rytsar. It would be my pleasure."

She turned to Thane and bowed to him. "What would you ask of me?"

Thane took a deep breath. Although he was certain Rytsar had other ideas in mind, he took the girl's hand and helped her to her feet. "I would like to speak with you."

The submissive cocked her head to one side in surprise, but answered, "Certainly, sir."

Thane smiled in response to Durov's shocked expression. "I'd like to know the submissive's perspective in such a power exchange."

Durov shook his head. "A gift wasted…"

Brad winked at the girl as she passed. "If you're looking for something more, darlin', come see me afterwards. I'm a virgin, too."

The submissive couldn't hide her smile and quickly looked back down at her feet as Thane guided her to a quiet area in the corner. He spent the next hour talking to her. He found it fascinating the way her eyes lit up when she talked about her various submissive experiences. It was equally surprising to learn that focused communication was an integral aspect of the exchange prior to beginning a scene.

After his experience with his own mother, whom he

referred to as only the Beast, Thane had doubted he could ever have a relationship with a woman. But this…this was a profound exchange between a Dominant and submissive, built on a foundation of respect and trust. Emotional commitment was not a required element.

According to the girl, some of her most memorable experiences had been with Dominants she'd not been collared by—including Rytsar Durov.

The idea was a foreign concept to Thane, but it gave him hope and direction. Relieving his sexual needs without entangling himself in unwanted relationships or having to resort to prostitutes was *the* perfect solution.

Better yet, he would have control over their pleasure, which he planned to explore extensively.

"Do you mind if I touch your marks?" he asked her.

"Please, Master."

"I'd prefer it if you call me sir."

The girl blushed. "Yes, Sir."

"What's your name?"

"I am called glee."

Thane smiled, liking the name. He reached out and lightly caressed the angry red marks on her skin. "These wounds, how long do they last, glee?"

She shuddered under his gentle caress and looked at him with what appeared to be growing fondness. "It depends, but each one is cherished by me."

"Why?" he questioned as he circled the outline of one with his finger.

She trembled, her attention now solely on his touch. "They are physical reminders of the connection I shared with my Dom. I suppose it's kind of like the hickeys you get as a teenager."

"Ah…" Thane let his fingers trail up her back to her neck. He tested his power over her by demanding, "Kiss me, glee."

The girl turned her head and leaned forward, pressing her lips against his. He instinctively flicked his tongue against those tempting lips and she parted them for him.

Thane felt blood rush to his groin as he explored the contours of her mouth. He broke the embrace, and stared at her for a few moments before asking, "Have you ever had an encounter here with someone who didn't use a whip or some kind of instrument?"

She giggled. "No, Sir."

"Would you like to try?"

The girl smiled in amusement, but her eyes grew bigger when she realized he was serious. "With you, I might."

"We'll consider it a date then."

"Not tonight?"

"No, as Rytsar so crassly indicated, I'm new at this dynamic and would like to do some research first."

"You are wise to do so, Sir, and I would be honored to be your first when you return."

Thane looked over at Durov. "So is he your Master?"

Glee giggled. "No." She pointed to another man who was caning an older woman. "That is my Master. He has given Rytsar free reign over me."

Thane frowned. "So your Master won't mind if you and I scene together?"

"Not if Rytsar has ordered it."

He shook his head in disbelief. "There's a lot for me to learn."

Durov came up behind him and slapped him hard on the back. "*Da*, you have much to learn but we must go now."

Thane took glee's hand and kissed it. "Until my return…"

She giggled again, blushing profusely.

Durov tsked in disgust. "There is no need for niceties, *moy droog*. You are missing the whole point."

"I disagree," Thane answered. "A woman deserves to be worshipped, especially if you plan to use and abuse her."

Durov rolled his eyes, but offered no witty comeback.

Brad remained silent as he followed behind them while the three made their way out of the warehouse.

"You are not allowed to speak of this place or what happens here to anyone. I'm sure now that you appreciate the dynamic, you can understand why it must remain a secret," Rytsar said as they walked.

"I could certainly see jail time happening if you weren't careful," Thane agreed.

"*Da*, there are many who do not understand BDSM."

"Well, I certainly didn't until tonight," Brad confessed.

When they happened across a payphone, Brad asked them to stop. "Just a sec, guys. There's something I need to do." Brad threw a bunch of change into the phone, dialed and then waited.

"Hey, Ma? I know it's late, but do you mind shipping me the old bullwhip? I think it's still hanging in the barn."

He paused for a moment. "Yeah, yeah, that's the one. If you could send it priority mail that would be great."

Another extended pause.

"You want to know why I need it?" He looked over at Thane and Durov. "Well...I've been stressing out over finals and thought a little bullwhip practice might take my mind off things."

He nodded as he listened to her talk for a while, gesturing to Thane and Durov to be patient. "Sure, a batch of peanut butter cookies would be great." Brad glanced at Thane. "I'm sure he wouldn't mind, Ma." He cuffed the phone and asked, "My mom wants to send you cookies too, and is wondering what kind you like."

Thane smirked, trying to hide a foolish smile, touched that Brad's mother had thought of him. "I have no idea, really."

Brad whispered, "She makes killer Toll House cookies, man."

"Fine, Toll House it is, then."

Brad spoke into the phone again. "Chocolate chip would be great, Ma. But get the package out tomorrow if you can. I'm dying over here."

After he hung up, Durov told Thane, "You are sharing those cookies with me, comrade."

Thane laughed. "A small price to pay for such an enlightening evening." He became quiet as he mulled over the events of the night while they made their way back to the dorm.

"Are you glad you came, *moy droog?*" Durov asked. "Despite the torture you were a witness to?" he added with an impish grin.

Thane put his hand on Durov's shoulder and answered solemnly, "It has been a rare gift—this night."

"Do not squander it."

Thane only nodded as he watched the Russian leave. He was overwhelmed by a sense of hope he'd never known before. Was it possible to overcome the damage done by his mother after the untimely death of his father?

To lead the semblance of a normal life…wouldn't that be a miracle?

He looked at Brad with a half-smile. "I never would have guessed waking up this morning, that this is how the night would end."

"Me either, bud. This has been one *crazy* night."

Thane looked at his watch. "And it looks like I can still get in a few hours of study."

He fully expected Brad to give him shit about it, but was surprised when Brad opened the door to their building, stating, "I think I'll join you tonight…"

"Hurry up, man!" Brad urged. "We're going to miss the start of the exam if you don't get your butt out to the bus stop now."

"I'll be there in a sec," Thane assured him. "Tell the bus driver to wait if you have to. I need to pay my bill."

"I'll be damned if I'm holding the bus for a slow-ass," Brad answered with a grin as he pushed open the door and headed out.

While Thane waited at the counter for the waitress to return with his change, he noticed a little girl with long pig tails struggling to grab a container of catsup from the diner counter. She was a tiny thing in a polka-dot dress, not looking to be more than seven.

The child's tongue stuck out from effort as she tiptoed with her arm fully extended, trying to grab the bottle. However, it remained just out of reach of her grasping fingertips.

Thane slid the bottle over to her, giving her a friendly wink.

The little girl grabbed it, clutching the bottle to her chest as she grinned up at him. "Thank you, mister!"

He returned her infectious smile, and chuckled. "No problem, kid."

"Guess where I'm going?"

He shook his head, charmed by the little brunette's enthusiasm.

Her hazel eyes sparkled with childish delight. "I'm going to Disneyland for the first time. Have you ever been?"

Thane shook his head. "Can't say that I have."

"Well, you should, you know! They have Mickey and Minnie…and Pluto. I love, love, love Pluto," she said in a dreamy voice.

"With Pluto there, I'm sure it's bound to be a good

time."

Thane heard a man's stern command come from the table by the window, "Get back here, young lady." He glanced over and saw the man glaring at him—obviously the child's over-protective father.

"Yes, Daddy," the brunette answered, skipping over to the table with the catsup bottle still clutched to her chest.

As the young girl slid into the booth, Thane overheard the mother say, "How many times have we told you not to talk to strangers?"

Thane could feel the heat of the father's distrustful stare burning a hole in his back as he turned towards the waitress, who was counting back his change. He laid two dollars on the counter for her, and thrust the rest into his jeans pocket.

As he passed by the family on his way out, the girl chirped, "Thanks for the 'sup, mister."

He couldn't help but smile. "Any time, kid."

"Not another word, Brianna," the father barked angrily.

Thane chuckled to himself, shaking his head as he went out the door.

You really need to chill, man. It's not like I'm going to molest your little girl….

COMING NEXT

Enchant Me: Brie's Submission

10th Book in the Series

Available Now

Reviews mean the world to me!

I truly appreciate you taking the time to review
Claim Me.

If you could leave a review on both Goodreads and the site where you purchased this book from, I would be so grateful. Sincerely, ~Red

ABOUT THE AUTHOR

Over Two Million readers have enjoyed Red's stories

Red Phoenix – USA Today Bestselling Author
Winner of 8 Readers' Choice Awards

Hey Everyone!

I'm Red Phoenix, an author who also happens to be a submissive in real life. I wrote the Brie's Submission series because I wanted people everywhere to know just how much fun BDSM can be.

There is a huge cast of characters who are part of Brie's journey. The further you read into the story the more you learn about each one. I hope you grow to love Brie and the gang as much as I do.

They've become like family.

When I'm not writing, you can find me online with readers.

I heart my fans! ~Red

To find out more visit my Website
redphoenixauthor.com
Follow Me on BookBub
bookbub.com/authors/red-phoenix
Newsletter: Sign up
redphoenixauthor.com/newsletter-signup
Facebook: AuthorRedPhoenix
Twitter: @redphoenix69
Instagram: RedPhoenixAuthor
I invite you to join my reader Group!
facebook.com/groups/539875076052037

SIGN UP FOR MY NEWSLETTER
HERE FOR THE LATEST RED
PHOENIX UPDATES

FOLLOW ME ON INSTAGRAM
INSTAGRAM.COM/REDPHOENIXAUTHOR

SALES, GIVEAWAYS, NEW RELEAS-
ES, PREORDER LINKS, AND MORE!
SIGN UP HERE
REDPHOENIXAUTHOR.COM/NEWSLETTER-
SIGNUP

Red Phoenix is the author of:

Brie's Submission Series:
Teach Me #1
Love Me #2
Catch Me #3
Try Me #4
Protect Me #5
Hold Me #6
Surprise Me #7
Trust Me #8
Claim Me #9
Enchant Me #10
A Cowboy's Heart #11
Breathe with Me #12
Her Russian Knight #13
Under His Protection #14
Her Russian Returns #15
In Sir's Arms #16
Bound by Love #17
Tied to Hope #18
Hope's First Christmas #19
Secrets of the Heart #20

*You can also purchase the AUDIO BOOK **Versions**

Also part of the Submissive Training Center world:

Rise of the Dominates Trilogy
Sir's Rise #1
Master's Fate #2
The Russian Reborn #3

Captain's Duet
Safe Haven #1
Destined to Dominate #2

Other Books by Red Phoenix

Blissfully Undone
* Available in eBook and paperback

(Snowy Fun—Two people find themselves snowbound in a cabin where hidden love can flourish, taking one couple on a sensual journey into ménage à trois)

His Scottish Pet: Dom of the Ages
* Available in eBook and paperback

Audio Book: *His Scottish Pet: Dom of the Ages*

(Scottish Dom—A sexy Dom escapes to Scotland in the late 1400s. He encounters a waif who has the potential to free him from his tragic curse)

The Erotic Love Story of Amy and Troy
* Available in eBook and paperback

(Sexual Adventures—True love reigns, but fate continually throws Troy and Amy into the arms of others)

eBooks

Varick: The Reckoning

(Savory Vampire—A dark, sexy vampire story. The hero navigates the dangerous world he has been thrust into with lusty passion and a pure heart)

Keeper of the Wolf Clan (Keeper of Wolves, #1)

(Sexual Secrets—A virginal werewolf must act as the clan's mysterious Keeper)

The Keeper Finds Her Mate (Keeper of Wolves, #2)

(Second Chances—A young she-wolf must choose between old ties or new beginnings)

The Keeper Unites the Alphas (Keeper of Wolves, #3)

(Serious Consequences—The young she-wolf is captured by the rival clan)

Boxed Set: Keeper of Wolves Series (Books 1-3)

(Surprising Secrets—A secret so shocking it will rock Layla's world. The young she-wolf is put in a position of being able to save her werewolf clan or becoming the reason for its destruction)

Socrates Inspires Cherry to Blossom

(Satisfying Surrender—A mature and curvaceous woman becomes fascinated by an online Dom who has much to teach her)

By the Light of the Scottish Moon

(Saving Love—Two lost souls, the Moon, a werewolf, and a death wish…)

In 9 Days

(Sweet Romance—A young girl falls in love with the new student, nicknamed "the Freak")

---

9 Days and Counting

(Sacrificial Love—The sequel to *In 9 Days* delves into the emotional reunion of two longtime lovers)

And Then He Saved Me

(Saving Tenderness—When a young girl tries to kill herself, a man of great character intervenes with a love that heals)

Play With Me at Noon

(Seeking Fulfillment—A desperate wife lives out her fantasies by taking five different men in five days)

Connect with Red on Substance B

Substance B is a platform for independent authors to directly connect with their readers. Please visit Red's Substance B page where you can:

- Sign up for Red's newsletter
- Send a message to Red
- See all platforms where Red's books are sold

Visit Substance B today to learn more about your favorite independent authors.